a time to mourn

A TIME TO DANCE

Ella Sailor

PRESS

Library of Congress Control Number: 2003102312
ISBN 1-591605-28-8

Xulon Press
www.xulonpress.com

To order additional copies, call 1-866-909-BOOK (2665).

To Jack
my husband, my friend
the love of my life

Contents

Contents

Chapter 1

St. Michael's

He was tired. The day had been too long … way too long … and disheartening; a simple fracture turned out to be bone cancer. The family needed someone to blame and he was first in line … *after all, an orthopaedic surgeon aught to be able to prevent such a thing,* he mused wryly. *I must be getting depressed; how can I suddenly be so cynical?*

He glanced at his watch … *eight o'clock … guess the three hours in Emergency are taking a toll. Too tired to cook … too tired to go out … too tired! Maybe I'll just go to bed.* He read for a few minutes before he dropped his head into his hands and sat motionless.

The scream of the siren broke into his thoughts. *The ambulance! Wonder if there's been another accident at the ski hill … hope those broken bones don't wind up cancerous. Guess they'll have to blame somebody else, since I'm not there.*

A still, small voice interrupted, *Why aren't you there, Doctor Braemer? After all, you are a surgeon - trained in sport medicine. There's only one intern left in Emerg and this could be serious. You need to go … quickly!*

I'm far too tired to be of help. Even as he muttered his excuse, he was picking up his bag and heading out the door. He pulled in behind the wailing siren and followed it into Emergency.

"Michael Braemer, I prayed you'd be here." The driver jumped from the ambulance and quickly opened the rear door. "Is she still with us?" he addressed the young doctor working feverishly over her.

"Jeremy," Michael recognized the young man as his intern, "what do we have here and how serious?"

"Plenty serious. Her heart keeps stopping. I think we have some broken ribs and at least one punctured lung ... maybe both. Her blood pressure just drops off ..."

"What happened to her?" Michael asked as they moved her quickly, efficiently into the Trauma Unit.

"I ran into her with the snow machine; I was on ski patrol," the young doctor confessed, his face ashen. "Good thing Pastor Bob's an EMT. We got her down the hill and ... and ... and ... she's not breathing anymore!" he cried, "Her heart stopped again!"

"Let me take over for you, Doctor," Michael sensed the young man was suffering more from stress than exertion. "Will you ask the nurse to get us some reinforcements ... someone from cardiology ... try Dr. Pascoe from neurosurgery; that's a bad hit to the head, bleeding pretty good! It could be a long night."

Throbbing pain overwhelmed her. Black heaviness gripped her mind ... immobilizing and imprisoning. Figures in white ... in green ... moving in the fog ... receding ... coming again.

Voices ... sometimes muffled ... sometimes sharp ... kind ... commanding. *A nightmare,* thought Rhea, as she struggled to waken. Then blackness.

More voices ... foggy figures ... more heaviness. *My head must be set in concrete,* she thought as she attempted to move her heavy left arm. Then she felt the needles, the tubes, the oxygen. "It really is a nightmare," she murmured; "a real, live nightmare."

"Whoa, take it easy, little lady," a kindly voice admonished. "You've been in an accident." The same kindly voice she had heard in the night. She struggled to see him, finally asking,

"Is there more than one of you?"

"Just one. Nobody wanted to clone me."

"Is my neck broken?" she asked, fingering the apparatus that held her head prisoner.

"Well ... yes ... and no. You have some cracked vertebrae."

"Which ones?"

"In your neck."

"Which ones in my neck?"

"Three, four and five," he answered. Then added, "Though I don't know what kept them from snapping altogether with the hit you took."

"What happened to me?"

"I understand it was a skiing accident. You were hit by the ski patrol. It must have been pretty direct considering ..."

"What else ....?"

"A couple of ribs ... punctured lung ... broken foot - four bones. Beats me how your boot got ripped off." Noticing her hand straying to the bandage around her head, he explained, "The gash in your skull seems to have been only superficial. Dr. Pascoe from neurosurgery gave you a pretty thorough going over."

"Do I still have hair?"

"You do," he smiled, "and eyelashes and fingernails.

All the really important stuff."

"And you? Are you my doctor?"

"I'm Dr. Braemer from Orthopaedics. I came by just as they brought you in. You're in the ICU at St. Michael's. I take it you know Dr. and Mrs. Wahl. They've been in many times over the last few days; they'll be stopping by again."

"Few days? I've been here ... a few days?" her voice trailed off as the medication took effect.

———

It had been ten days. Ten long weary days. But there had been gains - the move to a private room - the collar replacing the immobilizing neck apparatus - a bed that allowed her to change position. She was pleased to discover that except for a small strip near the hairline, her hair had not been shaved off.

Flowers lined one side of the room, covering the windowsill and bedside table. *I'll have to have someone read the cards for me,* she thought.

"Good morning," the cheery voice of the nurse, "and how are we today?"

Resisting the urge to say "Fantastic," Rhea managed, "I think we're moving in the right direction."

"Dr. Braemer has ordered a reduction in your medication. He would like another X-ray of your neck and your spine and ribs. He's in surgery today. You may see him later this evening."

Dr. Braemer, Rhea mused. She had asked Doc Wahl about him a few days ago. Doc Wahl, her father's old friend - now Chief of Surgery at St. Michael's - affectionately known as *The Chief.*

"Braemer's the best," the Chief affirmed in his usual gruff manner. "I moved mountains to get him here. I like his new methods: laser ... research ... technology. He makes the lame walk. You're in good hands; you won't find better!"

So he's coming tonight ... sure hope he makes the lame walk, thought Rhea, as she contemplated the huge cast on her foot and ankle, with pins protruding.

He stood looking out on the darkening street. It was raining again. He was suddenly tired. The day had been long ... stressful. Too many days ... too much stress ... too little sleep. Still, he looked forward to dropping in on Rhea - Dr. Rhea Rhymer, Director of Obstetrics and Gynecology. For several days following the accident he had been too busy to read the Sunday Post ... startled to find it on his desk, headline screaming: PROMINENT DOCTOR HIT BY SKI PATROL. He hadn't recognized the name on her chart. In the month that he had been at St. Michael's he scarce had time to meet his close colleagues. *Good thing I found out who she is,* he thought, remembering his simplistic answers to her questions, *lest I play the fool a second time.*

He turned slowly from the window as he heard her stir. The smell of flowers hung heavy in the air. It was not lost on him that the card on the huge bouquet of roses was signed in a too-familiar scrawl, "Jared." *I knew she had to be pretty under all that black and blue,* he mused, *or Jared wouldn't be sending flowers.*

"It's after nine," she said as he checked her charts. "Do you always work this late? Shouldn't you be at home with your family?" She was really doing well, alive, alert, bruises healing nicely.

He was amused and pleased that she expressed concern for his wellbeing. "Doctor, doctor," he chuckled. "She's not out of bed yet, and she's all ready to doctor!"

"Will I be able to ski again ... dance?"

"Whoa! Not so fast! There's only one Miracle Worker and I'm not Him. Let's just concentrate on healing some ribs and vertebrae. We'll work on the walk in a few days when we get you a walking cast, and take it from there."

Chapter 2

Between Law and Grace

S he stirred as they entered the room. It seemed a bit
unusual for Dr. Braemer to be doing rounds in mid-
morning. She had grown accustomed to his late afternoon
or evening visits. And the young man with him? She
recognized Jeremy Paulson, one of her students from last
semester - the one who had driven the ski patrol.

"Hello, Dr. Braemer … Jeremy," she managed. "It's
nice of you to come."

He spoke softly, haltingly, "Dr. Rhee, I am so sorry for
what I did to you. You have been so good to me … getting
me the job and all. I … I…" his words faltered and she
noticed the considerable stress lines for so young a face.

"I don't blame you for suing me," he said, "but I've lost
my job on the ski hill and I don't have insurance to cover
this sort of thing, and I would like to know …."

"He would like to know what figure you are looking for
to compensate for damages," Dr. Braemer finished for him.

She sat stunned for a moment as if unable to comprehend what had just been said. "Excuse me," she managed at
last. "I don't seem to be quite awake this morning. I'm not

quite sure what we're talking about. Jeremy, could you get me a juice or a coke from the nurse at the desk so I can come alive." A few sips later, still wearing a puzzled look, she continued, "Now, what is this about suing, and why do you think I would do that?"

"Your lawyer has sent me a notice of your intention," the young man offered painfully.

"I really don't understand. I don't even have a lawyer. I haven't been wide enough awake to think, never mind to sue anyone." Then after a moment she asked, "Do you have such a notice with you?"

He pulled the crumpled paper from his pocket and presented it to her. He did indeed have such a notice - from Taylor, Taylor and Moore. She recognized the firm as one her father had used five or six years ago. She could not remember the nature of his business, perhaps a property acquisition. Now she sat dumfounded as she read of their intended action on her behalf, citing both Riverview Ski Slopes and Jeremy Paulson as Defendants.

"Oh my! Oh my! This is a mistake! I am sorry ... so very sorry! I have not authorized such a thing. I'll see that it is stopped at once!" Her short, choppy sentences tumbled out quickly as she tried to hide the anger that she felt rising in her chest. *How dare they do such a thing? Who do they think they are to presume on me to go along with such an action?* Outwardly, she continued, "I'm not looking for compensation from you, Jeremy. We were both at fault and you are certainly forgiven for your part in this."

Both men were caught a little off guard. Dr. Braemer was visibly relieved; Jeremy, close to tears, stammered, "How can you do that, Dr. Rhee? Forgive? Just like that? I could have killed you. I nearly did. I went after someone with a broken leg. He was gone when I got there and I thought I was the only one left on the hill. I ..." his voice broke.

"That's true, Jer. I'm not minimizing the seriousness of the situation; I know I could well have died. But I can forgive you because God has forgiven me a great deal, and *to whom much is given, much is also expected.* I am thankful you had presence of mind immediately following the accident. I understand your quick action kept me alive until I arrived at St. Michael's and Dr. Braemer took over. God surely had His hand on me that night; He used you both to save my life."

They stood silently for a moment, then she continued, "Suing you would accomplish nothing, Jeremy. It could well ruin your career ... your life. The world would be poorer by one incredibly gifted doctor. Besides, Dr. Braemer tells me that there could well be no lasting effects from the accident. Does it get better than that?"

He looked up. Then, almost imperceptibly, "Thank you, Dr. Rhee. Thank you."

"Aren't you observing a knee replacement this morning?" asked Dr. Braemer. "You can't afford to be late," he smiled, then lingered a few moments after the young doctor disappeared hurriedly down the hall.

"I want to thank you, too, Dr. Rhymer. Jeremy came to me this morning prepared to drop out of the program. He had called his father when he lost his job and was facing a law suit. His father was less than charitable and called him a few choice names. He was pretty broken up. I suggested he talk to you about the situation; you seem like a reasonable person and it really didn't seem like you to do this sort of thing. Besides, I thought I had kept you too sleepy ..." he broke off, a sheepish little grin playing about the corners of his mouth.

"Rascal!" she countered.

"Jeremy mentioned that you had gotten him the job at the ski hill. How does that work?"

"Well, yes ... and no. Actually, we have a deal with the ski people. We supply the interns with EMT training and pay their salary. The ski hill supplies the equipment and the job. This gives our interns first-hand experience, a work-related job, some funds to help them keep going in their chosen field. Also we try to have at least one or two ski teams ... get them in competition with other ski teams ... gives them some wholesome activity other than hanging around bars and ... if you know what I mean? I guess you know that we don't take just anybody. It takes a little doing to get to train at St. Michael's. You've probably noticed that Jeremy is a particularly sharp lad, and a very nice one at that. Isn't he specializing in Orthopedics?"

"Yeah. He's working with me and he really is a going concern. Medicine would be poorer without his kind."

"About the job. I suspect they may take him back if I give them a call. I didn't want to get his hopes up because I don't know for sure. But they won't get a sharper EMT, and my bet is that from now on they won't get a safer driver!"

He agreed, then rose to go, adding, "See you a little later when I make my rounds."

———

She looked up from the clutter of files that covered her bed and night table. "Sandra, hold my calls, the doctor has just arrived - give me ten or fifteen minutes. Thanks," she said, replacing the receiver.

Then turning her attention to the two men who had just entered, she joked, "I must be in worse shape than I thought to need both a doctor and a pastor. Am I about to get *last rights?*"

They both smiled and assured her she was doing well. "Looks to me like you're doing a little too well," suggested Dr. Braemer as he noted the jumble of files, "What's all this?"

"Just administration. Nothing invasive," she laughed.

"We have an idea that we'd like to run by you," began Pastor Bob. "The ski team will be having its final run on Olympia at the end of the month. We wondered if you would like to join us. Dr. Braemer has consented to be ski doctor; he could also be there in case you needed help. I thought it might be healthy to revisit the scene before leaving it go too long ..." he trailed off, noticing the look of disbelief on her face.

"You'll have a walking cast by then," cut in Dr. Braemer. "I would be happy to have you ride with me and show me where to go. Pastor Bob will need to be back in town early Saturday afternoon ..."

She sat motionless trying to comprehend that they really intended her to get out of bed and head for the ski hill. *With a married man, at that!* Her thoughts were confused as she pondered why her pastor would be promoting such a thing.

Finally, she managed, "That's very gracious of you both to be thinking of me, but I ... really ... I ... I would feel like a nuisance with all this, and I am wondering ... I guess I don't feel it would be appropriate for me to go there with you, Dr. Braemer."

He flushed slightly, then quickly assured her, "None of us would consider it an imposition. If you change your mind, we'd love to have you come."

Noticing that Dr. Braemer was now perusing her chart, the pastor took his leave with a quick, "See you tomorrow."

"We'd like to take that cast off tomorrow and get an X-ray. It may be a week early for a walking cast, but I'm sure we can take the pins out and make a more comfortable package. I really do expect you to have a walking cast in the next week or ten days. And I would like another round of blood work. Then, as an afterthought, he asked, "By the way, may I ask why you keep having your blood checked for HIV?"

"Of course you can. I want to make sure I don't have it, for the protection of my patients and colleagues."

"Why do you think you might?"

"I just got back from Africa before the ski accident. AIDS is everywhere. Many of the young mothers are infected. I need to make sure ..."

He interrupted, "But your chart shows you have it checked every few months."

"That's because I work on the streets."

"You do what?"

"Work on the streets."

"What does that mean?"

"You know ... with the prostitutes, drug users, street people." She was enjoying keeping him on the edge.

"So what nature does your work take?"

She laughed. He had finally cornered her. "We've established a little clinic there, and we give out needles, condoms, birth-control pills, and medications. We have a place to deliver babies ... they used to find them in dumpsters and garbage bags; now we are able to place some with an adoption agency. For a while we were allowed to take these cases to St. Mike's but after a great hue and cry, we had to find other means. Some of the doctors help from time to time, and some of the interns. Pastor Bob has a real gift for ministering to these kinds of people."

"Well, I'll be," he said softly.

He finished perusing her chart; then, since it was on his mind, he asked, "Why do you think it inappropriate to come up the ski hill with me?"

His straightforwardness took her by surprise. She hesitated briefly, then simply stated, "You are a very attractive man, Dr. Braemer. If I were your wife I would hardly care to loan you out for the week-end, no matter how charitable the cause. It wouldn't be fair to me, either," she finished, flushing.

"Ouch! Where did you get the idea that I was married?"

"I'm not sure. Something you said ..."

"Well, I'm not married. I am very single. Does that make a difference in your decision?"

"What can I say now?" she laughed.

"Say 'yes.'"

She hesitated. "Well, okay ... yes ... if I can get around on my own...if I can walk by then."

"In that case ... you'll walk," he said playfully. "And thanks for finding me attractive."

Chapter 3

Olympia

❧

"Your foot is healing very nicely; your walk ... really coming along, but I don't feel especially good about letting you out of here just yet. What are your plans? Do you intend to go back to work right away?"

He sounds just like my Dad, thought Rhea. "Well, I would like to try at least a few mornings per week," she offered hesitantly. "I can hardly go on a ski week-end and not show up for work."

He found himself forced to agree. Then noting that he would be gone most of next week, he added, "Your home address and phone number don't seem to be listed in the hospital directory. Would you like to give them to me so I can find you on Friday?"

"Don't you have my cell number? You can find me anywhere with that? And I don't know where I will be that afternoon. I may not be at home."

"You have a problem with being picked up at home? Shall I pick you up on the street corner, then?"

"O my no ... not the street corner. You may not recognize me with clothes on," she quipped.

He was taken aback, then recovering quickly, he countered, "Come on now; how many have you operated on with their clothes on?"

"Not any," she laughed. Then suggested, "Why not pick me up at the Wahl's? You know ... the Chief and Joan's house. Joan wants to look after me for a few days to make sure I don't overdo it. They're my *other parents*, you know."

"Very well. I should be there around 4:00 Friday. Keep it down to a trot," he reminded her, noting she was already getting her things together.

In spite of her good intentions she felt her heart skip a beat as the polished black sports car, with skis mounted, stopped in front. She had never seen him in sport clothes and he looked boyishly handsome. The doctor image had disappeared and she was not quite sure how they would relate on a non-professional level.

After some debate, she had settled on a pair of burgundy pants and matching sweater. They were reasonably stylish, yet comfortable. Besides, burgundy looked good on her; it accented the reddish highlights in her dark auburn hair. Her father had always liked both of his *Rheas* in burgundy. A twitch of pain streaked across her otherwise happy screen for a second or two.

His intended greeting turned into a low whistle. "You were right," he quipped; "I may not have recognized you in clothes."

Pretending not to notice her blush, he continued, "I've never been up Olympia; hope you don't mind navigating," and picking up her bag, he offered his arm to help her to the car.

She was surprised at how easily they conversed - how comfortable they were with each other. He asked about her week. Was it difficult for her to return to work for a few hours every day? They spoke about the course he had taught over the week at Princeton. A very promising group of medical students. Several always stand out above the rest. *I bet you were one of those when you were a med student*, she thought as she listened to his commentary.

The late afternoon sun was blinding as they started up the mountain. Noting him shielding his eyes, she offered her Ray Bans. "Better the driver should wear them," she suggested; then added, "I guess the color is rather feminine but ... on you they'll look masculine." He smiled and accepted her offer.

"I must have left mine somewhere," he said. "I haven't found them in a month."

They stopped for supper at her usual spot - a small Austrian restaurant perched on the side of the mountain, nestled in spruce and ash. Rhea always thought it looked so at home that it might have grown there. She liked stopping at Wilhelm's, she explained, "The food is good, atmosphere relaxing, and besides, it's just about the right distance from town to make me feel like I'm on vacation."

Wilhelm greeted them warmly. A place by the fire for Dr. Rhee and her friend, and how good it was to see her alive and walking, he babbled on happily.

"The wiener schnitzel is delectable here, Dr. Braemer," she offered as they scanned the menu.

"Great, it's one of my favorites." Then, after a moment, he added, "People who know me really well call me *Michael.*"

"And people who don't know you very well, but would like to ... can they call you *Michael*, too?"

"Indeed, they can."

"Then *Michael* it is."

"And I hear most folk calling you *Dr. Rhee*. Is that how you like to be addressed?"

"It's mostly the interns call me that. Folk who know me really well call me *Rhea*." They smiled at each other sharing the humor.

"You seem to be good friends with Pastor Bob. How did you get to know him?" she asked.

"Well, he brought you down the hill in the ambulance and stayed with us all night while we worked and prayed. But I had actually met him in church a few weeks before that. He invited me to go out for lunch and we enjoyed each other's company. We've been keeping in touch and I'm appreciating him more all the time. We were both needing a good friend."

"Are you a believer, then?" she asked.

"Sure enough! I came to faith in Christ at summer camp when I was 10. Actually Jared and I were there together and we both came to the Lord following the campfire on the same night."

"Are we talking about Dr. Jared McCaig?" she asked with a note of incredulity in her voice.

"We are. Jared and I grew up together, started college, roomed together for a time. Why are you so surprised?"

She didn't know how to explain what she was feeling. Finally, she suggested, "Well, you are very different from each other; I have noted a bit of rivalry, or maybe competition there from remarks he's made in the last few weeks. It would seem like an unlikely match."

"You're right about that. We did challenge each other - maybe still do. Neither of us had a brother, so it was more like sibling rivalry. I hadn't seen him for nearly ten years, and was a little surprised to find him still competing with me."

"He's an excellent obstetrician and gynecologist," she offered, "and we do work together very well, though it took a while to get the teamwork going."

"Glad to hear it," he responded as they rose to go.

The ski hill was lit up for the evening run when they arrived. Skiers swarmed the hill like ants, Rhea thought. She was surprised to find herself a little fearful as she watched from the safety of the car. Though she remembered nothing of the accident, she felt a strange sense of foreboding. She had accompanied Pastor Bob on one last trip to look for a lost camera; then confident that they were the only ones left on the hill, she had raced him down. A few yards behind her, he had watched the whole scene with horror.

I know they wanted me to come back and face my fears, she told herself, *but it may be more traumatic for Pastor Bob than for me.*

She settled easily into her room. It had been a long day. The swimming pool outside her door boasted a hot tub and she decided on a quick soak before retiring. As she struggled into her swim suit she noted that the incisions around her ribs were still plenty sore. Fortunately, her old one-piece suit covered them quite nicely.

Glancing through the drapes as she prepared to leave the room, she noted the empty pool, then spotted Michael and Bob. She watched as they took turns from the high diving board. They were well matched ... well-built ... .muscular ... obviously enjoying each other's company ... like brothers. They swam effortlessly. She considered again whether she should hot tub ... lest she intrude on something special; still she felt like a peeping tom watching them through the drapes. At length, she decided to slip in quickly while they swam, and draping herself in a towel, she made her way to the tub. The cast fell off easily as she loosened the velcro strapping. She carefully eased her aching body into the hot water, laid back and closed her eyes.

Her thoughts continued on the two swimmers ... two very special men in her life. They were certainly equals - probably about the same age ... same height ... both so incredibly masculine ... personable ... thoughtful ... *So why do I feel such chemistry with one and not the other?* she wondered.

She woke slowly, hearing quick, agitated voices. "I must have fallen asleep," she gasped, trying to sit up. Her strength had evaporated and she felt weak and sick.

"We have to get her out of here," Michael said quickly; then turning to Rhea, "I'm going to lift you. Can you put your arms around my neck?" He lifted her gently as Bob draped the towel over her dripping body. Quickly, he carried her to her room.

"I'll need to check her blood pressure," he said as he dashed for his bag. "Can you get her something to drink?"

"Your blood pressure is dangerously low ... your heart racing. I'm concerned about that lung! Good thing we discovered you when we did! You're dehydrated ... need fluids ... need to get that temperature down. I should have cooled you off in the swimming pool ... didn't want to risk it." He spoke quickly, his short, choppy sentences betraying the anxiety he felt. He continued to lecture as he lifted her head and encouraged her to drink the orange juice. "And don't you ever go in there when I'm not here," he finished with an authoritative note in his voice.

You sure do sound like my Dad, Rhea thought to herself as she lay back. In a half whisper, she simply repeated, "Doctor, doctor."

"Mike, we need to get her out of that wet suit and into bed."

"Out of here, you two," she scolded, jokingly. "Give me a few minutes and I'll look after it myself."

"Maybe we should get dressed, Bob." Then turning to Rhea, "I'll be back in a few minutes and I'll stay until that blood pressure normalizes."

"That's not necessary. Why don't you two go and have a hot tub and a good night's rest. You'll need all the help you can get when you take on that ski team tomorrow. I really can take my own blood pressure, you know."

After considerable urging, they left her and retreated to the hot tub. They stretched out in the comfort of the hot water, enjoying being together, not feeling the need to make polite conversation. "No wonder she fell asleep in here," Michael commented. "We'd better watch it or we'll still be here in the morning."

Bob nodded and smiled. They relaxed quietly for a few moments, then Michael ventured, "Can we talk?"

"Sure enough."

"I don't know if this is a good time to ask, but can you tell me about the accident?"

"Rhea's accident?"

"Is that too painful to talk about?"

"Plenty painful. I'm actually wondering how I will react when I come by that spot tomorrow. I'm glad you're here, Mike." He paused. His voice quivered when he next spoke, "I coaxed her into making one more trip up the hill to get my camera. We found it right where I had left it ... on the outcropping where we had stopped to admire the view. We were about to start down when she whipped a snowball. You have to watch her all the time - she's just full of it!! I turned at the wrong time and she hit me square in the face, surprising herself more than me. She knew she was in for it, and took off down the hill with me in pursuit. We came to the 'Y.'" He paused again, his hands over his face, and then, "I saw it all. I'll never forget the sickening thud of the impact, her body hurtling through the air, flailing wildly down the hill, equipment flying in all directions; finally smashing into a tree, and lying motionless. I was sure she was gone."

Michael sat quietly. He had not realized the depth of the well he had opened. "I'm sorry," he managed at last. "I had no idea how bad it was for you. I saw the end product, but could hardly imagine how it came about."

Bob continued as though there had been no interlude, "I couldn't move. I'm an EMT and I couldn't think of what to do. I just stood there numb. Then I prayed, 'O God, O God, O God.' I could hardly believe the presence of mind of that young doctor on the ski patrol. He just whipped that thing down the hill and took charge. I finally got it together and went after him - got there in time to see him slit her suit and start applying CPR. She was alive - or almost! We slid her onto the toboggan and started down. Meantime, he ordered the lodge to alert St. Michael's. I'm still amazed that we made it to the hospital that night. I drove. He took charge of her in the ambulance. The rest is history ..." he broke off as if reliving the whole scene, then spoke again, even more softly, "I'm glad you were there, Doctor Mike. She might not have made it otherwise."

"Wow! Wow! That sounds pretty wild! I'm glad I was there, too. I had just gotten home and was wondering whether I was too tired to eat supper, when I felt this incredible urge to get back to the hospital. It was strange - like I couldn't help myself. I got there just in time - I pulled in behind you." After a moment, he suggested, "She's pretty special to you, isn't she?"

Bob nodded but did not reply.

After a few minutes, Michael probed, "You seem to have a close relationship?"

Again Bob nodded, then offered, "She's a very special little lady. So full of life, sparkle, love for everybody. We work together incredibly well. She organizes everything - the church - the hospital - the town. When I came three years ago, things at the church were pretty chaotic. She was away for a couple of months following her parents' death. She came over to meet me when she got back and we really hit it off. I wouldn't know what to do without her."

"May I ask if you're in love with her, Bob? I know my question is a little brash, but ..."

"I'm not sure how to answer that, Mike. I'm not sure what *in love* means. I think that has to involve two people. In that case, I would have to say 'no.' We have never had a dating relationship. Our associations always revolve around ministry of one sort or another ... not that we don't have a good time together ... just that ... well ... that's all there is. It took me a year to realize that was all there was going to be. I love her dearly, and I know she loves me, but she just doesn't have it for me. No chemistry. Like I'm a brother. She keeps me at arms length ... always calls me *Pastor Bob*... keeps it on a professional level.

Michael sat quietly, not quite sure how to proceed, then asked, "How would you feel if ... I mean ... how would you feel about ...?"

"... about your relationship with Rhea?" Bob finished for him.

"Well, I don't really have a relationship with her at this point, but I'd be lying if I said I wasn't interested."

"You don't think you have a relationship? If her eyes would ever light up for me like they do for you, I'd be married ... with kids!! I used to wonder if she knew *how* to flirt. Then I saw her with you. She knows how, all right, but she doesn't waste in on just anybody. I'd be lying, too, if I said I wasn't jealous. But since I have to be honest ... I have to say she's not my girl. How can I not give you my blessing?"

After a moment, he added, "I should warn you, though. I haven't seen her date anybody in the three years that I've been here. I guess I have wondered why she would need a husband, anyway; she seems so self-sufficient."

Michael was not prepared for his honesty and humility. He was overwhelmed at the love he felt for Bob. He had never had a real brother, and Bob was closer to him than he could have imagined a brother to be. He sensed his pain and felt at least partly responsible.

Suspecting as much, Bob continued, "I'm glad it's you, Mike. I couldn't watch her walk away with just anybody. Thanks for being so sensitive to my feelings ... and so up front about yours. I know God has someone for me ... somewhere ... sometime. In His time, He'll put it all together."

The distant rumble grew louder as doors banged and the skiers clomped in, shedding jackets and heavy boots. "Let's get out of here before they get in," Michael suggested. Then reaching out his hand to Bob, his voice husky, he simply said, "Thank you, Bob. Thank you." Then added, "We need to check on her before we go to bed."

She sat by the fire with a second cup of coffee. From time to time she glanced up from the magazine to watch the skiers on the slopes, yet she felt no compulsion to join them. The warm sunshine flooding in the window gave her a feeling of wellbeing and contentment. *A great day to be alive,* she decided.

"Well, just look who's up and about. You'll join us for lunch?" She jumped as she recognized Bob's voice.

"Lunch! I'm just finishing off breakfast," she laughed, holding up her coffee mug. "But I'd love to join you all the same."

"Good morning, Ski Doctor," she said, noting Michael's brilliant yellow outfit with the bold black lettering, 'SKI DOCTOR.' Obviously, he had done this before. She cringed inwardly remembering her remarks to him about the challenges of Olympia. She had suggested that the students hadn't nicknamed it *Olympia* for nothing. Her concern for his welfare had prompted her to ask if he was a really good skier. "Fair to middlin,'" he had replied, and she remembered thinking that he would have to do better than that.

The morning run had gone well. No serious incidents so far. She wondered how Bob had coped with the scene of the accident, but neither of them mentioned it, and she thought it best to let them have their privacy.

"Good to see Jeremy back on patrol," Bob commented as they ate hurriedly.

It seemed only minutes and they were gone - Michael back up the hill, with a quick, "See you at supper" - Pastor Bob heading home to complete preparations for the Lord's Day. *Wish I could be there for service tomorrow,* thought Rhea. *It seems like such a long time since I've been to church. Maybe I should have gone home with Pastor Bob.*

Chapter 4

Down from the Mountain

They sat facing each other at her favorite table near the fire. Wilhelm, with his usual fuss and flair greeted them warmly. "The baron of beef is very good tonight," he assured them, then added, "Doctor Ree's favorite, yes?"

As they waited for their order, she noticed the stress lines had disappeared entirely from Michael's face. *He really needed a week-end like this,* she told herself.

As if reading her thoughts, he said, "I haven't enjoyed a week-end so much in years. Six months of stress just drained away."

"It's good to see you so relaxed. You seem to keep a pretty wild schedule. Are you always like that?"

"No...well...yes. I guess the last ten years or so have been pretty hectic. I have received a number of research grants from some prominent universities. With that comes the obligation to teach medical students. It's a privilege, too. I enjoy the whole package, but since I prefer to keep up with surgical practice in the hospital ... it keeps me out of trouble."

"By the way, I need to say 'thank you' for rescuing me the other night. I'm embarrassed that it was necessary. Guess I'm not as fit as I would like to think."

He chuckled, obviously pleased that she had brought up the subject. "I'm glad I was there. You really shouldn't go up that hill without me, you know," he teased. Then added, "So you're a competitive swimmer?"

Noting the questioning look on her face, he explained, "the swimsuit you were wearing."

"Oh my, no! That harkens back to high-school days. It was all I could find to cover my scars."

"You had to cover up my fancy stitching?"

She laughed. "Well, I have a lot more healing to do before I go on display. And actually, I have a few muscles that will need to be tightened up in that area."

"You should heal without noticeable scarring." He went on to explain the methods they used to close the puncture caused by the splintered rib. "The incision we had to make shouldn't give you a problem, either," he added.

They ate slowly, savouring the warmth of the fire, and each other's company. She glanced up from time to time to find him watching her.

"Gravy on my face?" she asked.

"No. No, nothing like that."

Noting that she continued to look at him questioningly, he simply stated, "Rhea, you are a very beautiful woman. Every day you were in the hospital you seemed to get more lovely than the day before. I had a terrible time not saying so ... just as well I didn't since you thought I was married."

She smiled. "Thank you, Michael," she said, and he noticed that she blushed slightly.

"Tell me about yourself. How does a little lady like you get to be the Director of Obstetrics and Gynecology in a prestigious hospital like St. Mike's?"

"Well," she began, "My parents were medical missionaries, mostly in Africa, but they did establish medical clinics in other countries as well. I spent a lot of my formative years in Africa. Dad was a doctor, but Mom was a nurse and mid-wife. I helped her deliver babies in all kinds of questionable circumstances. I delivered a baby all by myself when I was 13 and nobody was home. The little girl that they brought in was probably about 12 and wasn't developed enough to deliver. It was scary, but I just did what I had helped Mom do and we all got through it okay. I guess my love of medicine was born there; also my desire to help the hurting ... the helpless. We didn't have a lot of reading material, so my brother and I spent a lot of time in Dad's medical books. By the time I got into pre-med I was really familiar with a lot of medical terms and practice. It wasn't nearly the challenge I had expected. I guess we all knew that I would eventually end up in obstetrics and gynecology."

His face showed his surprise. It hadn't occurred to him that she had grown up on the mission field. "So where did you learn to swim and ski?" he asked, puzzled.

"Actually we learned to ski and swim when we were children in Canada. Then my folks decided we needed to come home when my brother and I were in high-school. Jonathon was two years older and in Grade 11. He had gone to boarding school for two years prior to our coming home. Mom and Dad didn't think it the best plan, and decided to re-establish in Canada where we could be together as a family. It was a happy time for me, a real blast! I got involved in everything in high-school."

He smiled and nodded, remembering his own high-school days.

"So what brought you to St. Mike's?"

"My Father. He and the Chief had been looking for a small city or rural hospital where they could train young people in research and technology. Since the Government was planning to close down St. Mike's, they took it over. The Reimer Foundation has pumped millions into making it what it is. Dad knew I was looking to finish my time at Women's Hospital, and he really felt I would be happy here. They had no obstetrical department at that time, so I was the one who set it up."

"And you're enjoying the location ... the small city? It almost seems rural."

"The location was ideal for their purposes - just the right distance from either Toronto or Montreal, an airport with several flights daily, an hour and a half from the ski hill. Dad always felt that orthopedic surgeons should train in the vicinity of a ski hill."

Before he could question her further, she invited, "So ... tell me about yourself. You obviously ski and swim at a professional level, and must be renowned as a researcher and surgeon for the Chief to go after you the way he did. Is there anything you don't do well?"

"Nothing I'm going to tell you about," he said with a chuckle. "After listening to your exciting story, mine is pretty uninteresting ... mundane. Dad is an architect, Mom a nurse and music teacher. I'm three years older than my sister, Tracy. We always got along well and stood up for each other. She married about four years ago ... an old buddy of mine."

"So what took you into medicine ... with your Dad an architect?" she stopped as she realized she had hit a sore spot.

"Actually, I'm more like my Mom. She's compassionate, caring - a nurse. She's musical and loves the arts. My first year at university was devastating for me. Dad wanted me to be an architect and I tried ... believe me, I tried ... but it just wasn't for me. In the first semester I joined the ski team and we went to Austria and Switzerland during the school breaks. I watched a surgeon set a broken leg where the bone had come right through the flesh. I knew then that medicine was where I belonged. I took the course he offered in Emergency Medical Training, but I was afraid to tell Dad. I knew he would be disappointed in me." He broke off, realizing he had revealed more than he intended.

"That must have been very painful for you."

He nodded, then asked, "Do I understand you lost your parents a few years ago?"

"Yes," she said, a twinge of pain crossing her face. "It's very painful for me to talk about. Can we leave that for another time?"

"I'm so sorry. I lost some good friends a while back and I'm not anywhere near over it."

Then changing the subject, he asked, "So, how does a very beautiful and accomplished lady like you stay single?"

"Not by dating attractive doctors, for sure!" she quipped.

"Something wrong with doctors?"

"Not really.."

"So?" he agitated.

"So, the right one just hasn't come along."

"And if he did?"

"You're a rascal," she laughed. "Are you a cousin to Barbara Walters?"

"Doesn't it take a rascal to know one? What do you mean 'a cousin to Barbara Walters'?"

"You know, the journalist who interviews celebrities around the world, and gets them to say things they haven't even thought of yet."

He laughed. "You got out of that one nicely. But there is still a question on the table."

She gave him a questioning look as he continued, "Rhea, are you enjoying our time together as much as I am? Will you let me see you again?"

She had hoped he would want to see her again, but now finding herself slightly bashful, she managed, "I ... yes, Michael, I would like that; I am enjoying our time together very much ..." She stopped in mid-sentence.

"But?" he asked, sensing there was more to the story.

"Well, it's just that once I'm back on my feet I have a very loaded schedule."

"The doctors are all lined up? Do I need to take a number?"

She stifled a chuckle. "No ... no ... nothing like that. I'm just very involved in a whole lot of things - committees, meetings, the street ministry, etc. I have commitments that I need to keep. I guess I should ask how patient you are. After next week-end I won't have a lot of free evenings."

He hesitated, trying to determine whether she really wanted to see him, or was looking for a way out. Finally, he asked, "Can we get together over lunch? The week-end? What about Sundays?"

"I'm sure we can work it out. I'm really sorry my schedule is so full. I guess it was my antidote to grief; it seemed to hurt less if I was busy helping others. And ... I really didn't expect to have a gentleman friend drop into my life," she said smiling. "I'm off every evening next week and the week-end, before I'm back on my regular schedule, so if you have time ..."

"I'll make time. I'll be gone most of this coming week; should be home on Friday. Can we have some time together Saturday and Sunday?"

She nodded as he searched her face, *Does she really want to see me?* he wondered.

As if she had heard his thoughts, she leaned slightly toward him, her eyes soft and warm, "Michael," she said quietly, "I am enjoying getting to know you. If I didn't want to see you again, I would say so. I don't play games."

"Thank you for telling me," he said. "I appreciate knowing that."

"You have questions all over your face," she noted with a smile.

He hesitated ... wanting to know ... afraid of offending. "Dare I ask if you have other relationships ... if you are seeing anyone else?" he asked.

"I don't mind your asking. I haven't had a relationship with anyone since high school; in fact I haven't even dated since I came to St. Mike's."

"Why is that?"

"Probably a lot of reasons. Losing my folks left me pretty empty emotionally ..." she paused a few moments before going on, "and then the gossip factor is always a consideration ... but, more than that, I guess I just never met anyone that I ..."

"Not even Bob? May I ask how you feel about him, Rhea?"

"He's a precious brother. I don't think I have ever met anyone quite like him. The Chief heard him preach somewhere and encouraged the church to give him a call. He eventually came, after he had completed his doctorate. He's God's gift to this community, and for that matter to St. Michael's. He's powerful in the pulpit and on the street. I've really enjoyed working with him these three years. I love him dearly," she finished.

He was silent for a moment, then asked, "So you've known each other for three years and you love him, but...?"

She read his question at once. "But, I'm not in love with Bob. I know he would have liked that to change, but he is so much a brother ... I just couldn't think of him any other way. No chemistry, I guess I would say. He needs a wife, but I'm not her. I'm way too 'out in front'... not pastor's wife material at all. He could never handle me. There were times when I wished it were different - he would make a wonderful husband - but it wouldn't have been fair to either of us."

He nodded, relieved that she felt just as Bob thought she did. Then he confessed, "I'm really glad to hear that, Rhea. Bob and I have become really close and I appreciate him so very much ... I could never hurt him."

She had an impish look on her face as she confided, "I don't usually play cupid, but I do know someone who would make a perfect wife for him. I've been trying to get her to visit me for some time and I think I've finally got it arranged."

He looked amused as she continued, "My cousin, Lynda. She's a nurse, a year younger than me. She's been wanting to do her mid-wifery course here for the last two years and I think she's finally coming. She's very talented, musical, gracious ... everything a pastor's wife should be ... and she's *gorgeous!*

They laughed together. "So when do we get to meet this little vision of loveliness?"

"You don't. I'm keeping her away from you."

He grinned, obviously pleased that she thought him worth protecting.

"She'll spend the month of September with me in Africa, then come home with me," she continued. "Of course, I won't tell them about each other; that's too much like a set-up."

Then noticing the time, she exclaimed, "Michael, we need to go. We've been here nearly three hours." The restaurant was nearly empty. She noticed that Wilhelm was no longer in the kitchen, and young Willie had taken over.

They looked up as he approached their table. Had Dr. Rhee seen their newly decorated rooms, he enquired. She had not. Perhaps they would like to try one for the night.

Stifling her embarrassment, she responded, "Thank you, Willie, but you know I never have time to stay over night. And beside, Dr. Braemer is a colleague, not my husband."

He backed off as a much-amused Michael said under his breath, "We'll come back when we're married."

"You really are a rascal," she accused.

"You handled that very well." Then, making no effort to hide his amusement, he added, "I'd better get you home before they put us to bed."

"So where am I taking you?" he asked as they got under-way. "Do I get to take you home, or do I have to drop you on the corner?"

"You can take me home," she said, ignoring the amusement in his voice.

"Do you live in an apartment?"

"No. I have a house. I'll show you where to go."

"You live in a house? All by yourself?"

"Yes."

"Why is that?"

"Cause I'm not married."

"Rhea!" he exclaimed, with a note of exasperation. She had a way of making him ask for every detail.

She laughed. "It's too long a story to tell you tonight. I'll tell you all about it another time."

She admired the way he drove ... confident without being careless. They were almost home. She wondered how he would react when he saw her house.

"It really isn't as big as it looks," she apologized as he swung into the driveway. He sat staring ... speechless. *At least a half million*, he estimated looking at the beautiful structure set back from the street and banked by oak and spruce He was suddenly unsure of himself ... what to say, afraid to ask.

"We purchased this property the year before my parents died," she explained . We decided as a family to make

45

a retreat center where we could practise and minister to the hurting ..." she broke off as he sat silently ... looking. "The contractor had already started so I let him finish the first phase; it's more than I need, but a half-finished structure ..." again she stopped in mid-sentence as he continued to sit quietly.

Sensing he needed to respond, he finally offered, "It's very beautiful ... maybe a mite big for such a little lady." He was glad she couldn't read his thoughts - *Bob was right. Why would anyone as self-sufficient as this want a man?*

"Michael," she said, turning toward him. "I want to thank you for encouraging me to come this week-end. I haven't enjoyed myself this much in years." Then turning abruptly, she opened the door and started for the house.

Finally, coming alive, he grabbed her bag and followed. "Rhea, I'm sorry. Let me open that for you," he said, taking her key. He berated himself for being so clumsy. He had hoped to sit for awhile in the car ... take her in his arms ... hold her close. He had botched that pretty badly.

She was close to him now. He turned the key, then reaching out, he took her gently in his arms. "Rhea," he whispered, "I've so enjoyed getting to know you. Can I see you Friday if I'm back on time? Maybe we could go for supper?"

She nodded. "How will you get to the airport tomorrow?"

"I usually leave my car there."

"I'd be glad to drive you - deliver and pick-up," she offered. "Your car can stay here; I'm half way to the airport from your place."

"I'd really appreciate that, if it works for you. I have to leave around one." He pulled her close, wanting terribly to kiss her; then, deciding he had pushed it far enough for one day, he reluctantly let her go.

Chapter 5

A Healing Place

I t had been a brutal week ... long days ... short, sleepless nights. He didn't do well on these trips. He was glad he had finally finished at least one commitment. He smiled as his thoughts centered on Rhea. She had given him her unlisted number. That was satisfying ... he had succeeded where a whole lot of others had failed. He enjoyed calling her this week; she always seemed glad to hear from him. Now he looked forward to seeing her, having her meet him at the airport. If only he didn't feel so wretched!

They greeted each other warmly. He was surprised when she directed him toward her Mercedes ... probably five years old, he estimated. *Interesting,* he thought, *that such a little lady would have a full-size car ... and such a big house!* He shivered in the rain, realizing his top coat was in his own vehicle, and wondering why she hadn't brought it.

"I'm more comfortable driving my own car; hope you don't mind," she said as if in answer to a question. "You look terribly weary," she added with a note of concern in her voice; "Are you okay?"

"Not really. I have a nasty headache. I didn't eat or sleep well. Have you had lunch? Can I take you somewhere to eat?"

"Would you settle for a bite at my place? And maybe we can tend to that headache?"

"I'd love to eat at your place; and thanks for not sending me home. Do you have tylenol?"

She laughed, "Oh my! I'd never send you home ... I might put you to bed. I'm not much for tylenol, though. Can we try a hot soup and a snooze by the fire before we go for the drugs? I'm sorry my schedule got a little out of hand today. We had an emergency at work, and I didn't get home on time to make the lasagnas I promised to the folk down at the Ark - that's where they feed the homeless, you know. I try to help a couple times a month."

He listened quietly. *Wonder how she's going to work a date with me into all of this?* he mused.

As if continuing to read his thoughts, she added, "They'll pick up the lasagnas around 5:00; then we can either go out for supper or we can barbeque some steaks and eat by the fire. You look chilled; my guess is, you've probably eaten out enough for one week."

"You got that right. Staying in out of the rain sounds great!" he added as she swung into the driveway and proceeded around to the side of the house. The garage door opened and she pulled in beside his Corvette; the third bay was completely filled with packing boxes.

The house surprised him. It was warm and homey and hospitable. And familiar in a way that tugged at his heart. The furnishings were expensive, but not ostentatious. *Like Rhea*, he thought.

"Do you care for clam chowder?" she asked, "or could I make you some chicken soup?"

"Chowder sounds wonderful."

"Good, I've just finished a kettleful. It's all ready."

"Make yourself comfortable in one of the recliners, there," she invited, as she brought the chowder. "The arms flip open and you can set your mug in there."

"This looks like a whole kitchen," he noted as he opened the caddy.

"Indeed. And the other arm has a telephone, heater and vibrator. My brother and I gave these to our parents one year for their anniversary. They do about everything but dance. My Dad liked to retreat to his for an hour when he came from work. He always said that we might get battered by the world, but home should be a healing place."

There it was again, he thought; *that familiar note, 'home is a healing place.' Sounds like something Doc Matt would have said.*

"Would you enjoy a nap by the fire while I finish in the kitchen?" she asked as they finished the hot bread sticks and chowder. "If you're comfortable taking off your jacket and tie, I could get you a warm blanket ..." she paused to see how he was taking her suggestion.

"Doctor, doctor," he said with a warm smile. "I haven't been fussed over this much in years. It sounds good to me."

She retreated to the kitchen after turning on the CD player. "We'll keep it low to drown out the kitchen noises," she said. "Do you like classical?"

He stretched out in the oversize chair, feeling relaxed and comfortable under the warm cover. The sounds and aroma from the kitchen made him feel like a small boy again. *This is what home is supposed to be,* he thought. His mind drifted back over the last few months. He determined when he came to Riverview to buy a home rather than take another apartment. He searched for weeks. The real estate agent had finally found exactly what he had described. He remembered standing there ... looking at the emptiness; furniture would fill the empty house, he knew ... but it wouldn't fill his empty heart. It would take two to make it a home. He was tired of having no one to come home to, no one to care whether he was hungry or sick. He had returned to his suite disconsolate.

The night of the accident he had come from the hospital, tired, hungry, and more lonely than he could remember. He picked up his Bible and turned again to the second chapter of Genesis. He noticed something he had not seen before. After Adam had named the livestock, the birds and the beasts, he found no one suitable to be his mate. It was only at this point - when Adam realized his need - that God met him. God created a helper suited to his needs.

He had sat for a long time ... thinking ... praying earnestly for direction ... asking God to lead him to the one he had for him. He thought about his high-school days, the girls he had known, dated, been mildly interested in. He kept going ... college days ... graduate school ... no one!

Then the sound of the siren, and the feeling of urgency to get to the hospital! And the feeling that somehow this was a divine appointment. He arrived behind the ambulance. It had taken nearly two weeks before he wondered whether this was in fact God's answer to that plea - two weeks in which he watched Rhea come alive and grow more lovely every day. "Thank you, God," he whispered, as he had many times since then. He hoped the day would come when he could tell her about God's answer to his prayer. But not yet. *I wonder if she'll still want a relationship with me when she knows all about me,* he pondered as he drifted off.

He wakened as he heard steps in the kitchen and instructions being given in low tones.

Must be the pick-up from the mission, he decided. *Can it really be 5:00?* He felt rested, refreshed, his headache and shivers gone. *Home really is a healing place,* he thought as he lay quietly surveying the furnishings, the book shelf, the fireplace. *Funny*, he mused, *the empty spot above the mantel looks like ... maybe a picture has been removed!*

She tiptoed in and settled near the fire. "Good morning," she smiled, as he stirred. "You were really weary. How are you feeling? Supper's ready, except for the steaks. I didn't want to put them on till you were up."

"Can I do them?" he offered, as she moved a small table near the fire and prepared to set it. She willingly agreed, and heated the grill while he washed up.

"Rhea," he said, after he had offered thanks for the meal, "this is really special! You are so thoughtful! I feel like a little boy again, being taken care of. I haven't barbequed or had stuffed potatoes in years."

"I'm glad you're feeling better; I think we're all little people when we're sick. Thanks for letting me play doctor. I'm glad you were comfortable - being here, I mean."

The CD had switched from classical to old-time waltz and two-steps, enticing them to dance. "They're golden-oldies from my parents," she explained. "I loved to watch them dance ; they enjoyed each other so much."

"Do you dance then? Would you like to?" He asked hopefully.

"Well ... I used to, but I'm not sure what this will do," she looked down at her foot. "Maybe we could finish supper while we wait for the next disk. It has some slow waltzes; I might do better at a more sedentary pace."

"Your home is very lovely," he offered, "like you." Then asked, "What did you mean, it isn't finished?"

"Well, it would have had six bedrooms, a pool, hot-tub, exercise room, workshop, etc. It was far too large for one person, so I built only what I thought I could use and look after. I have two bedrooms, living and dining rooms, baths, family room, my office, a patio of sorts. I had to have it up to the standard imposed for this part of the city; otherwise I might have made it quite different. I have two more years to develop the rest of the property before the city comes down on me. The contractor who did the first phase of the house is anxious to complete it. And there is a developer who would like to get his hands on some of the property and I think he's behind the pressure the city is putting on me."

"So, will you finish it in two years?"

"I really don't know. I have sought advice and prayed a great deal. When I built three years ago, I hoped I might marry before the five years expired. If my husband lived somewhere else, I would sell and go. If he wanted to live here, we could finish the house together; that way he would feel like it was *our* home rather than mine ..." she broke off, embarrassed that she had revealed her heart.

"So this husband ... would he have to be a contractor? Or would the son of an architect have a chance?"

"You're embarrassing me, Michael. I hadn't really thought of choosing by occupation. Isn't it time to dance?"

He smelled clean and fresh, like soap and aftershave. She was delighted how easily they moved together ... how much her injured foot remembered. He held her close and murmured, "Tell me this is going to go on forever."

"Just the first 45 minutes of forever."

"Pity," he quipped.

His arms tightened as the waltz ended. She resisted slightly. "Am I doing something wrong?" he asked softly.

She shook her head. "Why do you ask?"

"You've been keeping me at arms length for quite a while."

She chuckled, noting his arms holding her too close to dance. "You're going to break my ribs," she warned, pushing back.

"Can I patch them up again?"

"Uh-huh. Just before I sue you."

They shared the humor as the music started again. *I wish this would go on forever, too*, she thought, and found herself giving in to the pressure to snuggle into his shoulder ... his neck.

"Rhea," he murmured, trailing kisses ... her temple ... her cheek ... the corner of her mouth; he paused as though waiting for permission. She turned her mouth to meet him. He kissed her then ... gently at first ... then long and passionately. "Rhea, beautiful Rhea," he whispered.

"Michael," she responded softly, as they held each other close, forgetting the dance.

Am I competing for your affection?" he asked, as she pulled away.

"No, Michael, no. I would never do that."

"So?" he questioned.

"It's just that ... well ... I really don't know you. I don't even know your middle name..."

"I'm Michael Lee Braemer." Then after a moment, "Surgeon."

"I'm familiar with the scalpel. It's the man inside that I want to get at."

"Are you afraid of me?"

"Not really ... it's ... the chemistry ... all those red blood cells ..."

"Doctor, doctor," he laughed. "Who else would worry about blood cells? What if I promise to make them behave?"

"Maybe it's not just yours I'm concerned about."

She felt his smile on the side of her cheek, as he suggested, "Then maybe we can agree together ...?"

She nodded. Then added, "Michael, I need to get off this foot. It's had quite a workout today."

"I'm sorry. I'd forgotten," he said, scooping her up and carrying her to the couch. "Let me massage it for you," Elevating it with a cushion on his lap, he worked the swollen joint slowly, soothingly, till he felt her muscles relax.

"Will I see you tomorrow?" he asked.

"I'm free. Afternoons off this week have been a big help. What do you have in mind?"

"I'll have to find a laundromat in the morning, so I'll have something to wear to work. I've been away two Thursdays in a row and missed my laundry time in the apartment block. Once that's done, I'm free for the day. Maybe we could drive up the river and explore, have supper together somewhere along the way." he looked at her hopefully.

"Sounds good. Want to come for breakfast and bring your laundry?" she asked. "My equipment is free and handy to the garage. You can start it before we eat and we'll go whenever it's done. It would give us a little more time," she added, "since it may be limited in the next few weeks."

He took his leave then, holding her close, kissing her gently. "I'm afraid to let you go," he whispered, "for fear I wake up and find this was a dream."

Chapter 6

Of Love and War

She hummed softly as she started the coffee and put out cereal, bagels, creme cheese, fruit salad; then smiled thinking of his call a few minutes ago. He would be a half hour later than planned; Jeremy had asked him to see a patient before he left for the day. He sounded excited - that *little boy* part of him she loved.

He dropped his bags as she opened the door and gathered her in his arms. As she snuggled close and lifted her mouth for his kiss, his eyes met hers - long and searchingly. After a moment he kissed her lightly, and let her go.

"What's wrong, Michael?" she asked, sensing that something was amiss. "Something wrong at the hospital?" He shook his head.

She showed him where to start the laundry and waited to pour the coffee.

He was too quiet. Something had definitely happened since his phone call an hour ago. Or maybe he had changed his mind about wanting to spend the day with her. They would need to get to the bottom of this.

"Michael," she began, "we don't have to do this today ... I mean ... if you've changed your mind ..."

"Rhea, No. Don't do this," he said, "I haven't changed my mind."

"Did something happen since you called me?"

"Yes, I guess I would say that."

"Well ... can you tell me about it?" She was at a loss.

He sat silently for a few moments, then, "Rhea," he reached for her hand across the table, "are you having a relationship with someone else? You can tell me, you know."

"Michael," she said indignantly. "That's the third time you've asked me that. I told you the truth the first time. Why would I lie?" Then after a moment, she asked, "Do you have someone in mind?"

He nodded.

"Well, you'd better let me in on this. Who are you concerned about? Bob Martyn?"

He shook his head. "No ... not Bob."

She determined not to ask further. The look on her face told him he would need to handle this carefully.

She found his silence unnerving. Finally, he asked, "Rhea, have you ever had a relationship with Jared?"

"Jared?" she echoed, the shock showing on her face. "No! Jared is a colleague ... nothing more!"

"Have you ever dated him?"

"Never. I've never liked him much. Why Jared? Why would you concern yourself about him?"

"He's keeps telling me to leave you alone ... you're his. This morning as I was leaving the hospital he caught up to me and started in again ... told me to keep my hands off you."

"O my!" she said; then thoughtfully, "How do you respond to him?"

"Well, this morning I told him it was too late ... way too late ... to keep my hands off. Mostly I don't say anything."

"Michael, is there some history with you and Jared that I should know about? Why does he feel free to do this to you?"

"Yeah. Guess I would have to say it's a way of life with Jared; we have a history of this sort of thing. It's almost too embarrassing to remember, never mind talk about."

She looked at him questioningly. "You'd better get on with it," she said. Then after a moment she suggested, "We need to eat our breakfast, and finish the laundry if we're going on that little jaunt. Could we talk about this on the way? I could make a picnic lunch ..."

She glanced at him from time to time as he drove. His blue jeans and crew-neck polo shirt did nothing to disguise his handsome boyish physique. At length she reached over and took his hand. He glanced at her and smiled, but she noticed the stress lines around his eyes.

"I've never been this way before; it's totally awesome!" she exclaimed as the road led through rock and shrubbery on the steep hills. From time to time they caught glimpses of the St. Lawrence River far below. At length they came to an opening that afforded an unrestricted view of the river. He swung in quickly and they sat for a moment awestruck at the view spread out before them.

They ate in a sheltered cove, the rock wall providing a back rest. Below them the giant waterway lay like a serpentine monster basking in the noon-day sun.

MThey sat companionably, enjoying the togetherness. He drew her gently back against his shoulder and held her close.

"Do you like me, Rhee?" he asked at length.

"Yes, very much."

"What do you like about me?"

"Everything ... except ... maybe ... your lack of trust in me."

"I'm sorry, Rhee ... I really am! I shouldn't have

listened to Jared. He's done this sort of thing to me for years."

"Has he ever lied to you before?"

"I don't know. I guess I didn't really care before now." He paused, as if wondering how to explain what he wanted to tell her, then went on, "He has always bullied me ... always been taller ... heavier ... more aggressive. I guess I allowed it because my Dad was like that and I grew up thinking it was normal."

"So ... did he think he could bully you out of a relationship with me?"

"Yeah ... sure ... I think so. We sometimes double-dated when we were in university. He would round up a couple of girls for an evening of fun. He always made it a point to tell me that he had taken out my date the next evening and what all he did ... as though somehow he had to make up for my lack of manhood ... show me up ... or whatever."

"How did you respond to that?"

"I guess I didn't . I was so busy I just didn't care. And besides, any girl who went with me one night and him the next wasn't of interest to me. I just let it go."

"Are you telling me that you and Jared ...?" she struggled for words, not quite knowing how to ask what she didn't want to know; "... that you and Jared ... slept around when you were in university?"

"No ... no ... I'd never do that. It was part of the rivalry between us; he would always challenge me to 'claim my manhood' as he put it, by spending the night with some girl or other; when I declined he would try to embarrass me in front of my date. I finally refused to double-date with him."

"How very painful for you," she interjected.

He went on as though she had not spoken, "I decided when I was a kid in high-school that I would wait for marriage. We had one of those *Just say 'no'* campaigns and I made a promise to myself and God. I'd be lying if I said I've enjoyed celibacy. Jared would come in at three in the morning, shower for half an hour and then sleep like a baby. I knew what he'd been doing. I'd be laying there ... awake ... lonely ... maybe even jealous ... not that I wanted to do what he did ... just that I longed for a relationship ... that would lead to marriage."

"Have you ever had a serious relationship?" she asked. "Have you ever been in love?"

He sat quietly, as though struggling with himself. Then, placing his hand under her chin, he turned her face toward him, and looking into her eyes, he said quietly, "Not until now."

Her eyes continued to search his with a questioning look. "I feel like I should have asked permission, Rhea, but I've fallen in love with you."

"Oh Michael," she whispered softly. "Oh Michael ... I didn't know I needed permission; I went ahead without it."

"Do you love me, Rhee?"

She nodded as he pulled her close. "Rhea, my beautiful Rhea ... hold me close ... just hold me," he whispered, as she snuggled closer and lifted her mouth for his kiss.

"When did you fall in love with me?' she asked, as they drove on.

"I'm not sure. I think when you were still in hospital ... you were so concerned about my working late ... that got my attention. Though at that time I thought maybe you were Jared's."

"Why was that?"

"Because of the way he talked. And ... maybe because of the flowers. I don't ever remember him buying flowers for a girl."

"Flowers? What flowers?"

"The big bouquet of roses when you were in hospital."

"Jared bought me flowers? Well, I'll be! I didn't really get to see much of my flowers; they were all gone by the time I was mobile. I did get his card - didn't know he had sent flowers too."

He went on, "Then, last week-end when I got to know you better ... the long talks we had at Wilhelm's ... I knew I was in love by then. I haven't ever met anyone like you before; I had already decided that what I wanted in a relationship didn't exist ... a fantasy."

"Oh Michael. That's beautiful! You're such a romantic!" she smiled. "I love you for being so honest ... about your feeling for me ... about Jared. I can see why it was so important to know whether I'd dated him. He certainly has tried hard enough over the last three years, but he's definitely not for me. I finally told him I was not 'harem material'. He was pretty ticked off, and pleaded innocent. He's a philanderer."

"When did you fall in love with me, Rhee?"

"I guess it crept up on me. I was attracted by your gentleness, your care for me in hospital. But I thought you were married, so I backed off. When I found out you were available and interested, I gave myself permission to ... well ... to feel again. I think I had been pretty numb for a long time. It wasn't long before I was thinking about you all day, and dreaming about you at night. I decided I must be in love."

"Down there," she said, pointing to a small fishing village on the river bank. He swung down onto the narrow winding road, as she continued, "Then, the week-end on the skill hill ... that was really special ... getting to know you a little better. Love is a funny thing. I always thought that when I met that special somebody I would have time to ... well ... to consider ... plan ... organize my thoughts ... get ready for a relationship or whatever. You caught me by surprise. I haven't been able to think since I met you," she finished laughing.

"I'm glad, Rhea," he said with a look of amusement, "because I haven't been much good either ... especially with Jared on me. I was afraid to admit to myself that I loved you so much for fear ..."

For fear ...?"

He drove quietly for a few minutes, then, "Rhea, would it matter to you if ... if I'm illegitimate?"

"Why do you ask? Are you adopted?"

"No. Yes. I don't know. I'm not sure. I mean ... not by my Mom. I'm sure of that. But I may not be my Dad's."

"Why do you think that?"

"Something my Dad said once."

"It won't matter to me, Michael. But I expect you'll have to find out for your own peace of mind. Were your parents married when you were born?"

"Oh yeah. They'd been married for a couple of years."

"You know the implications of what you're saying then? Your Mom had an affair?"

"I can't imagine that. I can hardly think about it. But I don't look much like my Dad. In fact I look an awful lot like Doctor Matt. His son and I were often mistaken for brothers."

"Wow. Was Doctor Matt that kind of a man? I thought he ... kind of ... discipled you."

"I know. I feel guilty even thinking that of him. But he took me under his wing so quickly and always included me in holiday gatherings and ... and besides that, my Dad hated him for some reason or another, that he never talked about."

"We need to talk more about our families, Michael, if we're going to get to know each other. I need to hear about your growing-up years, and tell you about mine. I need to tell you about my parents and my brother.

"I would like to know why you have such a hard time trusting me around other men. I would never do that to you. I'm very loyal. I would never betray your confidence ...

or embarrass you, or date anyone else while we are in relationship."

He squeezed her hand as they pulled up to a small seafood restaurant, but her words '*while we are in relationship*' hovered on the back burner of his mind.

Chapter 7

Of Debts and Debtors

❧

Pastor Bob was already in the pulpit and introducing his message when they slipped in the side door. They had missed the worship and singing but had finished their rounds on time to catch the sermon. Michael was pleased that Jeremy had wanted to join him. He looked forward to hearing Bob. His messages were in-depth, well researched, always relevant, powerful! He often found himself contemplating one truth or another for days afterward.

He wondered as they found a seat, where Rhea might be sitting, but decided not to disturb the service by looking around.

Today the Pastor's thoughts centered around God's incredible love for his creation. He explained how God had created mankind in His Own Image, for fellowship with Himself. Part of that image was the freedom to exercise free will - the right to choose. But man chose autonomy - he would run his own life and live independently. He outlined many ways that man has tried to run his own life, create his own religion, find his own way to God ... all doomed to failure.

Michael was fascinated as he described what sin is and how it works. "Some folk think sin is limited to overt behavior - lying, cheating, stealing, smoking, drunkenness ...," he went on, "and they are sinful practices, but they are only the webs. The spider, is the autonomous spirit that refuses to acknowledge either the Creator or His right to our lives."

He quoted from the first chapter of Romans, as he continued:

> For although they knew God, they neither glorified him as God nor gave thanks to him, but their thinking became futile and their foolish hearts were darkened. Although they claimed to be wise, they became fools and exchanged the glory of the immortal God for images made to look like mortal man and birds and animals and reptiles .... (Rom. 1:21-23)

> Furthermore, since they did not think it worthwhile to retain the knowledge of God, he gave them over to a depraved mind, to do what ought not to be done. They have become filled with every kind of wickedness, evil, greed and depravity. They are full of envy, murder, strife, deceit and malice. They are gossips, slanderers, God-haters, insolent, arrogant and boastful; they invent ways of doing evil ... (Rom. 1:28-30 NIV)

He went on at length describing the awful weight of sin in our lives, and the gulf that separates us from God. "We can never reach God by our own efforts, for the wages of sin is death - eternal death. So what could a holy God do to redeem the creatures he loved?

"He would pay the debt Himself, His own death as the perfect sacrifice for sin, would pay the awful ransom that holiness demanded."

"His death on the cross paid my debt," Pastor Bob continued, as his voice softened. "He freed me from the awful loneliness and alienation that I felt as the child of an alcoholic father."

As he began to tell his personal story, Michael noticed that a hush had fallen over the congregation.

"John 1:12 told me that if I received his sacrifice for me and confessed my sin, that I would become a child of God ... and that is what I am ... a child of the King. He paid my debt and took me into his own family," he finished.

The piano began to play softly as he concluded the message and invited any who felt the need to join him in the prayer room.

The doctors sat quietly, each absorbed with his own thoughts, as a soloist began to sing in a rich soprano.

That's her, Michael thought to himself, *that's the one who sang the first Sunday I came here.* He had not been able to see her somewhere in the back of the choir ; he couldn't see her now, either; the voice seemed to be coming from behind the piano. He had always intended to ask Bob about her.

As he pondered, the song came to an end, and as the words flashed on the overhead screen, she invited, "Perhaps you would like to stand and sing with me ..."

They looked at each other in surprise, "That's Dr. Rhee," Jeremy whispered. Michael noticed the tears as the young man excused himself, and added, "I'm going to meet with Pastor Bob."

Rhea's cell phone rang as she pulled into the garage.

She had not seen Michael in church but assumed he would be along for lunch as soon as he finished at the hospital.

"Hi, sweetheart, sorry I missed you after the service. May I bring company for lunch?"

"So you were there! I looked for you ... decided you must have been held up at the hospital. Of course you can bring company. Tell me how many."

"Just Bob and Jeremy. See you in a half hour?" he asked.

"Good enough," she replied, her mind already busy on preparations for dinner.

"Nobody makes roast beef and Yorkshire pudding like you do, Rhea," Bob complimented, surrendering his plate after the second helping. They all agreed heartily. Michael noted the warm and jovial familiarity between the two, and envied their three-year association. It was obvious that Bob had eaten here many times.

Jeremy sat quietly for the most part, overwhelmed with the warmth of the fellowship and good humor, but wondering when the right time might be to share his joy with Dr. Rhee.

"More tea?" Rhea asked as they pushed back their chairs.

"I really enjoyed your singing this morning, Dr. Rhee," Jeremy began.

"Yea, Rhea, you've been keeping that a secret," Michael interjected.

Jeremy went on as though there had been no interruption, "And Pastor Bob's sermon this morning was really powerful ... about the debt ... the weight of sin we carry. I've had a hard time believing that God really wanted to forgive me for the awful things that I've done; my folks never forgave me for anything. Then I went for prayer after the service ... and Pastor Bob and Dr. Mike explained to me about asking God's forgiveness ..."

"Jeremy, that's wonderful!" she exclaimed.

"Then they explained what it means to be born again. I'd heard that term used a lot and thought it had something to do with reincarnation, or whatever. I never knew that Jesus used it to describe the new life that He gives ... how the first time we are born physically ... into an earthly family ... the second time we are born spiritually. It's neat how we can ask the Spirit of God to come into our lives and He makes us a part of the family of God."

He was excited and happy as he went on, "And I really need to thank you, too, Dr. Rhee, for your part in all this. I guess I never thought too much about forgiveness until the accident ... when you forgave me and let me go free ..." he paused, searching for words to describe the depth of his feelings. "I guess I thought you must really have God in your life to be able to do that. It helped me to understand God's love for me ... because I saw it in you," he finished in a whisper.

Rhea sat silently. She was taken with his openness and his grateful spirit. "Thank you, Jeremy," she said at last. "I had no idea ... it's interesting what God uses to get our attention. He has certainly forgiven me a great deal. It was only right that I should forgive you that small amount." After a few moments she added, "About your folks ...?"

"I know I need to forgive them," he started, then paused. "I'm not sure what that means right now; I'll need to talk to somebody about that."

He looked at Pastor Bob who smiled and nodded.

Michael sat silently. He had not taken part in this exchange. *He's not the only one who should be talking to Bob about forgiving his parents,* his conscience reminded him.

"I guess I'd best get you home so you can get that sleep I promised," Michael addressed the younger doctor.

He lingered as the two stepped into the garage. "Thank you, sweetheart," he whispered kissing her gently. "I'll call you tonight, okay?"

"You share that recipe?" Bob asked mischievously as they drove away.

"Recipe?" Then realizing they must have seen him kiss Rhea, he laughed, "Not until I'm married."

Chapter 8

Of Men and of Angels

The sharp beep of the cell phone brought an end to her nap and a quick return to consciousness. That must be the hospital. She smiled as she thought how many babies are born on Sunday afternoons.

"Dr. Rhee, it's Valida. We have an emergency ... a man has brought his wife ... unconscious ... pregnant. She's not one of your patients. You haven't seen her before." She babbled on as Rhea's mind kicked into gear.

"Who's the intern on duty? Okay. Ask her to order the blood work ... we'll need an ultra sound. I'll be there straight away." Before hanging up, she asked, "Is Dr. McCaig on duty tonight?"

"He's in the delivery room."

"Ask him to wait for me when he's through. I might need his help."

The young mother's condition was more grave than she had imagined. In spite of her bulging abdomen the babe appeared to be very small. Her extremities were terribly swollen indicating advanced eclampsia. Equally troubling was the discoloration of skin around her face, neck, arms.

She continued to examine … her shoulder - black and blue … her back showing signs of bruising. *Looks like abuse, I'd best get some help with this one*, she told herself.

Pierre Doucette sat sullenly in the waiting room. He muttered angrily in French, though he had apparently conversed in English when he arrived. Rhea's French was fairly adequate and as she questioned him about his wife's symptoms over the last few months, he constantly affirmed that she always pretended to be sick so she would get attention. He was not responsible for her condition. She pretended her back was sore and she couldn't walk. He didn't do anything to hurt her. In response to Rhea's question, he didn't know her due date, but thought it might be as much as three months away.

"Your wife and baby are in very serious condition. We will need to operate immediately and take the baby. I will have the clerk bring the forms for you to sign."

He shook his head and folded his arms over his chest defiantly. He would not allow an abortion.

"We don't abort babies here," Rhea assured him. "We are trying to save both your wife and baby. If we do not act, you will lose them both."

He shook his head. "A big fuss over nothing," he growled in broken English.

"Valida, get me some help. I'll need someone from urology, someone from orthopaedics. Alert pediatrics. We'll need to get on this quickly. Has Dr. McCaig surfaced yet? I'll want him to scrub with me."

He emerged even as she spoke and was quickly apprised of the patient and her condition. Urology would take a few minutes to arrive. Pediatrician Merle Jacobson and Michael Braemer swung through the door simultaneously.

"Michael," she said in surprise. "I didn't realize you were on tonight."

"I wasn't," he said. "I just stopped by to check on a patient."

"Are we looking at a broken back?," she asked as he began to examine the young mother.

"You may have something there," he said. "Too bad we can't get an X-ray. Are we looking at spousal abuse?"

"It looks that way. And he's refusing consent to a cesarean. I've authorized a call to the police and it occurs to me that when they arrive he may be a little more likely to co-operate."

Her predictions proved accurate, and armed with authorization, the operating room buzzed with activity.

Michael watched as Rhea and her team prepared to do battle. He had often found himself wondering what she would be like under fire. Was she always as cool headed as she seemed. They paused briefly as she offered a prayer for guidance and competence for all concerned. He saw her exchange glances with each of the team in turn, then Jared. Without a word, his scalpel drew a long red line downward from the navel. Layer after layer of tissue was separated, until at last the small blue infant emerged in Rhea's hands. He disappeared into the capable care of Dr. Jacobson, and the cleanup and closure began. Michael couldn't help envy the way they worked together as one.

"What chance does the little one have?" he asked as they cleaned up.

"Maybe five percent," suggested Jared, looking at Rhea.

"One in a hundred; he had hardly any fetal heartbeat. He's been in distress far too long; for that matter, so has his mother. Her chances aren't great either. I shudder to think what might have happened had she gone into labor. The fetus was transverse. I suspect kidney damage - possibly kicked loose ... and then her back and shoulders ..." she looked at Michael.

"We'll get those X-rays as soon as urology gets through.

I hope her husband gets some time out of this. Maybe they can straighten him around in there."

"Well, tonight he's charged with assault; by tomorrow it may be manslaughter. Thanks for coming," she said as they walked out together. "May I treat you to a bowl of soup?"

"You bet!"

The cafeteria was almost empty. They settled into a quiet corner, enjoying the calm after the storm.

"That was a neat piece of work you did in there. I admired the way you worked together. Jared really is a good surgeon. Great teamwork!"

"Yes," she said, "we enjoy working together. He knows what he's doing."

"Will I get to see you this week?" he asked at length.

"My evenings are full. What do you suggest?"

"Can we meet here for lunch a couple of times - maybe Tuesday and Thursday?"

"No," she said.

"Well, that sounds pretty final. Can I ask why? Something wrong with the food?"

"No. The food's good. I just don't like to come here. I take a sandwich and eat in my office. It gives me time to think, get ready for the afternoon."

"Why don't you like to come here?" he asked with a slight note of exasperation.

"The noise, the smoke, the gossip … mostly the gossip."

"Do we have to be involved in that?"

"We'll be the centre of it if someone sees us together. Rumours will fly."

He sat silently for some time, then finally, "So you don't want to be seen with me; is that it? Are you embarrassed …?"

"Michael! Stop it!" she interjected. "Of course that's not the reason. Nothing about you embarrasses me. I am happy ... excited. I'm enjoying our relationship more and more."

"But?" he interjected.

"But there are a couple of reasons why I don't want the world to know. Having you all to myself is pretty special. I don't have to give an account for our time together, write a memo, report to council, justify it to anyone. We can just relax and enjoy each other.

"The other 'but' is that we don't know each other very well, and the stories that circulate could destroy our relationship. You're bound to hear the rumours that are going around about me."

"The only rumour I've heard is that you are the most eligible bachelor girl at St. Mike's ... and the most sought after."

"You're awfully sweet," she said kindly.

"I think you'd better tell me what the rumours are ..."

"I hate to tell you. Actually I was there when they started. We were having lunch in here and the discussion turned to various treatments for cancer of the prostate. Dr. Clarke turned to me and asked my opinion on something or another and I simply said it was out of my area of expertise. Jared piped up and said, 'Dr. Rhymer is only interested in female bodies.' The conversation came to a halt."

"Good heavens! What did you say?"

"I was in shock. Then muttered something like, 'Well, at least we have that in common.'"

"That was pretty quick thinking."

"When the others had left I ordered him up to my office. He was sincerely apologetic - didn't think before he opened his mouth - realized he'd gone away beyond the acceptable, but the damage was done. I'm an easy mark - single at 30, don't have a live-in, don't date, don't sleep around, work the streets ..."

"Wouldn't your relationship with me squelch the gossip about you preferring females?"

"Possibly. But I'm concerned, Michael, if you decided at some point that you didn't want a relationship with me ... I'm sorry ... do you understand what I'm saying? It would confirm for a lot of folk that I'm a lesbian ... and you wouldn't look too good either, not knowing any better than to date one."

"I keep getting the impression that you see our relationship as very temporary. I have no intention of ending our relationship. Please, Rhea, don't try to protect me ... just love me. I want to tell the world that you're my girl. And I want you to meet me here for lunch on Tuesday. Will you come?"

She sat quietly, considering; then slowly nodded.

"I'd like to check back on Mrs. Doucette and see if the wee one is still with us," she said as they rose to go.

"Mind if I come?" he asked.

Dr. Merle Jacobson met them as they entered the corridor. Shaking her head sadly, she remarked, "I am so sorry. It was too late ... way too late ... his lungs ... his heart ... poor little guy ... didn't even put up a fight."

They continued on to Intensive Care. Mrs. Doucette had regained consciousness briefly and asked for her wee one. Dr. McCaig had gently told her that the angels had come for him.

"Pretty creative for Jared," Michael suggested as they turned to go.

Chapter 9

Of Wars and Roses

It was early Monday when Rhea stopped briefly at Intensive Care to enquire after Mrs. Doucette. Her suspicions were justified - damaged kidneys - four cracked vertebrae - two thoracic, two lumbar. She was even now in surgery.

She sensed a slight stir among the staff as she swung through the door. "Wow," she said as she noticed the huge bouquet - dozens of deep red roses with cream centers - they nearly covered the front counter. "Someone deliver the triplets and not let me know?" she quipped.

"Seems to be for you," the receptionist answered.

All eyes were upon her as she quickly retrieved the card from under the plastic wrap. She stood uncertainly for a moment, then laughingly slipped her arms around the roses and lifted them off the counter. "Sorry, gals, these are not for sharing," she said, and headed into her office.

Michael, you are a rascal! she thought to herself as she stood contemplating whether to tuck the card into the bouquet, or to put it in her purse. She could imagine the rush to examine it as soon as she stepped out. Did she really want that? Did Michael? She concluded that he did. She smiled as she looked at his masculine scrawl, *My love always, Michael.* It would certainly give a message to Jared. She stood for a few moments admiring the blooms, then tucked the card deep among them and turned on her computer.

He returned her call late in the afternoon. "I heard you were in surgery all day," she said, then quickly added, "Michael, the flowers are absolutely gorgeous, and you are a rascal! What a stir you have caused in my tranquil little world!"

He chuckled. "Glad you're enjoying them. Do we have a date for lunch tomorrow?"

"We do, unless the triplets arrive on schedule. They'll have to come first, I'm afraid."

"I've already had a call from our mutual friend?"

"Must be Jared. He was in and checked out the roses."

"Yep. Wants to know what I think I'm doing sending you roses. Wants to have a talk."

"You really need to do that, Michael. Why don't you have him for supper at my place some evening when I'm out. I could set the table and put something in the oven. Let's talk about it."

She watched him make his way through the lineup in the cafeteria. He always moved so confidently, sure of himself, yet never pushy or rude. She had found an empty table for four and placed her jacket on the chair next to hers to reserve it for Michael. Dr. Clarke approached, tray in hand, and she nodded approval. Without notice or approval Jared materialized and claimed the chair across from her. Noticing her jacket on the empty chair, he asked, "Expecting someone?"

Too bad I couldn't get a table for two, she thought, as she answered, "You bet!"

The atmosphere was noticeably strained as Michael joined her with their tray of sandwiches and coffee.

"I notice you're walking pretty good on that little foot," Dr. Clarke addressed Rhea. "Must have had a pretty good surgeon on that one, eh?" he said with a glance at Michael.

"You got that right; he makes the lame walk," she smiled.

"I note he thinks his expertise entitles him to certain benefits," remarked Jared with a strong hint of sarcasm. Then turning to Rhea, "You might like to know that I have a fair amount of expertise myself ... in certain areas ... and if you ever have need of a good gynecologist ..."

"I am so sorry," Rhea cut in, "that I cannot make you the same offer ... not being either skilled or knowledgeable in the area where you have the greatest need. However, allow me to recommend Dr. Pascoe; I'm sure he can look after all your needs."

The other two men at the table erupted in laughter, recognizing that she spoke of the neurosurgeon. "You little wretch," Jared managed a chuckle.

"I'm sorry," Rhea said through her laughter. "I really am. It's just that you leave yourself open ..."

"Dr. Braemer. Calling Dr. Michael Braemer, please report to R12," the voice crackled over the PA system.

He rose to go with a quick smile at Rhea. "I'll call you tonight."

So much for lunch in the cafeteria, thought Rhea, as she deposited her tray and headed back to the office.

The conversation in the front office ceased as she entered. All four girls attempted to look as busy and preoccupied as possible. Rhea surmised they had checked out the card in the flowers and were discussing the situation. Since there were several elegible Michaels on staff, she assumed they would be out-guessing one another. *They should just ask Jared,* she mused with a smile.

At four o'clock Michael called. "Are you free for supper?"

"Sorry, not tonight. How about tomorrow? Before we go to prayer? Pastor Bob asked if we would like to sing on Sunday. Can we get together at my place after and try a few numbers?"

"Super! Sounds great! Five o'clock tomorrow then. I'm looking forward."

Chapter 10

A Helper Suitable for Him

❝**I** really haven't played in years," he argued as she insisted he try his hand on the piano.

"We'll need to remedy that right quick," she suggested as he tried a few scales. She noticed the competent way his hands took charge of the keyboard. "Well, I see you've done that a time or two."

"Yeah. Mom kept me at it for years … and years … and years."

"So, how far did you go in music?"

"Stopped just short of the exams for the Toronto Conservatory."

"Wow! No wonder you're so accomplished. Why did you not finish?"

"I had too many other things going, and I didn't really intend to make a career out of it. Besides, my Dad really never appreciated it too much. He thought I was too effeminate as it was. I really enjoyed playing and singing as I was growing up, but it wasn't the be-all and end-all of life for me."

"You play so effortlessly," she noted, "like you swim."

Then placing the music before him, she added, "Sing with me."

They sang then. *Amazing Grace, how sweet the sound* ... his deep, rich baritone blending with her full soprano. As the song ended, he caught her in his arms, and they both laughed softly. The hour flew by. Still they sang, enjoying each other, the harmony of their gifts, and the warmth of their fellowship.

"I heard you sing the very first time I came to church, you know," he told her. "You were hiding in the back of the choir. I thought our voices would blend, and I waited to hear you again, but it never happened ... until last Sunday. I always intended to ask Bob who it was, but never thought of it when we were together. I've really enjoyed this time together tonight. Can we do it again? Can we sing together often?"

"Whenever you like."

"I leave for New York on Sunday afternoon, Rhee, and I'll be gone for a month this time. If I come home for a week-end in the middle of the month, can we spend the time together?"

She hesitated for what seemed to him a long time. "That would be really stressful for you," she ventured, "having to work such long days and then travel on the week-end." She paused again, then added, "What if I came to see you in New York?"

"You'd do that? You'd come and see me in New York ... for a week-end?"

"Why not? I could fly in. You'd have to get a room for me somewhere. Can we talk about it some more before then?"

Lord, you really have prepared a helper suitable for me, he thought to himself as he kissed her goodnight.

Chapter 11

New York

He could hardly bear the suspense as he parked the car at La Guardia. His heart felt like a trip hammer ... still 15 minutes before arrival. *What if she didn't come? When he talked to her yesterday, she assured him she'd be there.* His thoughts flew back and forth. Would she like the adjoining rooms he had reserved in the hotel on the water-front? It seemed forever since they'd been together. Maybe she'd changed her mind. But they had talked every day. She enjoyed the flowers he sent last week. They had caused the usual stir. He smiled, remembering her description of the event.

He spotted her as she came through Customs, a week-ender in each hand. He noted how together she always seemed; her shoulder bag accenting the stylish pants and jacket. She had the gift of looking professional, without losing her loveliness, he thought.

"I can hardly believe this is for real," he murmured, holding her close.

"Me either," she assured him. "This is a first for me."

"I thought we might dine and dance at our hotel tonight,"

he suggested as they drove. "They have a very lovely dining room and ... unless you'd prefer to do something else. Too bad we didn't know about this a year ago ... maybe we could have gone to Carnegie Hall."

"Oh my!" she laughed. "I don't need all that. I just came to see you. The supper in the hotel sounds wonderful. And the dancing too. I had a really late night on the street last night, so I'll need to get to bed sometime before midnight."

"Do you mind that I reserved adjoining rooms?" he asked. I thought it would be better than running back and forth from the campus ... but if you're uncomfortable ...?" He paused, looking at her, then added, "I want you to know I still intend to keep my commitment."

"Commitment?" she asked.

"To make the red blood cells behave."

She laughed. "Thank you for being so up front; the rooms are a really special idea. They'll give us more time together. Maybe we'll get to share a little ... get to know each other better."

She gasped as they pulled into the underground parking lot at the lavish hotel. "Michael, this is way too posh," she stammered.

"Wait till you see the inside," he laughed. "Did you bring a dress?"

"Nothing that will go with this!."

He turned from the view of the harbor as the door opened between their rooms. She had changed into a plain white organdy that flowed softly, accenting her femininity. He gave a low whistle. Why did it always take his breath away to look at her?

"Michael...Michael," she whispered, slipping her arms inside his jacket as he pulled her close.

The elegant dining room lived up to its reputation - extravagant furnishings, low lights, soft music, and delectable cuisine.

They dined leisurely ... savouring the time together ... looking forward to the remainder of the week-end.

"I understand this is a special day for you," she said as she reached into her small beaded bag and handed him a small package, "Happy Birthday, sweetheart."

"Rhee! How did you know?" he asked in surprise. Then surveying the tasteful wrapping, he commented, "It's beautiful, Rhea; it bears your signature."

"I hope they'll suit your taste," she commented as he opened the gift, "they can be exchanged, I'm told."

"Ray Bans! Sweetheart! You are so perceptive!" She noticed his eyes were rather misty, as he gently took her hand and put it to his lips. "I am deeply moved."

"I've been noticing your earrings," he said as they danced. "They're most unusual, sort of a reddish tint to the gold. Are they from the Middle East perchance?"

"They are, they're from Jordan," she said, surprised. "They were a gift from my folks; I don't wear them often, just on very special occasions."

"And this is special?"

"Very special. Thank you for all the thought you put into making it so."

Back at their table, she leaned toward him and asked, "Michael, were you worried that I might not come?"

He looked down, then back at her. He didn't know how to answer. "Why do you think that?"

"Our last couple of phone calls ... you seemed anxious ... stressed."

"I guess I can hardly believe that you love me ... that much ..." he broke off .

"It's one of the reasons that I came, Michael. The other reason is that I couldn't stay way from you any longer."

He reached across the table again and drew her hand to his lips. "I love you, Rhee."

"And I love you," she whispered.

She slipped into a jogging suit before joining him at the small table in his room. The view of the harbor from the tenth floor was breathtaking.

"Juice, coke, gingerale?" he asked, opening the small fridge.

"Coke sounds good."

They sat silently, admiring the view; each absorbed with private thoughts. Then, "Tell me, Michael, what did it feel like growing up as Michael Braemer, Jr.?"

"I'm not sure how to answer that. Some days were really good; others the pits. I've already mentioned that I have a lot of my Mom's genes - that was a constant source of friction with my Dad. He wanted me to be more like him, but it just wasn't there. Tracy seemed to have more of his genes. She's a mathematical whiz, took accounting and works for their firm. He always pitted me against her, used her as an example of what I should be like. It's a wonder I love her so much; it could just as easily have turned the other way."

"That's painful, Michael. Why do you think he's like that?"

"Probably something from his childhood. He never talked about his family; they may have treated him like that.

"He was incredibly determined that I would be an architect. I really tried to get interested; I wanted his approval so badly. It just didn't work. I was totally miserable that whole first year at university. Then I switched to health sciences. I went home for Christmas with fear and trembling. He spoke of nothing else but how we would work together next summer; I realized that the huge package under the tree contained a draft board and accessories.

"It was Christmas Eve when I walked into his study and told him I just couldn't be what he expected of me. He sat staring at me, his mouth open. Then I dropped the bomb shell; I had switched to the health sciences in the fall.

"For a moment he sat … stunned. Then - I'll never forget his words - 'You ungrateful wretch! How dare you do this without my permission! Get out of my sight - out of my house - you are no son of mine!'

"As I got up to leave, I said, 'I'm sorry, Dad … sorry I've been such a disappointment as a son.'

"He just repeated what he had already said, 'You're no son of mine.' Then he added, 'And you don't need to think that my money is going to fuel your nonsense. You'll never amount to anything.'

"I've thought of that so many times since; the whole world could applaud me, but in his eyes I'll always be a failure."

By now Rhea was sobbing, her face in her hands. "Oh Michael … Michael," was all she could say. He stood up and lifting her gently, carried her to the sofa. They cried together, their arms around each other.

"He stormed out of the house, and as I went to my room to pack my things, I heard him drive away."

"So what did you do, Michael? On Christmas Eve?"

"I kissed Mom and Tracy - they were both crying terribly - and I drove all night and part of the next day to get back to Montreal. Doctor Matt had invited me to accompany the ski team to Austria, leaving on Boxing Day; I thought I might still have a chance.

"The road was terribly icy, freezing rain. Accidents were everywhere. I finally pulled over and sat and cried and prayed. I think that was the night that I really committed my way … my life … to Christ. I asked him to protect and guide me, and Mom and Tracy ... and Dad, too ... and to help him to see things differently."

"Do you know what happened after you left?"

"Mom left. Tracy told me. Dad came home just as she was getting in a taxi and heading to the airport. He tried to stop her, but she wouldn't listen. Tracy said that she and Dad just sat and cried together. The turkey was all stuffed in the refrigerator, and all the Christmas goodies, pies and stuff. Neither of them knew where Mom went or if she'd be back. They finally put the turkey in the freezer, and went out for Christmas dinner."

"What a horrible way to celebrate the Prince of Peace," she managed through sobs. "Did you get to go to Austria?"

"Yes. I called Doctor Matt as soon as I arrived on December 25; told him I had changed my mind. He was happy to include me, since they still needed an EMT. He was really good to me all the years that I interned. He showed me how to apply for bursaries and scholarships, and which summer jobs would be best to further my studies. He always treated me like family, and his son and I got along better than brothers. After I got my MD, I was able to study under him again, since I was specializing in orthopaedics; we actually did some research projects together."

"So where is he now?"

"I came back from France, all excited to share my findings with him, and was told that he and his wife had been killed by a landmine in the Congo ..."

She sat bolt upright, "Are you talking about Dr. Matthew and Rheanne Reimer?" she asked wide-eyed.

"You know them?" he asked surprised.

"You're talking about my Mom and Dad!   And Jonathon! You know Jonathon?"

They sat silently. Stunned. Amazed. The implications of this new discovery were overwhelming.

"No wonder I fell in love with you so quickly," he mused. "You seem so familiar, the way you talk and walk, the way you cook, the way you care, even your home is familiar in a way that tugs at my heart. And you look like your Mom ... your hair ... your features. Why didn't I see it before?"

"Maybe because you weren't expecting it. Maybe because my last name is different."

"Why is that?"

"Rhymer is our family name from the old country. My Dad and his brother, Uncle Gus, both changed to Reimer when they arrived in Canada. Something to do with the way Immigration interpreted it, or whatever. When Jonathon and I decided to go into medicine, Dad thought we should both change back to the original family name before our degrees started rolling in. Jonathon decided to stay a *Reimer*, but I changed mine."

"Why did he want you to do that?"

"I guess because we worked overseas in questionable political circumstances a lot of the time. Dad was a really wealthy man. When he was a young doctor, he bought a piece of land in Texas, with the intention of building a hospital. They found oil. He invested wisely and never looked back. He has helped build clinics in quite a number of Third-World countries. He felt that if he were ever taken hostage, they might come after me for ransom, if they knew I was his daughter."

"So what about Jonathon?"

"Actually, I worked overseas with them much more than Jonathon. He seemed to prefer more civilized situations, like New Zealand and Australia."

"Jonathon and I were really close," he said after a lengthy silence. "We're a lot alike in many ways. We double dated occasionally, casually. He always said that I needed to look up his sister, that she was exactly what I was looking for. I probably would have, except that she was always out of the country. Didn't you ever come home? How come I never met you there?"

I don't know. I came home often. You were never there. I was there for most of the holidays, Christmas, New Years, sometimes for Thanksgiving. I must have been at home the Christmas you're talking about. Looks like we just missed each other, like ships in the night. Dad always teased that his latest intern was just the man for me. It was a standing joke between us. He was most anxious that I marry. He always said that the more educated and accomplished a woman is, the harder it is to find a man. He knew my expectations were pretty high; and that the choices become fewer as we get past the 20's."

"What if we had met then, Rhea? Do you think we would have fallen in love?"

"It's really hard to know. We were both so busy we may not have noticed each other. Or we may have felt an obligation to court because you were Dad's intern and I was his daughter. I believe God is in control of our lives and His timing is perfect. We will always be able to look back and know that we fell in love without any obligation or prompting. I love the way you pursued me, Michael. I still like it, you know," she said snuggling into his neck.

"And I still like to," he assured her."

Her earring caught on his shirt, and she slipped them off and placed them carefully on the small end table beside the sofa.

"You really are a lot like Jonathon," she said after a lengthy silence. "You really could be brothers." Then she sat upright again, and stared at him, her eyes wide. "O Michael, what if ... what if ..."

"No ... no ... please God, no. I couldn't bear it, if it were true. Do you think it possible, Rhee, that your Dad ... and my Mom ...? You know your Dad. He wasn't like that, was he?"

"Not by the time I knew him. But who knows what he was like when he was young. We can find out, though. His DNA is on record. It may prove he's not your father, but it won't tell you who is. I think you'll just have to write to Michael Braemer, Sr.

"We need to get some sleep, Michael Braemer, Jr.," she said smiling. "I just don't have as much stamina as I used to have before the accident. And it was after midnight when I got to bed last night ... the street clinic was overcrowded..."

"I don't like you working the street," he said. "We need to talk about that sometime. What would you like to do tomorrow? Want to sleep late, order breakfast and eat here?"

"Yes, yes and yes. And can we go for a long walk, along the waterfront, or in a park, or? And maybe a swim and a hot tub before supper?"

"Sounds great. But I would like to take you shopping, Rhee. You remember the other day when you were chilly and I put my leather jacket around your shoulders. It just matched your hair, except for the pretty little highlights. And I was wondering ... would you let me buy you one like mine? Would you wear it? Is your hair going to be that color for a while?"

She laughed merrily. "Well, it's been this color for the last 30 years, why change it now? And I'd love to have a jacket like yours."

"So, we'll walk, and we'll shop, and we'll swim, and we'll hot tub, and then...?"

"And then we can have supper. And can we talk some more? I have some things I want to share with you about my parents. This has been a week-end of surprises. Do you think you can handle a few more?"

Chapter 12

Dead or Alive?

S he woke when she heard his shower, and struggled to
see the bedside clock -already nine. The coffee smelled
wonderful. Michael must have turned it on when he got up.
She lay for a few moments thinking about their conversa-
tions of yesterday. What an amazing turn of events. So
many questions answered ... but the one big one still hanging over them..

Forcing herself out of her reverie, she stepped into the
shower. The hot water felt good, revitalizing. She looked
forward to spending the whole day with Michael. *He just
can't be my half-brother, please God, no,* she found herself
praying silently as she took the blow-dryer to her hair.

"What are we wearing, Michael?" she called.

"I'm in walking shorts. Okay with you?"

"You bet."

She emerged a few minutes later. "Oh my! Breakfast
for a royal household ... eggs benedict, fruit salad, rolls,
muffins. I'm still full from last night."

"It's one gorgeous day out there," he said as they
finished eating. "Ready for the waterfront?" She noticed he

had the new sunglasses in hand.

They strolled hand in hand, exploring the small shops, stopping for a sandwich and coffee, and feeding the gulls.

"Tell me," he began as they faced each other across a small stone table, "what surprises await me concerning my future in-laws?"

She laughed. "You slipped that in there nicely. You may change your mind."

"Try me."

"I really am afraid to try you on this one. I'm afraid you'll think I'm a real basket case."

"Try me," he suggested again.

"Well, it's just that ... I really think ... I don't know how to say this ... but I don't think that my Mom and Dad were killed in that land mine; I think they're alive somewhere."

He sat speechless for a few moments. She searched his face for signs of shock ... disbelief.

"Why do you think that?"

"Well, some things just don't add up."

"Such as?"

"I wasn't notified till almost a week after the accident. When I got there they showed me the place where the land mind blew up the jeep. The grave was in the same area. They claimed the burial had taken place the next day, because of the extreme heat, and that there had been only body parts. When I enquired about having them exhumed and cremated, they were adamant that it would not be allowed. I pressed for identification. How did they know for sure that it was Dr. & Mrs. Reimer and their driver that had been blown up? After a day or two, they produced Dad's wallet. It was in good condition but had nothing in it but his identification, and the instructions to notify me in case of accident or death. It simply said to notify Dr. R. Rhymer, at St. Michael's Hospital, with address, phone and e-mail numbers. No mention of the fact that I was his daughter. I wondered about

Mom's personal effects, their clothing, and whatever. They wanted me to believe that everything had been blown to bits. When I pressed them, they gave me part of a white cotton shirt, like a doctor may have worn. It was blood stained, and they assured me it had been Dr. Reimer's. They offered to wash it for me, but I declined. I had it checked against his DNA when I got home, and it wasn't his."

"Does Jonathon know about all this?"

"Yes. Of course."

"What does he think?"

"I told him when he arrived in the Congo a few days after I did. He thought I was onto something at first, but after he talked to the army officials, he began to think I was simply in denial ... that I couldn't deal with losing our parents. He doesn't know the mindset there like I do. I spent a lot more time there than he did. They can be so convincing.? They actually had him believing that the wallet had been thrown clear without any damage, while everything else and everybody ..."

"So what do you think happened to them?"

"I think they were kidnapped. With the continual fighting going on there, it seems reasonable to me that there would be a lot of wounded gorilla fighters in the hills and jungles. Finding a doctor, or anyone with medical knowledge, would be pretty well impossible. It may, or may not, have been a planned operation. Maybe they just came upon them by chance when the first jeep hit the land mine." She paused, keeping her eyes fixed on his face. "So, do you think I'm right off the wall?"

"Actually, you make really good sense to me. Have you ever run this by the Chief?"

"Yeah ... sure, when I first got home. He thought I might well be right, but that we would need more evidence to act on it. I've never gotten any more evidence. I actually thought that if Dad was alive and well, he would find some way to get in touch. Of course, he had his usual ton of supplies along, and they wouldn't need anything for a very long time. But he would run out at some point and they would have to let him order from outside the country."

"Wow! How long has it been now? Did you say three years?"

"Almost. I know that's a long time. But I still think that if I had a word from him, something that I could go to the authorities with …?"

"Who would you contact?"

"I don't know. I would need advice. I've thought of the Government, or Fifth Estate; I'm sure I could stir up enough interest to put pressure on the Congolese Government."

"You are something else, Rhee! You are really something else!"

"Be honest with me, Michael. Do you think I'm right off the edge?"

"Definitely not!. I think it bears checking out. How do you think your parents would fare in the jungle for three years?"

"Dad would have a ball. He'd have a captive audience for the Gospel. Mom would do okay, too, if they are both well. I would fear for her if something happened to Dad. She would, of course, worry about us, and how we would deal with their sudden disappearance."

"How did you deal with it?"

"I cried all the way to Africa. We had often talked about all of the things that could or might happen to one or the other of us on these trips into no-man's land. I thought I had quite a realistic view of separation and death. I was sure I could handle whatever might come my way. It all went out the window when I heard about Mom and Dad. I found that I don't handle grief very well at all. But I'm convinced I'm not in denial…" She laughed. "I really do sound like a nut case, don't I?"

"No, Rhee ... no you don't."

"I'm sorry, but I really needed to tell you about all this, especially since you knew them and had heard how they died. Have I ruined our lovely day? Can we put it on hold for now and get on with more pleasant things?"

"Yes. But we won't forget about it, Rhee. Maybe we need to go and get that jacket."

Chapter 13

Of Men and Boys

"This has been a wonderful week-end, sweetheart," she said as they cuddled on the sofa. "That chef has probably prepared seafood once or twice before. I am so ... o full and so ... o comfortable."

"It has been a wonderful time. I'm so glad you came," he murmured, planting a kiss on her forehead.

"And that jacket, Michael. It is fabulous! You shouldn't be spending that kind of money on me, you know. The other day, Reba...you know ... the big southern lady from Radiology ... came in just after the roses arrived. She was too cute. She just said, in her best southern drawl, "Doctor Rhee, you-all better marry that boy pretty soon; cause he gonna be broke soon 'nuf."

"And you said?"

"You just might be right about that."

"Did you mean that, Rhee? I mean the part about the marrying?" She looked up at him as he went on, "Do you ever think about the future, about us together?"

She nodded. "I've hardly been able to think of anything else.."

"Is there some reason why we can't get married...I mean unless I'm your brother?"

She nodded, as he looked at her questioningly.

"What reason?"

"You've never asked me."

"RHEA," he said in exasperation. "You little rascal. I was afraid to ask you."

"Why was that? Did you think I would say 'no'?"

"No. You wouldn't say 'no.' You'd just say, 'Michael, don't go there,'" he mimicked her tone.

"Are you mocking me out? I could never marry a man that makes fun of me."

"Could you ever marry a man if he didn't?" he teased.

"I probably could if he asked me."

"Well, you'd better get ready, because he has every intention of doing so."

"Promises, promises," she laughed.

"O Rhee! Rhee! Rhee!" he whispered softly. "Can we talk about this really soon?"

"Do you feel like you know me, sweetheart? Or do you have questions? Are there things you would like to know about me?"

He hesitated for a moment, then ventured, "Yes, there is something. You've mentioned a time or two that you had a rather serious relationship in highschool. Can I ask about that?"

"Sure. Though I don't know if I would call it a serious relationship; I guess it probably was pretty serious for a 17-year-old. We came back from Africa when I finished Grade Eight in the English school system. When I got back to Canada, it was pretty much equal to a Grade Nine, so I went into Grade 10. I was a little younger than everybody else in the class. Jonathon Fields had been elected class president for the term, and since I was on the student activities committee, we met together to plan and organize events. He was tall, over six feet, blond, blue-eyed, well-built, played football. We took to each other from the beginning. We had a blast pulling off the things that we came up with. He really enjoyed the limelight, and I work well behind the scenes.

"The next year, I was class president and he was vice-president; our final year we reversed roles again. By that time, we were really good at all kinds of events, and kept the whole student body involved.

"Besides that, we both worked as lifeguards on the beach for two summers. We just enjoyed being together, working together. We were a good team."

"Well, were you boy and girlfriend?"

"I guess we were. Everybody thought we were much more serious than we were. Neither of us dated anyone else, but we were never serious about each other. When he'd bring me home, he'd give me a hug and a quick kiss. We kind of took each other for granted. In fact, it was really funny the week of our senior prom. He never asked me to go with him, just took for granted that we would be going together. So did I. Then a day or two before, I got to wondering ... we were to lead the Grand March together, but was I his date? Sure enough, the day before the prom he called to find out what colour of corsage I wanted. I was both relieved and amused."

"So what happened to the relationship?"

"I'm not sure. After graduation was over ... the last summer before we all left for college ... he became much more serious about our relationship. He worked with his Dad that summer in the law office. His Dad thought he should give him an inside look at his future. I think he did errands to the court house, land titles office - sort of a courier- served writs of summons, and all that sort of thing.

I saw a different Jonathon than the care-free boy of school days. He talked a lot about the future, settling down to a law career with his Dad. He knew I was heading into medicine and wondered if I would be establishing a practice in town or working in the local hospital. I couldn't assure him of either of those things. He knew my Dad's bent to helping a hurting world and from his questions and comments, I realized his parents really disapproved of us. They saw us as always traipsing around the globe ... rolling stones that never gather moss. And with their bent toward the good life, social elitism, the limelight, and all that goes with it, I suspect the pressure was on him to let go of any relationship with me."

"So did he?"

"We spent a lot of time together that last summer. Just the two of us. Swimming, playing tennis, the occasional movie. When my brother Jonathon was home we would double date occasionally. A night or two before Jonathon, I mean Jonathon Fields, left for college, he asked me to go out for supper. By this time, I was really beginning to care for him. I expected he would end the evening by asking me to keep in touch when we went off in separate directions. He was very quiet, almost depressed, not at all like his usual self. He had reservations at a lovely resort area, where we ate and then danced on the patio under the stars. He was in tears by the time the dance was over. I had never seen him like this before and didn't know what to say.

"When he took me home, he opened the trunk and gave me a lovely bouquet of yellow roses. Then he walked me to the door, kissed me on the forehead, and, with tears running down his face, turned and walked to the car. I haven't seen him since."

"You didn't get in touch?"

"No. I deposited the roses on the table and fled to my room. I'm sure I cried all night. In the morning my Mom took me out for breakfast and a long talk. She was very comforting, but tried to make me realize that God was using

Mr.& Mrs. Fields to save us both from future heartache. I realized they had probably been praying for an end to the relationship, too, knowing full well the different directions we were heading. I hated to admit they were right."

"And he hasn't contacted you since then?"

"Yes. Twice. He called St. Michael's when my parents' death was on the news. I had already left for Africa and they forwarded his message by E-mail. They apparently had a memorial service for them in the church we used to attend. They wondered if I would come.

"Then he called when I sent in my registration for *Homecoming*. He noticed that I would be coming a day early and asked if he could take me to supper the night I arrived. They were planning to re-enact the Grand March and he wondered if we could lead it together for old-times sake."

"And the answer was ...?"

"Yes and yes."

He sat quietly for so long that she finally asked, "Does that bother you?"

"Yes. I would have to say it does."

"I made that commitment before I knew you, Michael. I had no reason to refuse. I can hardly back out at this stage. Knowing how the Fields do things, they will have advertised it all over by now - the Grand March, I mean. What bothers you? Is it the supper date?"

"The whole thing bothers me."

"I'm sorry. I don't mean to give you stress. I have no intention of renewing more than a casual friendship with Jonathon. He mentioned that his parents had invited me to stay in their home while I'm in town. I declined. They know my coming to the reunion will cause quite a stir after all the press coverage of my folks. They would like to get in on as much as possible. It didn't, and doesn't, appeal to me to be used in that way."

"I know your intentions are good, Rhee, but you were pretty fond of this guy, and ..."

"Michael, Michael," she laughed. "Do you really think I could just slip into a relationship with someone who hasn't seen fit to contact me for ten years, and then does so only when my parents die, or I'm coming to town? I haven't seen him in 13 years. I'm sure he's a very fine young man, but honestly, I need more than that in a man ... a whole lot more."

"He may have been a very fine young man when you last saw him, Rhea, but now he's probably a very well-heeled lawyer."

"I'm sure he is. But why would I want a well-heeled lawyer, when I'm in love with a well-heeled doctor?" she asked, leaning over and kissing him lightly on the cheek.

"I know I need to let you go. We both need to know that it's over between you and Jonathon. I'm just finding it a little threatening ..."

"Let me put it this way - does it really make sense to you that after I've waited all these years for the right one to come along, that I would play around with someone else? I've known all this time that Jonathon was there. I could have gotten in touch any time that I chose. I didn't choose. I thought he was probably married by now, and it didn't matter to me."

"I'm glad you're in love with me," he whispered softly, holding her close. After a few moments, he asked, "So when does this event take place?"

"I'll be leaving next Thursday, back on Sunday night."

She felt him draw in his breath sharply.

"I'm not going to spend the week-end with Jonathon," she said indignantly. "I don't make a habit of spending my week-ends with men in distant cities." She pulled away from him as she spoke.

"I know, Rhee. I know that. Please ... let's not allow

this to come between us."   She allowed him to pull her close again.

"My flight is at 2:00 tomorrow, Michael. How do you want to spend the morning?"

"Do you want to worship?"

"That would be wonderful. Do you know of a church?"

"There's a lovely chapel just off campus. I went there last week. It's warm and friendly, and the doctrine is sound. Want to go to the early service, and have brunch later?"

"Sounds great," she said sleepily.

Chapter 14

Born to Privilege

"That was one beautiful worship time," she commented as they sat over brunch in the hotel. "Pretty incredible music for such a small chapel. It reminded me of the Africans; they just love to sing."

"So we're going to sing together sometime, Rhee?"

"Whenever you like."

"You're such a team player, Rhea. You were a team with Jonathon, a team with Jared, a team with Pastor Bob. Are you going to be on my team one day? Or am I going to be on yours - following you around the world?"

He stopped as she looked at him in surprise. "I thought I was already on your team, Michael...that's why I'm here..." she finished in a whisper, tears suddenly stinging her eyes. She felt as though he had suddenly slapped her.

"Rhea, I'm sorry. I didn't mean to sound so harsh. I mean ... I guess ... well, I know you have a hard time working me into your schedule. Sometimes I feel like I'm another obligation that you have to attend to."

She had quit eating and sat quietly, looking down, afraid to look up for fear her eyes might spill over. "I'm sorry, too,

Michael. Sorry that you see my love for you as another obligation. I'm must be blowing it somewhere. I've tried to explain so many times that these obligations were taken on before you were in my life. I need to be faithful to my commitments. Shouldn't it give you a sense of security to know that if I'm faithful in the little things, that I would be faithful in the bigger things - like my relationship with you?" She looked up as tears spilled down her cheeks and she reached for her napkin.

"Besides," she continued, "I've already told Pastor Bob that I will only continue in music and teaching until the beginning of the fall term. I thought we might want to decide together how we will serve.

"And I have already cut back on the street ministry to one night a week."

"That street ministry really bothers me," he cut in. "How could anybody organize such a thing - women working on the streets at night with all of the drug users and prostitutes? I have a few questions for anybody who would put together such a thing."

"Fire away, Dr. Braemer. You're looking at her."

He stared open mouthed. "You organized all this ... this ... this ...?"

"Somebody needed to do something. People were dying on the streets. The young were getting pulled into all kinds of misery at earlier and earlier ages, babies aborted and tossed into dumpsters, others left in garbage bags.

"It's always been a mystery to me; some young couples who want to have a little one so desperately can't conceive. But the young girls on the street ... they are abused, wasted on drugs, yet their emaciated bodies conceive. Sometimes they already have AIDS.

"We have such a small city, and the problem is already so bad. Who should do something about it, Michael?"

"You can't rescue the world, Rhea. You've taken on half

the continent of Africa. You're only one little person ... powerful little person, I have to say!"

"I really don't want to rescue anybody. But I can brighten my little corner. If I can teach others to help themselves, give hope ..." She paused. Clearly she wasn't getting through.

"Is there anything in Riverview that doesn't bear your fingerprints, Rhea?"

"Nothing I'm ashamed of."

"Nor should you be. I'm sorry, Rhee. I guess I just don't understand your passion."

"Who do you think should help the poor and the disenfranchised, Michael. They can't help themselves and they can't help each other. Dad always used to say that we are born to privilege; and with privilege comes responsibility. Look at us, Michael. We have it all - health, education, money. We can study whatever we want, get involved in sports, travel, music, the arts. I don't miss what I give away."

"I hear you sweetheart. I'm willing to take another look at your work on the street."

"I would like you to come with me sometime, and see what goes on. I'm willing to look at other options if you're adamantly opposed to it, but I'll need to get some things in place before I withdraw from the frontline."

"Would you really do that, Rhea?"

"I'd really like you to come with me some evening? Then we'll talk some more."

He nodded. "I agree; I'd like to see for myself what goes on there."

"I'd like to talk about our finances, too, Michael."

"Really! Do you think we won't have enough to live on?" he asked with a note of incredulity in his voice.

"No," she laughed. "It's what we should do with what we have, that I think we need to talk about. I have a lot of property, investments, money. I inherited from my folks, as well. If it turns out that they are still alive, we will have an interesting time sorting things out."

"Wow," he said. "That never occurred to me."

"Both Mom and Dad had pretty fair-sized insurance policies. Jonathon and I asked the insurance company to invest the monies in our names. I was able to convince Jonathon that if our folks were suddenly to appear, we would be liable to return the monies. This way, it should be a rather simple process to simply sign it back. There really must be a question in his mind about Mom and Dad, or he wouldn't have agreed to that."

"Wow," he said again. "You have certainly had a lot on your plate these last three years."

"Michael," she said earnestly, as she leaned across the table toward him, "do you really think you want to be involved with me? It seems to me that your life as a single has been pretty uncomplicated. You have only yourself to worry about; if you want to do something, or go somewhere, you just go ahead with it. Do you really want the responsibility that goes along with me, and maybe with my family?"

"I'm getting the impression that you see me as pretty self-centered. Actually, I'm getting the impression that I *am* pretty self-centered. But I haven't seen anything so far that would scare me off. I want you in my life, Rhea, and whatever that means, I'm willing to work with it."

"Thank you," she said, taking his hand across the table. "We need to check out, and I need to head for the airport. Will you pick up my earrings from your coffee table?"

Chapter 15

Jonathon, Jonathon

"Paging Dr. Rhea Rhymer, calling Dr. Rhymer, will you please report to the Information Desk. Calling Dr. Rhymer," she heard as she entered the terminal.

Jonathon Fields, I hope you're not behind this, she thought as she made her way to the desk. She suddenly felt herself being whisked off her feet and whirled around.

"Surprise! Surprise!" She steadied herself as she recognized her brother, Jonathon.

"What are you doing here?" she asked. "I thought you were in Australia."

"It's a long story. I can tell you over dinner. I've been here since yesterday and I've been having a ball. By the way, the hotel clerk, Mrs. Bellamere, remembered me. She gave me the room next to yours."

"How did you know when I was coming and where I'd be staying."

"That was easy," he laughed, "I still know you pretty well. You're not the only one who knows how to figure out these things, you know. Mrs. Bellamere graciously let me know that you'd be checking in around noon. From there it was a small matter to check on which flight came in just before 12. No sweat!"

"You really are very sharp."

"I come from a long line of them," he mimicked.

"But I can't have dinner with you; I'm already spoken for. Would you settle for lunch and the afternoon together?"

"Yea, okay. But who's the date? Anybody I know?"

"Oh sure ... Jonathon Fields."

"No kidding. You and Jon finally have somethin' goin'?"

"No. No. Definitely not. I haven't seen him since the summer we graduated. This is just for old-times' sake and it was arranged months ago. Actually, I have something going with someone else ... and it's getting really serious."

"No kidding. Anybody I know."

"Yes. You know him really well. But you must realize this is privileged information. Very few know that we are seeing each other and I want to keep it that way until we're engaged."

"Wow," he exclaimed, letting out a low whistle. "So it's *that* serious! Is this lucky man a medic of some sort ... a doctor?"

"You bet he's a doctor! About the lucky thing ... I'm not so sure."

"So, are you going to let me in on this top secret?"

"Dr. Michael Braemer."

Another whistle. "So he finally took my advice. I told him years ago to look you up and marry you. How did he find you?"

"The Chief finally succeeded in getting him to come to St. Michael's. He probably saved my life the night I had the accident. He describes it as my 'crashing in on him,' which is just about the truth."

"Wow. Are you carrying this grateful thing a little far?"

"You're the second one to suggest that; the other one

was Jared. It makes me smile. Anybody who knows Michael the way you do, must surely know that most eligible females would love a chance at him. He has all the qualities I've been looking for in a man. And I didn't know that he had interned with Dad, or that he knew you, until last week-end. We were both surprised and delighted to find out who we were," she laughed.

"And how about you, Jonathon? I'm sure you didn't come from Australia just for this reunion."

"You're right about that. Actually, the Chief has been asking me to come for the last few years. Says he could use a good oncologist at St. Mike's.

"So? Why haven't you come before? And why now?"

"Well, I've always been interested, but I was enjoying my work in Sydney; also I've had another very special reason for hanging around this last year."

"Tell me about her," she teased.

"She's a doctor. Thought I ought to keep the tradition," he said with a slight smile, "but I guess it's not going anywhere. She's specializing in pediatrics, and I wonder some days if she knows I'm alive. When I tried to tell her about my dream to return to Canada and work in a small research hospital, she didn't have time to hear me out."

"Oh Jon, I'm sorry!"

"So, I'm here for a few weeks to finalize details with the Chief; then I'm going back to finish my term at the hospital and pack my belongings. I should be here by the end of August."

"That's wonderful, Jon ... it will be just wonderful to have you nearby. I've missed you terribly. But I'm sad for you. Is there no chance that this will work out for you and ... guess I don't know her name."

"Dr. Lucinda Robinson. I call her *Luci*, and sometimes *Lady Rob*. Guess that comes from Dad always calling Mom, *Lady Rhee*. She's very lovely ... an ash blonde ...

about your height ... and shape ..." he laughed. " Guess I sound like a man in love; I fell pretty hard."

"Oh Jon ... dear Jon. So you're just going to walk away from her?"

"Probably. I'm not sure she'll notice ... that I'm gone, I mean. I really don't understand what happened to us. We spent a lot of time together, had a lot of fun. We never talked about the future ... she would just change the subject ... but she seemed to really love me. This last while she just filled her life with work. I was there whenever she needed me to take her to the airport, or pick up her dry-cleaning, but our times together were non events."

"So you think she's afraid of commitment?"

"Maybe. Or maybe I'm not what she wants to commit to. I'll see her again when I go back, but these two weeks away will give me some thinking time, and I'm hoping she'll be evaluating her feelings while I'm gone. I really can't go on like this any more."

The card said,. "Welcome to Homecoming, Ladybug. Shall I pick you up at 6:00?" The familiar scrawl, "Jonathon."

"Ladybug," she thought, remembering how he had named her that after a particularly successful football game. She had led the cheerleaders, all dressed like ladybugs. Now she stood a long moment looking at the bouquet on her dressing table. *Yellow roses. Yellow roses, indeed!* She wasn't sure she had gotten over the last bouquet of yellow roses. More seriously, was he trying to revive a childhood relationship ... from thirteen years ago? She had been so sure of herself when she told Michael about him.. Now she found it unnerving. How should she respond to him? How would he respond to her?

She wouldn't have long to find out; better get showered and changed. She hoped her choice of an off-white, linen sheath, with gold accessories would fit whatever Jonathon had in mind. She berated herself for not asking what to wear.

The slight knock sent shivers up her spine. *Rhea, get a grip,* she told herself as she opened the door.

Whatever greetings they had intended evaporated as they stood silently looking at one another. "Jonathon! Jonathon Fields! You are even more handsome than I remembered!"

"And you, Dr. Rhymer, are more ravishing ... more beautiful!"

She admired his well-tailored sportcoat and slacks. He was indeed what Michael would call 'well-heeled.'

"I hope you're not in a hurry this evening," he commented, as they turned onto the Old Beach Road. "I thought we might spend some time reminiscing and catching up on each other's lives."

"Sounds wonderful. I have all evening," she responded, then wondered whether they were at this moment heading back down memory lane. They were getting dangerously close to the resort where they had spent their last evening together ... thirteen years ago ... dining and dancing. *Surely he wouldn't do that,* she thought.

The resort had been refurbished and was larger than she remembered. They were obviously expected and ushered onto a delightful garden patio overlooking the lake. The scent of flowering shrubs and hanging baskets hung heavily in the air, and mingled with the poignant smell of gingerroot and spice. The aroma of steak barbequing piqued her senses and stirred her appetite.

"I hope you don't mind my bringing you here," he offered once they were seated. "I felt that I needed to apologize for the last time."

"It's a lovely spot," she assured him, "so serene and...well ... rather intoxicating. I remember it as being very romantic."

She met his eyes across the small table. They were warm and inviting, and she realized that she had put her finger on the pulse of his intentions. O God, *I'm getting in a little deep here,* she prayed. *I need an opportunity to tell him about Michael.*

"Maybe you'd like to tell me about the last time we were here, Jonathon," she invited.

"I recall you seemed to be rather distressed. Was I responsible for causing you ...?"

"No ... certainly not. I was plenty distressed ... depressed ... and yes, it did have a lot to do with you, but it was not of your making. I had envisioned quite a different kind of evening. I've always been sorry that I blew it so badly."

"I'm sorry. I shouldn't have asked. We don't have to go there if you'd rather not."

"I need to go there, Rhea. I brought you here to apologize ... to explain what happened ... maybe to clear the air and leave us both feeling better about the special relationship we enjoyed during those years." She nodded as he went on, "I was in love with you, Ladybug. I fell in love that first year we worked on projects together. You were so full of life ... ideas ... enthusiasm. There was nothing about you that I didn't admire. But I was 16 years old, Rhee. I had just gotten my driver's licence. It was a bit early to be so in love ..." he stopped as his eyes misted over.

You never told me how you felt, Jon. Not in three years. We were always so casual with each other ... more like buddies than a dating couple. Do you remember our prom? You never even asked me to be your date. A day or two before, I remember wondering if you intended to take me. Then you called and asked what colour corsage I wanted, but you never did ask me to be your date. We just took each other for granted."

They sat laughing, then, "I am sorry, Rhee. You deserved better than that. I would do things a little differently if I had another chance. You know what they say about hindsight always being 20/20. Can I ask what you plan to wear tomorrow night, so I get the right colour corsage?"

"I'll be wearing white. Why don't you choose. It'll be a surprise."

"You really want to trust me with that?"

"I do."

"You know, Rhee, the years we dated were the most special of my life."

"They were special to me, too, Jon. On my way over I found myself remembering you with a very grateful spirit. I was such a newcomer ... almost a foreigner ... rather naive, as I recall. You just accepted me the way I was, and showed me the ropes. I'm sure it was your acceptance of me that gave me credibility with the student body. You were always out in front, sought after, applauded. You made those years a joy for me ... when they could have turned out quite differently."

"Thank you for being so generous. I remember that time quite differently ... all the guys trying to date you, carry your books, buy you hot dogs at the games, walk you home. It was a nightmare for me."

"You're exaggerating," she laughed. "I never even liked hot dogs, and I don't remember walking home with anybody but you."

"That last summer ... I knew I was in love with you. I wanted terribly to talk to you about our relationship and I brought you here."

"So what happened?"

"My folks. They were not impressed. I guess they realized that I had been getting pretty serious about you as the summer wore on. I'm sure they thought that as we each drifted off to a different university our relationship would die a natural death. They rightly perceived that I was taking steps to keep that from happening.

"Dad came home early from work that afternoon. They sat me down and told me in no uncertain terms that I was to break off our relationship; we were heading in different directions and would ruin each others lives."

Rhea smiled. "It is as I thought. We were never under any illusion as to how your family perceived ours. They saw us as wanderers, traipsing around the globe. They were right about our choosing such different directions, Jonathon. We may well have ruined each other's lives. Our world views are really worlds apart," she laughed.

"I never saw your family that way, Rhee. They always treated me so warmly, like I was family. I never really knew how to treat a girl, so I watched your brother, and tried to treat you like he treated the girls at school. I didn't get to know him well, but he was a role model for me in many ways."

"The night we came here, Jon, I felt so badly for you. I wanted to comfort you but I didn't know what to do. You were so very distraught; I had never seen you like that before. I guess I expected that we would talk about our futures, where we would go to school, when we would be home on holidays, if we would keep in touch … that sort of thing. I was just devastated when you dropped me at the door and left without even asking me to keep in touch. I remember dropping the roses on the table and running to my room. I must have cried all night."

His eyes misted as she continued, "In the morning Mom took me out for breakfast and a long talk. When I got home the roses had disappeared. I assumed Dad took them to the hospital, but he never said and I never asked."

"So what did your Mom say?"

"About the same as your folks. You know Mom. She's so spiritual about everything. She felt that the Lord may well have been using your folks to keep us from a lot of heartache in the future. I knew she was right, but I hated her for saying it. Thinking like an adult when you're seventeen and in love is really hard."

"Tell me about it!" After a moment he asked, "So you were in love with me, too, Rhee?"

"I sure thought so at the time ... whatever a teenager perceives love to be. I have to tell you, though, Jon, that there is somebody special in my life ..." She broke off as he caught his breath sharply.

"I was afraid of that." Then reaching across the table, he picked up her left hand, and noting the absence of a ring, he asked, "How special? He doesn't seem to have staked his claim."

She flushed. "All in good time."

"So who is this guy? I suppose he's a doctor?"

"Yes, he is a doctor ... par excellence!"

"Ouch! How is a lowly lawyer supposed to compete with that? May I ask his name? Is it that guy that saved your life after the accident?"

"How do you know all that?"

"I make my living knowing other people's business, you know; besides, I read the papers."

They both laughed. "So?" he asked, "Is it him, that Dr. Braemer?"

"You guessed it; but ... may I ask you to keep it quiet for now?"

"Sure, but why? Has he asked you to marry him?"

"No. But he will. And I'll say 'yes'."

"So what's he waiting for?"

"Me."

"So you're not sure about him?"

"I'm sure about him, Jonathon. I'm wildly in love with

Michael. But we only met when I woke up after the accident; that's hardly four months ago. I move very slowly on things that are important to me."

"So when I called you to arrange for tonight, you didn't even know him?"

"That's true."

"So would you have been open to a relationship with me, if he hadn't crossed your screen?"

"That's hard to know. If I am to be really honest I would have to say ... O dear ... I'm afraid I'm going to say this badly; I guess I have a problem with a man who says he loves me but can stay away from me for thirteen years. I need more than that; I need someone who can't live without me ... who can't let me out of his sight."

"I feel like that Rhea. I've followed your movements around the world. I have a whole scrapbook of your achievements and accomplishments. My Mom came across it one day and she just stood and looked at it. She was almost in tears. This ... this Braemer ... is he like that? How can he let you come to see me? He must be one cocky rascal ... sure of himself!"

She smiled remembering Michael's difficulty in letting her go. "He's not like you're imagining at all. He's warm and kind and generous. He also knows that I have a lot of commitments to keep ... commitments that I made before he came along. This is the only one with an old boyfriend," she laughed. "Besides, he needs to know that he's the only man in my life ... that I really have forsaken all others."

"I know who he is, you know. He was on the debating team at McGill when I was there. Some atheistic students were debating the existence of God. Braemer was on the team that the Navigators had organized to take them on. He's one sharp cookie!"

"I didn't know that he ever debated. Thanks for sharing that with me. But tell me ... help me understand why you never tried to get in touch with me, since you seemed to know where I was all the time."

"I tried ... again and again. You were always somewhere else and didn't respond. After a while I was afraid to. You're such a well-travelled, international ... and I'm such a small-town, provincial ..."

"Poor you," she laughed. "Never having the chance to live in the jungle and dine on live termites. You've been deprived!"

He went on, "The longer I waited the less-likely I saw my chances of having a relationship with you. Besides, I was afraid my folks may be right - not that you would ruin my life - but that I might ruin yours. Looking back, I think it was probably the main reason I listened to my parents. I knew you had your eye on the other end of the world, that you would probably practise medicine around the globe ... to expect you to be satisfied here in small-town Ontario ... I really would have ruined your life, wouldn't I, Rhee?"

"I don't know, Jon," she said thoughtfully. " It would certainly have been different."

"Shall we dance before we have dessert?" he asked, noting that she had pushed her plate back.

"Love to. That steak was perfect - way too large for me."

The lake lay shimmering in the afterglow of the sunset as they stepped onto the outdoor pavilion. *It's almost dark,* thought Rhea, noting the moon already on the rise.. *Have we really talked that long?*

She slipped easily into his arms and they moved together in long-remembered harmony.

"Moonlight ... soft music ... a beautiful woman ..." he murmured softly as he pulled her close. *Way too close,* she found herself thinking..

"It really is intoxicating, isn't it?" she responded, realizing that he knew full well what he was doing when he brought her here. "Do you come here often?"

"No. I hadn't been here since the night we came together. Then I came last week to check it out; I wanted to bring you here. I liked what I saw, so I made the reservation. I'm glad you were able to come tonight. Friday nights are probably a zoo in this place."

The music had slowed and she felt his arms pressuring her to rest her head on his shoulder. She lowered her eyes to avoid his gaze. Long-forgotten memories flooded her thoughts and bombarded her emotions. *I shouldn't have come,* she told herself.

"What's wrong, Ladybug?" he whispered gently. "Are you afraid you still love me?"

She didn't trust herself to respond. "Look at me, Rhee," he continued. "Look into my eyes and tell me you don't love me."

"I do love you, Jonathon," she responded tearily, "but I am very much *in love* with someone else, and I am going to be his wife."

"Rats," he muttered as he followed her back to the table.

"Would you mind if we drove and talked for a while?" he asked later as he turned on the ignition, "or am I already over my limit?"

She smiled consent.

The breeze stirred her hair as he nosed the convertible slowly along the Old Beach Road. The lake rippled and glistened beside them in the moonlight, while cottage lights seemed to dip and dance as they reflected from across the bay.. At length he pulled into a small cove overlooking the lake. His silence left her uneasy; she had only seen him this way once before.

"You wanted to talk?" she broke the silence. "Anything in particular?"

"Yes, several things in particular."

"Go for it."

"Rhee," he began, rather uneasily, "we need to talk

about us."

"There's a *you* and a *me*, Jonathon, but there is no *us.*"

"I can't believe that you would commit to a guy you hardly know - for only four months, is it? Honestly, Rhee, we've known each other for sixteen years ..."

"No we haven't, Jonathon. We met sixteen years ago, but we only knew each other as teenagers. Our relationship was very superficial; it revolved around sports, fun, and school. We never had a serious conversation in all that time. You really don't know me ... maybe you never have. I'm not the pigtailed cheerleader with pompoms in hand leading your parade.

"Look at me, Jonathon. I'm 30 years old. I'm a doctor. I deal with birth and life and death ... sometimes all three in one day. I've spent half of my life in the Third World, dealing with poverty, disease and death. Do you know about such things, Jon, in your world of high privilege and plenty?" She stopped, suddenly realizing she must sound rather judgmental.

"No, Rhee, I don't know about those things, but I know about you. I would never try to stop you from doing anything you wanted to do." He had turned toward her, his arm carelessly across the back of the seat. Now his arms encircled her and pulling her to him he murmured softly, "I love you, Rhee. I've never stopped loving you. We belong together. Marry me, Ladybug, marry me."

She stirred uneasily as the incessant buzzing roused her. *6:30* she muttered, fumbling for the phone. *That must be Michael.*

"Good morning, Rhea," she heard in answer to her "hello."

"Good morning, sweetheart. I saw you had called last

night but I didn't get in until 2:00. Thought you would probably appreciate my waiting till morning."

Silence! "Michael, are you there?"

"Yes. I'm here." Another silence. Then, "Rhea, are you sharing rooms with Jonathon?"

"Yes. Yes, I am. How do you know about Jonathon?"

"I gather I wasn't supposed to."

"It doesn't really matter. He wanted to surprise you when he comes home with me, that's all."

"Home with you!! Rhea ... for heaven's sake! How do you expect me to deal with that?"

"Sweetheart, I'm sorry you're so upset. I had no idea. How did you find out anyway?"

"The desk clerk told me. She said you have adjoining rooms and if you weren't in yours, maybe I could reach you in his."

"Possibly ... but we've hardly been in. I don't understand why you're so upset, Michael.

It's only Jonathon. I wouldn't object if you shared rooms with Tracy ..."

"Don't be ridiculous," he cut in, "Tracy's my sister."

"And Jonathon ... is my brother," she finished lamely as the phone went dead.

"Oh, Michael, sweetheart," she said aloud, suddenly wishing she had been fully awake when he phoned. Quickly she dialed his cell number. *It sounds so empty*, she thought as she counted to seven, then hung up.

"So just how many sweethearts can you handle in one twelve-hour period?" She looked up to see her brother in the doorway. "That must have been one incredible supper ... I waited up till after midnight. Just what time did you get in, Missie?"

"Hold on there, big brother. It's been a few years since I answered to anyone ... especially you," she laughed. Then added, "We'd better get showered and get some breakfast.

We have an early appointment with Jonathon Fields."

"Jonathon Fields? Why? What have we done?" he jested.

"We had a long talk about Mom and Dad last night. He has kept up on all of the news and data concerning them and he agrees there is no evidence that they actually died over there. His legal firm does a lot of international lobbying for the Government. He thinks they might be able to put a little pressure in the right place to get some action on it."

"Do you think he's capable of such a thing?"

"Well ... we'll have to decide after we meet with him today. I would have to say that even in highschool he accomplished everything he set out to do. My guess is that he's one very competent lawyer."

Chapter 16

Fields and Fields

The imposing glass and brick structure was new since Rhea had last been to Bridgeport. THE FIELDS BUILDING could have been a lavish hotel or shopping mall, Rhea thought as she noted the crystal chandeliers, palms and sparkling fountains in the main lobby.

"Definitely designed to intimidate," Jonathon commented as they stepped off the elevator into the oak-lined labyrinth. The 10th floor was reserved entirely for the offices of *Fields, Fields and Associates*.

"I'll tell Dr. Fields you have arrived," the receptionist said pleasantly. In seconds Jonathon swung easily through the oak doors and welcomed them himself. *He plays the part of the prosperous lawyer very well,* thought Rhea ... *impeccably dressed, distinguished, terribly handsome.* Then smiling to herself, she mused, *Maybe I'm making a mistake after all.*

"Your offices are very lovely; they reflect you very well," Rhea remarked as he seated them at the small oak table near the window and ordered coffee and rolls.

"Coming from you, I'm going to take that as a compliment," he responded. "Tell me how you see that."

125

"Well, let me see," she said looking around, "I think the paintings and sculptures speak of your love for the arts, and your knowledge of things international; the windows ..." she gestured with a sweep of her hand taking in the curved expanse of glass covering the two corner walls, "... the windows speak of your love for the beauty of the valley - the river, the town - and rather keep you in touch with the comings and goings below; and ... let me see... the oak finishings and furniture, and the touch of hospitality would seem to represent both the solid part of your personality and your generous nature. Don't you think so, Jon?" she finished, addressing her brother.

"You've said it very well, Sis," he replied suddenly coming alive.

"Your compliments are very generous," he said, obviously moved.

They were both surprised and impressed at the amount of material he had amassed in the past three years. His files bulged with newspaper clippings, news reports from the internet, transcripts of international newscasts, research and maps of the area in which the alleged accident had occurred, research on the various factions in the Congo, hospitals and clinics in the various areas where Dr. and Mrs. Reimer had worked.

"Why would you do all this?" Jonathon Reimer asked with a note of incredulity.

"I loved your folks," the lawyer responded. "They always treated me like a son. I have a personal interest in this case and I would love to pursue it. I e-mailed Rhea when she was over there at the time of their disappearance and offered my services, but she tells me she didn't get my message. She must have been in the outback somewhere."

The two doctors sat silently, each wondering what the outcome might have been had Rhea received the communication at the time. Three years of agony may have been averted for all concerned, if it could have been proved that they had been abducted.

"So what would you see as the next step?" Jonathon ventured.

"I would need to have your permission to go ahead; then I would poke around a bit and look for some hard evidence that they are alive. I expect to be in South Africa in late August and early September. I'd like to slip into the Congo and ..." he broke off as they exchanged glances, then added ..."Is there any chance that either of you could meet me there?"

I'll be in several African countries for the entire month of September," Rhea offered. "Actually my cousin, Lynda will accompany me; I'll be instructing the last phase of a couple of courses I started last year. If I know soon enough, I can arrange for a few days to meet you in the Congo."

"One thing about this bothers me," her brother began; "If Dad is alive somewhere, why haven't we heard from him? You know Dad, Rhea, he's so innovative and knows the African ways. If he's there somewhere he would have gotten a word to us somehow."

"I've wondered the same thing, Jon. But if they're way back in the sticks, with a ton of supplies and medications, they wouldn't need to send for supplies for a couple of years. They'll need to eventually, and I'm sure they'll pressure Dad to get more where that came from. I still hope we'll hear from him before long." Then turning to the lawyer, she asked, "Would a request for medical supplies constitute hard evidence?"

"It would indeed and it would give us a bargaining chip ... no more help from Canada unless they release your folks. So ..." he looked from one to the other, "are we going to go ahead with this?"

"Let's do it," Jonathon volunteered, looking at Rhea, who nodded slowly. "What would you like for a retainer?"

"I'm sorry, I should have mentioned that," the lawyer replied. "I would really like to do this out of my personal interest. If you would look after the disbursements ..."

"No, Jonathon, we can't do that," from Rhea.

"No way. You've already put a great deal of time into this," her brother remarked. "You put me to shame. Give us a day or two to transfer some funds. Would 20 grand do for a start?"

"No, don't do this. Half of that would be too much," the lawyer objected, as they shook hands and took their leave.

The light on her phone signalled a message waiting, as she opened the door to her room. *It might be Michael,* she thought as she quickly dialed the front desk. Her heart sank. Mrs. Margaret Fields had left her number. As Rhea changed into shorts and walking shoes, she pondered the call from Jonathon's mother. Probably another invitation to something or other. She took time to decide how she would respond, then reluctantly dialed the number. She declined the invitation to Sunday dinner, but yes, she would meet her at 3:00 o'clock in the hotel for coffee. *She definitely has something on her mind,* Rhea decided as she prepared to join her brother for lunch on the wharf.

She took time to quickly dial Michael's cellular number. He was not standing by..

"What are you wondering, Jonathon? You keep looking at me with that look in your eye."

"I'm wondering how you feel about Jonathon Fields. He's obviously in love with you, isn't he? And do you think he's doing this investigation to gain your affection? Has he asked you to marry him?"

"Hold it! One question at a time, okay!! So which one would you like me to attempt first?"

"Do you think he's in love with you?"

"No. I'm sure he thinks he is, but I maintain that he doesn't know me anymore ... maybe never has. He might be in love with the teenager I was when we saw each other last."

"So ... did he ask you to marry him last night?"

"Jonathon! You are awfully nosey. Why do you think you have to know the details of my personal life?"

"So, the answer is 'yes' then"

"Yes. He did ask me to marry him, and don't you tell a soul. Do you hear me?"

"I thought you were in love with Dr. Mike?"

"I am in love with Michael."

"You're not going to tell him about Jonathon's proposal?"

"Oh, brother. Stop it. Of course I am ... sometime ... certainly not now. He hung up on me this morning. I tried to call him twice; he doesn't answer."

"Why was that?"

"Well, I wasn't quite awake when he called at 6:30 this morning.. He tried to call me last night and the desk clerk said I was not in my room. She apparently asked if he would like her to call Jonathon's room since I might be there. He was very upset when he called this morning. Of course he didn't know you were here and, I'm guessing, but I think he may have assumed I was sharing rooms with Jonathon Fields. By the time I figured that out, he hung up."

"Wow, I can't imagine Mike doing that. He's always so gracious, caring, careful not to offend. Of course, I've never seen him in love. I can't even imagine it. He seemed so cool ... downright indifferent toward the opposite sex. We would go out together with a couple of girls ... attractive girls ... and just have a ball. He seemed to really have a good time, but he'd never call her, or make an effort to see her again. One gal cornered me in the cafeteria and asked me what was going on, and if she had offended him or whatever. She was a really lovely gal and was quite taken with him. Honestly, Rhee, I can't even imagine what you're telling me."

"So ... what do you think I should do? You know Michael a lot better in some ways than I do. Give me some advice."

Her brother sat deeply in thought for a few minutes, then asked, "Are you wondering whether you should marry Jonathon Fields?"

"No. His family is too superficial for me. I don't think I could ever fit in there. Why do you ask that?"

"Jonathon could give you everything you ever longed for, Rhea. He'd shower you with all the treasures money can buy."

"You said it, Jonathon. He could and would. The only problem is that I'm not longing for what money can buy. I have everything I need."

"So, what is the difference between these two men? They both love you. They're both very nice people, educated, handsome, kind, wealthy, well able to provide for you. Why are you so sure you are in love with Michael?"

"Some of it I can't explain, Jon, like the attraction, the chemistry. But some of it is really practical. Michael and I share a common love of medicine. We both love God, people, the Church. That oneness of purpose would be missing if I married Jonathon Fields. I would never be a partner with Jonathon. He would make the decisions for our lives and tell me later. I would be a china doll for him to show off. I'm not good at that. I'm way too practical ... and frugal in my own way. He thinks he would never try to stop me from anything I wanted to do. That's ludicrous. The first time I got involved in street ministry, or helping the homeless, his family would be so embarrassed!! It would never work, Jon."

"I think you may be right. I just want you to be sure about your feelings for Michael. I think he's pretty fragile emotionally. Probably because of the thing with his Dad."

"So do you have some advice for me right now?"

Again he sat silently for a few moments, then suggested, "Maybe give him a few days to think it over. He's pretty level-headed. I think he'll come around and give you a call."

"I've got to get back and change before I meet Jonathon's mother at 3:00. Thanks for the advice; thanks for listening."

Chapter 17

One More 'Fields'

S he rose quickly as Rhea entered the lobby. "Thank you for agreeing to see me," she said, extending her hand.

She's just come from the beauty parlour, Rhea thought, noting the blonde hair elegantly coiffed, her still-trim figure accentuated in the latest fashion from Vogue. *She could be downright beautiful,* she mused, *if she could just get rid of that determined look.*

"You look like a lady with something on her mind," Rhea offered as they sat over coffee.

"Yes, yes. I would have to say that I do. I....I....I must say this is very hard for me. I need to talk to you about Jonathon."

"Jonathon?"

"Yes, my son! First I want to say how sorry I am for ...for..."

Rhea waited, as the older lady fumbled for words, and her eyes filled with tears.

"I'm sorry we advised Jonathon badly concerning his relationship with you. We thought it would be best with each of you going your own way and all ...," she broke off again, then regaining her composure, she continued, "but he hasn't been able to ... he doesn't seem to ... he just isn't looking for anyone else. I feel we made an awful mistake. I think he still loves you, Rhea."

"Mrs. Fields," Rhea began, "we were very young, too young to consider a serious relationship. You were only exercising parental discretion ... keeping your son from making a choice that may have proved detrimental to both of us."

"We thought so at the time, but now ... now ... it has been so many years since then. He dates here and there but scarcely a second time. He was terribly excited to find that you would be at the homecoming. I haven't seen him like this since you left. He loves you, Rhea. And you ... you are still single, too. Could it be that you ...?"

She stopped as the younger woman looked up in surprise. Rhea sat quietly, her thoughts careening wildly in several directions at once. "Why do you think that Jonathon still cares for me?" she managed.

"He has a whole scrapbook of you. He follows your accomplishments with interest. More than that, I see him looking at pictures of you ... then I know he still loves you. He is still angry with us. He has never been the same since ... since ..."

"I am sorry to hear that, Mrs. Fields. Sorry that Jonathon has not found someone to love. I'm sure his differences with you have nothing to do with me."

"But I'm sure that they have."

"What is it that you want from me, Mrs. Fields?"

"Well ... I .... Oh, dear ... this is very hard for me. Would you ... could you reconsider ...?" She paused trying to read what she saw in Rhea's face.

"Mrs. Fields," Rhea began slowly, "I am very straightforward, not known for beating around the bush. It is no secret that I have never been your favourite person; in fact you have never liked me, or even attempted to get to know me in the three years that Jonathon and I were friends. I am not naive enough to think that anything has changed since we haven't seen each other all this time."

"Yes, yes, something has changed - my attitude. I am sorry that we didn't get to know you. Jonathon always wanted us to have you over; we didn't think it was good for him to be so serious about you when he was so young - to have only one girlfriend. We tried to discourage him, but he became even more determined. We would like to make it up to you. We would like you to come over so we can get to know each other."

She would like to use me to restore her relationship with Jonathon, Rhea thought as she asked, "Does Jonathon know about this? Does he know that you're talking to me about this?"

"No, no. He mustn't know. He would be very upset. I must ask you not to tell him."

"I can't promise you that Mrs. Fields. I will not offer the information, but if he should ask me, I would need to be honest."

"Can I ask you again, Rhea ... will you come to dinner on Sunday?"

"I am really sorry that I cannot come," Rhea replied, feeling sudden sympathy for the older lady. "My schedule is packed; in fact, I am due at the hair dresser in 20 minutes."

"So you won't consider seeing Jonathon?"

"Well, of course, I will. We will be together all evening, and then most of tomorrow. I'm looking forward ... it will be a special reunion."

They sat in silence for a few moments. It was not what Mrs. Fields had hoped for, but it was not an outright rejection.

"You know," Rhea offered at last, "you really don't need to go to bat for Jonathon. He's a big boy ... knows his way around ... knows how to go after what he wants." She wondered what his mother would say if she knew about last evening. Then looking at her watch, she added, "I'm sorry, I must be off."

Chapter 18

Betrayal

The sense of betrayal was beyond anything he had experienced ... the feeling of loss without precedent. Numbly he held the cell phone - its tinny ring echoing the emptiness of his heart. His finger refused to click the button. How could she do this to him!!! He had shared his heart with her. They had been so close. He could still feel the warmth of her body snuggling close to him, her lips on his neck, her fingers playing in his hair. He could hear her soft whisper, "I could never go with anyone else, Michael; I could never betray you like that. I love you, sweetheart. I'll always love you."

He wondered wryly how Samson had coped emotionally when he found Delilah had betrayed him to the enemy. "At least I still have my hair," he muttered to himself as he glanced in the mirror.

She had seemed so careful about spending the week-end with him in New York; and he had been careful to protect her privacy, her values, her reputation. Now he wondered how much of her was real.

She had cheerfully confessed to sharing rooms with an

old boyfriend. How dare she compare his relationship with his sister, Tracy, to hers with Jonathon! And how was he to cope with her bringing him home? "Does she really think I want to meet him? I suppose she thinks we'll be friends!! Oh, God, help. I can't handle this!"

His body shook with dry heaves but the tears refused to come. He was numb. Classes would begin in 20 minutes. *Better get over there and organize my materials*, he thought, fumbling with his shirt.

He muted the cell phone, dropped it into his attache case and headed for the classroom. By 5:00 he was dry-mouthed and shaking. *Better get a sandwich*, he thought to himself, suddenly realizing he hadn't eaten yet today.

His days became empty and meaningless. If only he could sleep. If only there were some way out of this life, except the obvious.

The hardcopy draft of the letter to his father lay on his desk. He had intended to get Rhea's opinion on what he had written before he sent it off. Now he swept it into the wastebasket. *What do I care who fathered me*, he muttered in despair.

Call display told him Rhea had called seven times. He couldn't bring himself to respond. *What more could she possibly have to say?*

Chapter 19

Homecoming

The familiar *tap tap tap* on the door set her heart thumping. *Why is this happening to me?* she asked herself.

He emitted a long, low whistle as she opened the door.

"I hope you still like purple," he said extending the boxed corsage. "I know it used to be one of your favourites."

Exquisite purple orchids peeked up at her. They would be gorgeous on her white gown. He had included a matching boutonniere for the lapel of his white dinner jacket. She affixed it for him, hoping he would not notice her trembling fingers.

He whistled softly as she turned from the mirror with her corsage in place. "You are absolutely stunning. I won't be able to take my eyes off you."

The evening flew by flawlessly in a blur of activity. The Grand March, the sumptuous banquet, the decorations, introductions, old friends, accolades; and always Jonathon by her side, smiling, nodding, making introductions, proud, and oh ... so protective! She caught glimpses of her brother Jonathon from time to time, surrounded by adoring females.

Midnight came too fast. Tomorrow would be another full day, beginning with the parade and ending with the square dance late into the night. Rhea did not plan to take it in. She would definitely need some rest before she participated in the worship service on Sunday morning.

"I'm afraid I need to go, Jon," she said, "I'm feeling rather depleted."

He apologized and quickly took charge, escorting her through the milieu and into the quiet of the outdoors. They drove in silence, enjoying the star-studded evening, the gentle breeze, and the companionable mood.

"I need to take you to your room," he said as he parked in a five-minute zone. Then added with a twinkle in his eye, "Don't worry, I won't come in."

He unlocked her door, then turning to her, he asked, "Are you square-dancing tomorrow night?"

"No, I think not."

"Good. Can we have some time together then?" Noticing her hesitation, he assured her, "Rhea, I promise I'll be good. You can trust me. Please ... let's be friends. Can we have dinner together?"

"Jon ... I ...," she looked down wondering how to refuse without hurting his feelings further. "I ... really ...," she began again.

"Please don't say 'no'," he coaxed, taking her in his arms and giving her a quick hug. "Will you at least sleep on it, or pray about it?" he teased.

"I already did. The answer was 'no.'"

"Rhea!"

She laughed. "Okay, then, we'll have supper together tomorrow, but I'll need to be home at least by 10:00."

"See you at six then."

She smiled and shook her head as she heard him whistling his way down the hall. "Rascal," she said to no one in particular.

"It's been another great day," he said as they scanned the menu. "Rhee, I'm so glad you came. I guess I need to apologize for crying all over you the other night. I promise I'll not repeat the performance."

She looked up in complete surprise.

"I want us to be friends, Rhee ... even if you marry Michael ... and I want you to know I'm not working on your parents' release to put pressure on you," he hesitated as the waitress approached to take their order, then added, "please say we can keep in touch."

"Jonathon," she said with deep emotion, reaching across the table and placing her hand on his, "you move me to tears. I knew you weren't just trying to get my attention with the thing about my parents. I know you too well for that. I hope you and Michael with be friends."

"Tell me about him. Help me to understand what there is about him that made you fall so *deeply in love*," he chided.

"Can love be explained?" she asked, looking up almost shyly through her lashes. "I didn't fall for him because he saved my life, or because he's a handsome doctor. I've probably worked with a hundred of those in my day. When I started to regain consciousness, I could hear him giving instructions to his team. His voice was quiet, kind, direct. When he examined me he was gentle and thorough. I was so drugged I could see him only in a blur, but I began to want to see who he was. I concluded he must be new at St. Mike's since I didn't recognize his voice.

"It was a few more days before I actually came alive a

little. He was making his rounds late one night and I was concerned for his welfare. We'd had a few couples break up because of the over-involvement of the husband at the hospital. I suggested he needed to be at home with his family but he stated rather matter of factly that they were a long way away. I took from that he was either married or separated. I really didn't want to get involved with him, though he had certainly gotten my attention. The resistance I had built up just melted away one day when he told me rather point blank that he was *very single.*

"Humanly speaking, we have a lot in common - our faith, ethics, love of medicine, music, sports - we both love to ski and swim, travelling, teaching, love of home and family. When I met Michael it was as though I had loved him for years - I just didn't know who he was."

"Wow! I had no idea it had gone all that deep. Knowing you, I should have guessed at least that you wouldn't have made such a decision lightly. He's one lucky rascal!"

"I really can't explain the *falling in love* part, except that we both knew what we wanted, the time was right ..." her voice trailed off.

They ate quietly, each absorbed in their own thoughts. Then looking up he asked suddenly, "Rhea, I need to ask you something. Has my Mother been in touch with you since you arrived?"

"Oh, my," she managed, the surprise showing on her face.

"So she has?"

"Does it matter to you, Jonathon?"

"You bet it matters. And she asked you not to tell me, right? That's why you're hedging?"

"You must be an incredible lawyer!"

He laughed. "Nice try! She's terribly disappointed that you refused Sunday dinner, and she doesn't give up easy. Is that what she wanted?"

"You're really hard to deal with you know. I feel like I'm on the witness stand."

"Just answer the question and I'll let you off," he laughed.

"Actually, the subject of Sunday dinner did come up."

"So?"

"Please, Jonathon, I really don't want to talk about this."

"Did she tell you to keep away from me?"

"No, quite the opposite. She apologized for the way she had treated me in high-school and asked my forgiveness."

"Are we still talking about my mother?"

"Of course. She felt they had made a mistake in separating us and mentioned that since we were both still single ... maybe ...," she hesitated as he put his hands over his face.

At length he looked up, and in a choking voice he managed, "Hindsight is always 20/20.

"I'm sorry," he said, wiping his eyes. I promised not to do that." She sat silently as he tried to regain his composure, then, "I think I hate her sometimes, you know? Her endless control of my life. I know it was her doing to separate us. Dad really liked you. He knew I loved you but he would get so tired of her endless schemes that he would just give in to avoid the hassle. I went through periods of hating them both for what they did to me.

"I never played football again after you left. It seemed so ... empty ... pointless without you providing the adrenaline there in the stands ... or heading the cheer leading."

"Jonathon! What about your football scholarship? What did you do with that?"

"I turned it down. Mom had a jolly fit. I really didn't care. Actually, I felt good about watching her rant and rave, knowing she couldn't force me to do her will. I accepted the academic one and it almost paid for my first year at university ... though I didn't do very well. Guess I was just in a state of depression. Life had really lost its meaning for me.

"By the way, the barbeque is at my house tomorrow afternoon, you know; I didn't tell Mom about it or she would have tried to help. There'll be about 20 of us from our graduating class. I'm having the most of it catered. Your brother should come, too, if he'd like to."

"Jon, that's special of you. I didn't recognize the address, so I didn't know it was at your house. We need to leave around 4:00 to fly away by 5:00. Hope that works for you."

"Rhea, I need to go back to our relationship. Tell me ... how long did it take you to get over caring about me?"

"I still care about you, Jonathon. I don't expect to get over that. But the way I care has changed. The first month or so after I started university, I kept waiting to hear from you, hoping you'd call or drop a note. I cried sometimes - feeling lonely, rejected, frustrated at the turn of events. Finally, one day while I was having devotions, I realized I needed to get on with my life. It turned around at that point. I quit waiting and really got down to my studies. Things went much better after that.

"I found myself avoiding relationships like the plague. I would either compare my would-be suitors to you or to my brother Jonathon, and then reject them outright." She laughed, then went on, "So you've influenced my love life for the last thirteen years."

"So ... this Michael ... he measured up?"

She chuckled. "When I met Michael, I forgot all about you! Sorry ... but it never occurred to me to measure him against anyone. He was in a class all by himself."

"Wow. So you really have it for this guy." She nodded as he sat silently for a few seconds, then he continued,

"Rhea, I've often wished over these years that we had gotten pregnant when we were in high-school. There would have been no opposition to our getting married ..."

"Oh my, Jonathon! Oh my!" She sat a few moments as if in shock. "I would never have married you if you had gotten me pregnant. My relationship with you was built on total trust. I never felt afraid to go anywhere with you at any time. You were so gentle and treated me like a lady. You were my hero. If you had violated that trust ... I can't even think of it. I could never have trusted you again."

"So you wouldn't have married me? What would you have done with the baby? Abort it?"

"Heavens, no! I would have been a little single Mom with an awfully cute little Jonathon or Julie. Probably my Mom would have helped me, and I would just have gotten on with my studies."

He sat looking at her, his heart in his eyes. "You are one exceptional woman, Rhea Rhymer."

"Jonathon," she ventured at length, again reaching across the table and placing her hand on his, "You need to come to grips with your feelings about me, and let them go."

"I've tried, Rhee. God knows I've tried. I've dated here and there but I keep seeing your face and it all goes awry. How do you suggest I do this?"

"You might start by getting rid of the scrapbook, and any pictures and mementos you have of our years in high-school. You can hardly forget me if you keep feeding your thoughts and emotions on memories."

"I'm not sure I can do that yet, Rhee."

"Oh, Jonathon. Why not give it to me."

"Will you destroy it?"

"No."

"Will Michael object?"

"I don't think so. Maybe one day we'll show it to our

grandkids."

"I'll think on that, Rhee."

"I need to go, Jon. Will we see you in church tomorrow?"

"Yea. I understand you're singing. I don't want to miss that. Though I haven't gone in years. It was just another control thing of Mom's."

"Dear Jon. Church is more than that... so much more. But I'm glad you'll come tomorrow. Actually Jonathon has consented to sing with me."

The church was packed, standing room only, as Rhea and Jonathon made their way to the podium. Jonathon spoke briefly, thanking them for their concern, support and prayers during the painful loss they had experienced nearly three years ago. He introduced their special number and they sang together in harmony.

Rhea was overwhelmed with emotion as she recognized so many old and dear friends of her folks. Many of them were in tears as they listened to the duet. She felt again their care and concern for the awful loss they had experienced. She wondered how they would respond if they knew what investigations were going on behind the scenes and the possibility that Matt and Rhea might still be alive.

Mr. and Mrs. Fields sat stiffly in their usual spot, the second row on the right. *Some things haven't changed*, thought Rhea, but was that just a little bit of emotion she was seeing on both of their faces? *Perhaps some things have changed after all.*

She noted Jonathon Fields sitting alone near the back. He glanced up from time to time, his eyes full of tears. *Jonathon, dear Jonathon, God has somebody special for you … just the right girl to be your running mate. Trust Him with your life, please Jon.* Then she added a prayer that God would make him willing to accept God's plan for his life.

Chapter 20

Home Again

"That's been one full week," Jonathon commented, as they put the finishing touches on supper. "I'm glad the Chief and I connected so well. I'm really looking forward to getting back to Canada and getting my life together, and I'm glad I have a full month to make the move from Australia. I'll miss it though ... and I'll miss Luci ..." he broke off wistfully.

"We both seem to have a love life that isn't going anywhere," Rhea responded. "I sure wish I knew what to do about Michael."

"He'll come around, Rhee," he offered, putting his arms around her and planting a kiss on her forehead. "Anyway you'll always have me," he added with a grin.

"Michael," Rhea screamed, as she pushed Jonathon away and ran for the door. Jonathon turned to see Michael leaning on the door frame and slowly sinking to the floor. A few long strides and he had him in his arms and carried the limp form to the armchair.

He ran for his bag as he barked instructions to Rhea, "Call 9-1-1. We'll need intravenous ... he looks dehydrated

... oxygen ... some blood work. She dialed quickly, asking if Dr. Jeremy Paulson was in Emergency. His voice was calm and businesslike and Rhea knew her requests would be attended to thoroughly and at once.

"Would they bring him in?" he wanted to know.

"Probably not," from Jonathon. "Not until we know what he has; it could be something he picked up from the many international students in New York. Could be meningitis. He seemed to go down so fast ... his temperature dangerously high ... his blood pressure dangerously low.

"We need to get him into bed. He can share the guestroom with me," offered Jonathon. "Good thing those twin beds are adjustable; he's sure having a time trying to breathe." They busied themselves making him comfortable, sponging his face and chest in an attempt to lower his temperature. It seemed only minutes before Jeremy arrived with the intravenous and oxygen. The blood work was dispatched to the lab as the three doctors stood guard over the comatose patient, marvelling that he had driven from New York, recognizing God's intervention in directing him to Rhea's without accident or incident.

"Good thing he didn't head for his apartment," Jeremy offered. He would have died there alone ... if he got there at all." They nodded in agreement.

"What do you think might be the problem, Dr. Paulson?" asked Jonathon, after they had checked his vital signs again.

"Hard to know. Maybe meningitis, or maybe some type of viral pneumonia. There's just so many strains of that stuff going around out there. Either could have left him dehydrated and unconscious, but his lungs sound really strange, his breathing shallow, his colour bad ... my guess would be pneumonia." He looked at Rhea.

"I think you're right on the money, Doctor," she nodded.

"It'll be a while before we get the lab report. Why don't

you two get your supper and I'll keep watch here," suggested Jeremy. "Maybe we could pray first."

They bowed together in prayer, seeking the healing power of God, thanking Him for the collective wisdom He had bestowed upon them as physicians, asking for His guidance. Rhea felt the heaviness roll away as Jonathon committed Michael to the power of God and to His divine will.

Supper had been reheated and as they began to fill their plates, Jeremy's urgent voice broke in, "Doctor Rhee, I think he's quit breathing; can you come?"

She struggled to shed the heavy bonds of sleep. *Funny,* she mused, as a vague state of consciousness returned, *I feel as though I'm being watched.* Suddenly sensing movement, she opened her eyes to find Michael watching her.

"Where am I, Rhea?" he asked weakly as he pulled down the oxygen mask, "and why all this?" he indicated the oxygen, intravenous, and blood-pressure monitor. "Am I at your house?"

"Michael ... you're awake!" She slid off the twin bed where she had dozed for the last two hours. "Yes ... yes, you are at my house. How are you this morning?"

"What am I doing here? How did I get here?"

"You drove here last night. I presume from New York. You were very sick when you arrived and just passed out."

"I drove here? from New York? I sure don't remember that. I remember leaving for home sometime in the afternoon," he paused, confused. "So what's all this?"

"You were very sick ... dehydrated ... high temperature ... low blood pressure; we thought you might have meningitis, so we just kept you here. Actually, you have a type of viral pneumonia that is very quick acting.

Your blood is very low, Michael. We think you need a transfusion to get you back on your feet. I called your folks. Your father tells me that you share a common blood type and he would like to ..." she paused as Michael grimaced. "They'll be here this afternoon," she finished as he lay looking at her.

"He doesn't have to come all that way to give me blood. My type is really common. Actually, Jeremy has the same type."

"Yes, I know, Michael, and Jeremy has already offered. He donates all the time. But your folks wanted to come anyway. It wasn't up to me to refuse his offer."

"Are you my doctor, Rhea?"

"No. I'm the nurse."

"So who's responsible for all this?"

"Dr. Jonathon Reimer. He came home with me from the homecoming. He was here when you arrived. Jeremy was just finishing his shift and brought the equipment and supplies, so we all worked on you together."

"Oh ... Oh my!" He paused to process this new information. "So where are they now?"

"Jeremy went home about midnight. He wanted to come back and stay with you for a while today. Jonathon just went to bed around 6:00 when I got up and traded places with him."

"It took all of you to look after me?"

"Yes, Michael. Please put that oxygen back on. Your breathing is really shallow. You're exhausting yourself with all the talk." He lay quietly, his eyes closed.

She brought a basin of warm water and a washcloth. "Your temperature was pretty high in the night," she said as she began to gently wash his face, his neck, his chest, arms, hands.

His eyes scarcely left her face as she finished the sponging and drying, and smoothed his hair. "I'd no idea you knew how to nurse," he offered.

"Necessity," she smiled, "the mother of invention."

"Rhea," he said as she straightened the sheets, "Are you angry with me?"

"No, Michael. Should I be?"

"You have every right to be."

"We'll talk about this another time, Michael. I'm sure we'll straighten it all out. Right now, you're way too sick to expend this kind of emotional energy. Can you take a sip of this orange juice?" She slipped her arm under his shoulders and helped him sit up.

He lay back exhausted, the effort obviously too much for him. "So my folks are coming today?"

"You may want to discuss your Dad's offer with Jonathon. We were of the mind last night that you would need something to give your system the kick start it needs for recovery. We'll have the blood checked thoroughly to make sure we don't give you something else that you don't need." She paused, then continued, "I really think you are far too sick for company right now. You need all the rest you can get. How do you feel about that?"

"Relieved!"

"Good. Then we won't let anyone in until at least tomorrow or Monday. Your folks will be staying with the Chief and Joan. I'll call and tell the Chief what we've decided. I know he'll get them to co-operate with the visitation thing. Sleep now," she added as she moved toward the door.

He drifted off. Muffled sounds coming from the kitchen always gave him a sense of home and security. He found himself wondering whether one day she would be making happy sounds in *their* home rather than just in *hers*.

"Boy, Dr. Mike, you've had a tough go," Jeremy stood reading the chart. Thought we'd lost you a few times, there."

"Why was that?"

"Well, you quit breathing; heart slowed away down. Dr. Reimer and Dr. Rhee are some team! They must have worked together before. They know what they're doing in an emergency. It was a joy to watch them ... even in the circumstances. We worked on you for hours. Just when we thought you were stable, you'd quit all over again."

"Wow. I had no idea."

"Sure a good thing you came here," the younger doctor continued. "You may have died if you'd just pulled into your parking lot, or even gotten to your apartment."

"I don't remember a thing, Jeremy. Can't remember coming here."

"I think the Lord directed your subconscious. He brought you to a place where you'd be cared for. And both doctors were here. That Doctor Reimer can sure move. I'd never met him before, but I understand he's going to be the new oncologist at St. Mike's. I'm sure looking forward to getting to know him. Guess he's going back to Australia in a week or so to get his stuff."

Michael's face showed his surprise. "He's a great guy, and an excellent doctor. I hadn't heard he was coming here, but it's great news. So sorry I gave you all such a bad time. When am I out of here?"

"Out of here? Man, I'd just relax and enjoy!" Jeremy quipped with a twinkle in his eye. "There isn't a single guy at St. Mike's that wouldn't change places with you. By the way," he added after completing the chart, "I left some blood for you this morning when I did my rounds. I thought in case you needed it before your Dad ..." he stopped as he noted the look on Michael's face. "You don't have to use it, you know ... just a precaution."

"Michael, ol' boy, so glad you're still with us," Jonathon burst into the room in his usual exuberant manner. "I've been waiting to set eyes on you again, but really ... you certainly got my attention last night."

Michael grinned. "We just do whatever it takes. Thanks for being there, buddy."

"Now that's more like it," he commented looking at the chart. "Mike, I want you to have a couple units of blood, and that right quick. I'm not sure what happened here. It seems to me that something has lowered your resistance ... allowing the virus to take hold."

"You don't think the pneumonia caused ...?"

"Not likely. I suspect a pre-condition. Your blood was really out of whack. I'm amazed you got here. Your guardian angels were certainly working overtime. I'd like to do some serious investigating when I get back from Australia at the end of August ... unless of course you have somebody else ..."

Michael shook his head wearily, "No ... no ... I don't know any doctors. I've never been sick enough to need one," he smiled.

"I understand we now have Jeremy's two units on hand," Jonathon continued. "Since he's all checked out, I suggest we go ahead at once. Once your father arrives we'll stock up a little in case we need to do this again. Are you okay with that, Mike?"

"May I see the chart?" Michael asked, reaching for the clipboard. "Wow! Guess we'd better do something," he agreed, handing it back. "Can't imagine how I got that bad that fast"

"You look a lot better this morning; even a little colour," Rhea noted as she checked his vitals.

He laid his hand on hers as she checked his pulse. "Rhee," he said, putting it to his lips. "Can we talk now?"

"Will you eat some breakfast then?"

"If you get rid of this intravenous, I'll eat or die trying."

She smiled and perched on the edge of the bed. "Talk away," she invited.

He looked into her eyes several times; they were especially warm and friendly, though her manner had been cool and professional. "Rhee," he began, then faltered. She waited. "Rhee," he began again,. "I need to ask your forgiveness for my behaviour last weekend. Will you forgive me for not trusting you - yet one more time?"

"I forgive you, Michael. Neither of us knew that my brother would be there, so I can understand what happened. Mrs. Bellamere was so excited at seeing both of us together after so many years, that she just told anybody who would listen ... and the fact that we were staying in *her* hotel ..." her voice trailed off ..."What I'm struggling with, Michael, is ... is your refusal to let me explain, or to answer my calls. I called seven times, Michael. Tell me ... explain this so I can understand."

He lay quietly, his eyes closed. When he looked up, they were full of tears. "I don't know what happens to me, Rhee. I just can't handle emotional pain any more; I just run away, withdraw, hide."

"But if you would have listened to me Michael, you wouldn't have had the emotional pain. You woke me out of a deep sleep and by the time I realized that you thought I was sharing rooms with Jonathon Fields, you hung up on me. I don't know how to deal with that; it leaves me with a lot of questions ..."

"Are you wondering if that's what happened with Dad?"

"Is it?"

"I don't know," he replied thoughtfully. "I don't think so. If Dad had ever tried to contact me, I would have answered.

I would have been apprehensive but ecstatic. I did write him, you know. I actually tried to call you on Thursday night to get your input on what I'd written. That's when the hotel clerk told me about you and Jonathon. I had a pretty miserable night. Actually I had a pretty miserable couple of days. I finally made myself settle down and think. Then I realized that even if you were sharing adjoining rooms with Jonathon Fields that I could trust you. You said you would never cheat on me, and I decided it was time to believe it. I had trashed the letter a few times, but finally decided to send it anyway. Dad e-mailed me right back and said ..." his chin quivered as he continued, "and said I am his son."

"Dear Michael," she whispered, squeezing his hand. "I'm so glad for you ... for us."

"For us? Does that mean you still love me?"

"Of course I love you!"

"Even after this?"

"Dear Michael," she stroked his cheek, "Love can't be turned off like a water tap. Neither of us is perfect. We just need to learn to deal with the problems as they come up."

"Will you hold me, Rhee," he asked, pulling her toward him. She leaned over and took him gently in her arms. "I'll never refuse to take your calls again, sweetheart," he offered. "Can we make that a promise between us?" She nodded eagerly into his shoulder, as he continued, "I should probably have called you and apologized for my behaviour but it seemed so trite; I thought I'd best come and see you and ask your forgiveness. Maybe that's why I wound up at your house, even if I was out of my mind." She smiled as he promised, "And I'm making a commitment to never mistrust you again."

She sat up. "Oh, dear Michael," she said with a startled look on her face, "You're going to have lots of opportunity to practise that one. I'll be meeting Jonathon Fields in the Congo for a few days in September."

She let him pull her close again for a few moments, then, "Michael, it's time for some breakfast. How about a glass of juice and some hot cereal? Jeremy and Jonathon will be home in a couple of hours. I suggested they bring Pastor Bob along for Sunday dinner; he's been calling and wanting to see you, but I've been holding him at bay. Maybe you could get up for a while and join us at the table." She looked at him questioningly.

"Yes, yes and yes," he responded cheerfully. Then added, "Thanks for staying with me today, Rhee."

"Oh, yes, I forgot to mention that I've invited your folks for breakfast tomorrow. They'll probably stay with you for a few hours while I slip to the hospital. I thought you might like a little time…"

His eyes were soft and warm as he looked at her, "You are one special girl, Rhea Rhymer," he responded with deep emotion..

Chapter 21

Braemer and Braemer

"**D**o come in," she welcomed cheerily offering her hand. "I'm Rhee Rhymer." Then looking at the distinguished gentleman with sandy hair and grey-green eyes, she commented, "There's no mistaking you, Mr. Braemer; I have one just like you in the dining room."

Michael stood unsteadily to meet his folks as they approached the breakfast table. His mother embraced him tearily, his father shook hands warmly and Rhea noticed that he was not far from tears himself.

Conversation was light as they enjoyed the fruit salad, baked omelette, breakfast sausage and rolls.

"More coffee?" Rhea offered, as she brought the carafe.

"Now, young lady, I'm going to get right to the point," the elder Braemer spoke suddenly, though Rhea noticed a twinkle in his eyes.

He's so like Michael, she thought. *How could he ever wonder if he was really his father's son?*

"Why yes, Mr. Braemer, please do come to the point," Rhea replied smiling.

"I'm not impressed ..." Rhea noticed Michael's mother tugging at his sleeve, but he pushed her hand aside and continued, "... with your medical staff ... not allowing me to see my son for nearly two days. And another thing, why is he here in a private situation when he should be in the hospital and being taken care of properly? And further-more, I came as quickly as I could to give blood for my son, and they haven't taken it yet. I need to go home this after-noon."

Michael sat silently, regretting the outburst, feeling for Rhea, wondering how she would respond.

"Whoa, there!" she laughed. "One thing at a time. Firstly, the decision to allow no visitors was a joint decision of the doctors looking after Dr. Braemer. His blood was so low and his system so weak that even a few cold germs could be potentially fatal. This is a 'doctor' town and when doctors speak as a team they carry a lot of weight. You can see him today only because his blood has recovered with the transfusion from one of the young doctors here. Believe me, he looks a lot better today and is able to be up for a short while."

Mr. Braemer looked at Michael, who nodded his agree-ment with Rhea's explanation.

"Now, where were we?" Rhea continued. "Oh, yes, why is he here instead of in hospital? That's a rather interesting question. Dr. Braemer stopped in here on his way home from New York on Friday evening. He had just come in when he suddenly collapsed - comatose - unconscious. Dr. Reimer was here at the time and we weren't sure what we were dealing with. He was very dehydrated and we suspected he might have meningitis, so we called the hospi-tal for everything we needed to make an accurate diagnosis, plus intravenous, monitors and medical paraphernalia. Once we determined he had viral pneumonia, we just kept him here. We both know your son and thought he would prefer staying here to hospitalization."

"She's right, Dad. I'm in excellent hands, and I'm very comfortable ... at home."

"So, you refused my blood?" he asked, turning to Michael.

"No, no, of course not. It just takes a few days to have it checked out, especially over the week-end. I expect we'll hear from them today. Are you still prepared to give in case I need some more?"

"Absolutely," he affirmed as Rhea jumped up to answer her cell phone.

"Yes, they are still here. Why don't you join us for coffee and you can see him here?" she said into the phone. "Yes, they'll be here all morning with Michael. I'll be heading to the hospital in a half hour or so."

"That was Dr. Reimer," she said, answering the questioning look in Michael's eyes. He's coming by to see your Father..." she was interrupted by the ringing of her cell phone.

"Rhymer," she answered noting from the call display that the hospital was on line. "The trips! Right on schedule! Fantastic! Is Dr. McCaig available? Ask him to scrub with me on this one. I should be there in 20 minutes."

She moved quickly, slipping the cell phone into her medical bag, as she spoke, "I'm so sorry to run. Dr. Reimer will be here in a few minutes and he will answer any further questions you might have, Mr. Braemer. Perhaps you would be good enough to help Michael back to bed, or ..." then looking at Michael, she asked, "or maybe you'd like to relax in the family room for a while."

He nodded, obviously pleased that she had remembered him, even in her busyness.

"He will need to drink at least two glasses of fluid," she held up an eight-ounce glass, "between now and lunch ...

water, juice, gatorade ... not tea or coffee."

His mother nodded and Michael looked amused, as she added, "See you at noon."

"What was all that about? And just who is this little lady?" his father asked as the door closed behind Rhea.

"Is Miss Rhymer a nurse? asked his mother sweetly.

"No. Actually, Rhee is a doctor. She heads the Obstetrics and Gynecology Department; they specialize in multiple births. She talked about the trips being right on schedule. That's her pet name for triplets. It's the second set of triplets this month."

"Oh my ... oh my ... oh my!' his mother exclaimed, as if in disbelief. "She's hardly more than a girl!"

"Well, I'll be!" was all his father could muster.

They were interrupted by the arrival of Dr. Reimer, who seemed to pull in just as Rhea left.

11:35, Rhea noted as she swung easily into her garage. *Hope Michael and his folks had a great time together. Wonder why Jonathon wanted to see Michael's Dad. Sure hope there's nothing wrong with his blood.*

Her cheery, "I'm back," was welcomed with subdued greetings from the three in the family room, she noted. She busied herself in the kitchen, trying not to eavesdrop on the quiet conversation.

"Sweetheart, can you join us?"

Sweetheart! she thought. *He must have told his folks about us.* "Yes, I'll be right there," she replied, "I'm just putting the soup on to warm."

Michael held out his hand to her as she entered the room. She noted his tear-streaked face, his Mother's red eyes, tissue boxes here and there. She allowed him to pull her gently onto the arm of his chair.

"Michael," she said putting her hand on his forehead, "You look absolutely spent. Shouldn't you be in bed?"

"In a minute, okay? Sit with me a bit." He slipped his arm around her waist and held her close. "I've just told my folks about our relationship."

"We're just delighted," his mother cut in.

"Indeed, we are," his father affirmed. Then added, "I understand you're Matt and Rheanne's daughter, and that.... that Dr. Reimer that just diagnosed my cancer is your brother. I must say ..."

"Cancer! Oh no! Oh my! I am so sorry. So very sorry. Do they know what kind?"

"Well, my PSA count is around 20, sounds dangerously like prostate cancer according to Dr. Reimer. He says I need an examination to confirm. Suggested I see my doctor as soon as I get home. We've been talking here with Michael; he suggested maybe Dr. Clark would take me on since Dr. Reimer will be away for a few weeks."

"Dr. Clark would certainly be the one. He's very competent ... wouldn't be at St. Mike's otherwise. Jonathon is just moving back here from Australia. He'll be joining our team of oncologists. But isn't this a little far for you to come, especially if you need radiation or ...?"

"We'd be glad to make the trip, or stay in town, or whatever is required," Michael's mother offered quickly, "just so he gets the best treatment," she brushed away a tear.

His father chuckled, "And especially if I get the same kind of treatment I see my son enjoying."

Michael and Rhea exchanged a smile. "Time for you to go to bed, Michael. Have you been drinking enough?"

"Oh, my, no," his mother confessed, "we've forgotten all about it. I think he had a glass of juice, though."

Michael smiled as Rhea helped him up. "Doctor, doctor," he chuckled.

"It feels good to lie down again," he said as she tucked

him in, and smoothed his hair. "I don't think I'll be well for a long time."

"Shall I get Jared to look after you next month when I leave for Africa?" she asked with a mischievous twinkle in her eye.

" I guess I'll get better by then," he decided grinning.

"So you knew my folks," Rhea began as she poured tea. "How did that come about?" There was a little silence, then Mr. Braemer cleared his throat, "We ... uh ... we were friends way back in our college days. Actually Lillian here and your mother roomed together, and Joan Wahl, too, when they went through nurses training."

Rhea noticed that he stammered rather uncertainly. "Oh really," she encouraged. "Of course I've known the Wahls all of my life; they were appointed our guardians when we were born, but I'm not sure I ..."

"No, you've never met us," he looked down as though not wanting to meet her gaze, "I'm afraid I played the fool." Lillian buried her face in her hands and he put his arm around her before he continued. "Your father and Herb Wahl and I were good friends; we all started university together. We ... uh ... we had a lot of fun together, we were all athletic. We often dated together. We were all believers and attended the college chapel. I met your Mother there and we dated a few times. When I found out she had two room-mates I arranged a date for the six of us," he paused looking down.

"So that's where my folks met?" Rhea asked.

"Yes. I'm afraid so. Matt looked across the table at Rheanne in the restaurant and never took his eyes off her all night. I was pretty ticked off. It made no difference to him that she was my date. She apparently returned his interest.

164

They danced and talked and laughed together as though the rest of us didn't exist. And it didn't end there. They were enthralled with each other. In no time, they were engaged."

"Oh my! I had no idea!"

He continued, "I was so angry, I moved out of the apartment. Herb tried to reason with me but I wouldn't listen. I never spoke to your Father again. He had taken what I made myself believe was mine, and without even a word of apology. Not that I had fallen in love with your Mother - just that he took her. Meantime, Herb and Joan had started dating regularly. I finally admitted to myself what Herb had told me all along ... that Lillian and I had enjoyed each other's company and that I found her very attractive. It took months before she would even consent to have coffee with me."

Lillian looked up tearfully.

"Of course we've always stayed good friends with the Wahl's," he continued, "not that we're close ..."

I'm glad to hear that," Rhea commented, not quite sure where to go from here.

"Then your Dad became a doctor, started making his mark around the world. I found myself resenting his success. Lillian always wanted to renew her friendship with Rheanne. I was still too angry to let her. Now I guess it will never happen ... I do regret ..." he broke off suddenly as Rhea drew her breath in sharply.

"I have played the fool; I have sown the wind and reaped the whirlwind. My grudge has cost me 12 years of my son's life. I was so angry when he refused to work with me, and I found he was working with Matt Reimer. Like rubbing salt in an open wound. I wanted to kill Matt Reimer. I refused to admit to myself that I saw all along that Michael was not cut out to be an architect; his gifts were always in music and patching up the hurting. It angered me further; somehow it made me feel left out ... like my two buddies being doctors and having so much in common. Michael always had so much in common with his mother, and I took it out on him."

Lillian sobbed brokenly at this last confession. "Oh Michael, Michael, if only ..."

"He is my son, Rhea. He told me the two of you were wondering. How else could he have gotten where he is without inheriting my stubbornness?" He chuckled.

"And now my son wants to marry Matt's daughter! And his son diagnosed my cancer! Does God have a sense of humour or what?"

"How did you know that we are Matt's kids?"

"I recognized Matt and Rheanne in the picture over the fireplace. And I asked Michael. He told us you and Jonathon are the children in the picture. It wasn't hard to figure out the rest. I asked why he came here when he was sick, and he just said it was the most healing place he knows of. His Mother prompted him a few times before he admitted being in love with you and wanting to marry ..."

"I'm glad I let Jonathon put the picture back over the fireplace when he came this time. He was quite determined. I had taken it down after my parents disappearance ... I couldn't bear the pain ...."

"So how do you feel about having your family ...," she faltered, then started again, "how would you feel about having Matt's daughter as a part of your family?"

"Wonderful!" from Lillian. "Rheanne would be delighted if she were here."

"Well, I'm glad I got to know the two of you a little bit before I found out who you were. Though I must say that most of my antagonism evaporated when I heard of Matt and Rheanne's death. I am pleased to find my son in such pleasant circumstances, with such a fine family!"

"I do love your son, Mr. & Mrs. Braemer. He is like you both. You have every reason to be proud ... so very proud ... of him."

"God has been gracious to me. He gave him back to me this morning," he offered in a tearful choking voice. We prayed together after we talked. We asked each other's forgiveness and asked God to restore the years the locust has eaten."

"So you will plan to marry soon?" Lillian asked between sniffles.

"I don't know," Rhea smiled. "He hasn't asked me yet. I think he really wanted to know that you would accept me, that he would not rupture your relationship further. He really loves you both, and his sister. He has longed for relationship with you, but didn't know how to go about repairing the damage."

As they rose to go, Rhea asked, "You'll join us for supper, I hope? Joan and the Chief will be here. Do I understand you're staying the night?"

"Yes, yes, we'll be staying. Michael has his examination this afternoon. I believe Dr. Clark will be seeing him. And we'd love to come for supper," she glanced at Michael Sr. for his approval. "What can we bring?"

"Not anything, please. Joan will supply the salads and dessert. The rest is all looked after. Michael will be delighted to have you all here together. I'm hoping he'll be strong enough to be up for a while. Jonathon will be joining us, too."

They took their leave with hugs for Rhea. "Oh, God, how good you've been," she prayed as she watched them leave. "You never cease to amaze me!"

Chapter 22

Like Father Like Son

"Michael," she spoke gently, "are you awake? You haven't had any lunch. Can I get you a cup of soup?"

He smiled, opening his eyes just slightly. "I'm awake. I'm just enjoying listening to you moving around my room." Then taking her hand and putting it to his lips he asked, "Will you sit with me a minute?"

"Of course I'll sit with you," she said smiling. "Then I wonder if you would have a bite to eat, and maybe you'd enjoy a warm soak in the tub."

"Mmmm, sounds good, but I have something else on my mind."

"What's that?"

"Sweetheart, did my briefcase come in from the car?" She shook her head. "Would you mind to get it for me?"

He raised his bed until he sat upright, as she arranged the briefcase for his convenience. Then opening it slowly, he pulled her into his arms. "Rhea, my beautiful Rhea, will you marry me?"

"Michael," she sat up quickly, looking into his face to see whether he was serious. "Oh Michael," she repeated, the shock showing on her face. "You know I will. Why ... right now?" She stopped with a puzzled look on her face.

"Oh, sweetheart, I've wanted to ask you for so long, but I ... first of all I didn't know if you'd want to marry into such a fractured family, or if ... if you'd want to marry me if my folks wouldn't accept Matt's daughter ... and I needed to know who my father was." His voice faltered as he continued, "But now that we've got all that straightened away ... Oh, Rhee, I'm so sorry to ask you like this, but I just can't wait any longer. I'm so sorry your ring wasn't ready when I left New York. Meantime ..." he produced an ornate jewel box from his briefcase and handed it to her, "meantime, I didn't forget your earrings."

"Oh Michael, dear Michael, you are adorable. Yes, I'd love to be your wife." She gasped as he opened the case. "Oh Michael! Oh Michael! Oh Michael! It's exquisite! Wherever did you find a chain to match my earrings?"

"There's a little Arab shop in New York that deals in gold from Jordan. I have to admit to scheming to get those earrings and take them to him, to see if he could duplicate the fine spun gold and still insert the diamonds. I was over-joyed when you forgot them in my room."

"My darling, if you don't quit with the gifts and the roses we won't be able to afford to marry." She pulled back from him as he tried to hold her close.

"Why are you pulling away from me? Let me hold you."

"Because your motor is starting to rev and you have pneumonia."

"Sweetheart, you rev my motor from across the room," he murmured pulling her back into his arms.

"Who do I have to ask for permission to marry you?"

"Probably the Wahls and Jonathon. Both will want to

have a say. My guess is that both Jonathon and the Chief will give you a hard time; Joan will be her delightful self."

"Can I do that tonight while they're here?"

"Oh, dear! In front of your folks? If you want to risk it."

"Could be fun," he said mischievously.

"That was delectible," Lillian commented as she laid down her fork.

"Delectible, nothing," snorted Michael Sr. "It was just supercilious ... fantastic ... satisfying. Lillian, it's been a while since we had roast beef. And that Yorkshire Pudding ..." He stopped as if savouring the taste in his mouth. " We Braemers know enough to find a good cook and marry her before she gets away." He looked at Michael and winked.

"Indeed, we do," Michael picked up on the joviality. "Now I have both an announcement and a request."

Rhea flushed slightly as he continued. "We're so glad to have you here, Mom and Dad, and Dr. and Mrs. Wahl, and you, too, Dr. Reimer. It would seem to be a good time to tell you," he reached over and took Rhea's hand, " that the lovely Lady Rhee has consented to be my wife."

"Oh, Michael," from his Mother.

"Rhea, that's wonderful," from Joan.

"About time," from the Chief.

"Well, I'll be," from Jonathon.

Only Michael's Father sat silently as if too stunned to speak.

"Now," Michael continued, "Rhea tells me that I need permission from both her brother and her guardians, and so I ask for her hand in marriage." He sat down, looking from one to the other questioningly.

"Well, I'll be," Jonathon repeated, as he quickly looked down to hide the deep emotion he was feeling.

"I'm delighted, just delighted. Yes ... yes ... you have my permission to marry our lovely Rhea," Joan smiled warmly.

The Chief cleared his throat, began uncertainly, then began again. "Of course ... of course you have my blessing. 'He that finds a wife finds a good thing,' the Good Book tells us, and I would have to say you've certainly found the best. Matt and Rhea would be proud!"

"Thank you, thank you both," Rhea noticed that both Michael's voice and his hand trembled slightly. She waited, wondering what Jonathon would say.

The silence seemed interminable. Finally having recovered his composure, he began, "Well, Mike, my old buddy, my good friend." He stopped as if making a point. Then began again, "So you want my permission to marry my little sis." Michael nodded, smiling, as he went on, "You must realize that she is a prize." Michael nodded again. "She is love personified ... she is beautiful inside and out. Not only that ... she is very educated ... a doctor ... a department head, no less. She has a very responsible job ... she earns a good salary ... she teaches ... she sings ... she is a nurturer ... a good cook. She always has a bed for me when I come. When I come to her place, I am at home. Now, tell me, Michael, why should I give up all that ... give her to you ... for nothing?"

The seriousness he projected into his monologue was cut short by Rhea's burst of laughter, "Here come the camels!" She looked at Michael. "I warned you he'd want to bargain!!"

The Wahls, who obviously knew the story were now enjoying the fun, and Jonathon could no longer keep a straight face.

"He sold me for ten camels to an African chief when I was only ten," she explained to Mr. & Mrs. Braemer. If Mom and Dad wouldn't have arrived at the right time, I'd be gone."

"There'd be little Rheas all over Africa," Jonathon grinned, "and all of them doctors!"

The laughter and banter continued until Jonathon finally conceded. "I told you ten years ago to find her and marry her," he grinned, "You'd better get on with it before I change my mind."

"So when will the wedding be? And will you live in this house? Lillian asked.

"I want to know when he had time to ask her," Michael's father cut in.

"Well, I asked her this afternoon, sometime between my nap and my bath. It was really hard to find time in my busy schedule." The group chuckled as he turned to Lillian, "Mom, why don't you come and join us for Thanksgiving and we'll have some of those details worked out. Actually, we probably won't announce our engagement till then anyway."

"Why is that, son?"

"Well, her ring isn't ready yet, and by the time it comes she'll probably be in Africa. She'll be there for the whole month of September."

"Yes, yes, you must come for Thanksgiving," the Chief added his voice. "Come for the Friday evening when we have our fundraiser - a lovely banquet and dance - tickets are only a hundred dollars. Our project this year is new equipment for the Department of Orthopedics. That's Michael's department, you know. Got to get some new equipment to keep up with all that research. Then stay over with us and we'll all have Thanksgiving together. Should be a great time. Bring your daughter and son-in-law, too."

"Oh, that sounds wonderful, doesn't it dear," Lillian looked at her husband, "if you're well enough by then."

"Well enough?" the Chief's face showed concern.

"Dear, we don't have to go into that right now, and spoil such a lovely evening," Michael Sr. addressed his wife, "and besides I want to know how they met, and how long they've known each other."

"Actually, Dad, I only met her last March when she crashed in on me."

The Chief took up the story, "Rhea had been up the hill with the ski team when she was hit by the ski patrol. Michael was working in emergency when she came in, and probably was the one responsible for saving her life."

"She certainly got my attention," Michael quipped.

"A gal has to do what a gal has to do!" Rhea laughed with a shrug of her shoulders.

"Well, so you've known her since March," Jonathon chided. "What's the rush? Why the proposal from the sick bed?"

"I knew that one was coming," Michael countered. "I thought it best to ask her while you were here and I could get your permission. Then, of course, there's that wretched lawyer snapping at my heels."

"Now, Michael ..." Rhea began.

"Don't 'now, Michael' me. I know about the yellow roses."

"How do you know?"

"The hospital called just after you left. They wanted to know if you wanted them delivered here."

"And you said?"

"I said if they couldn't find a patient who needed some flowers, there was a dumpster out back."

"Michael!!"

"Just kidding. Actually I told them you were on your way and would deal with them."

"That's a good boy!"

"So how did you deal with them?"

"Actually, I left them on the counter for the staff to enjoy. They really are lovely; far too lovely to throw out."

"What a wonderful happy family time," Michael

confided to Rhea as she straightened his bed. "just what I always thought a real family would be like. Our family's going to be like that one day, Rhea."

"Of course, my love," she smiled and kissed him on the forehead.

Chapter 23

For Better - For Best

"You're up bright and early," she smiled as he joined her for breakfast.

"Morning, sweetheart. Did I sleep all day yesterday?"

"Most of it. You were exhausted from all the activity when your folks were here. You were up a long time. And this getting engaged is exhausting business!"

"You can say that again. What day is it?"

"Wednesday."

"I thought Jonathon wanted to be on his way to Australia by the first of the week. How come he's still here? Is it because of me?"

"I don't know, Michael. He hasn't said one way or the other."

"But he knows I have to leave here when he goes, so ..."

"Possibly. But it's not all bad. He would love to see you up and about before he leaves, and it does give us some time together that we wouldn't have otherwise."

"Such eternal optimism! What a family I'm marrying into."

"It's a pristine day out there. Are you up to a small walk

in the back yard?" she asked as they finished their coffee.

"You're really going to let me out?" he teased.

"Well, I think it would accomplish a couple of things. It would give you some fresh air and exercise ... and we can look at the property. We'll need to decide what to do with it once we marry, and if we want to live here."

"At this point I can't imagine living anywhere else, sweetheart. Remember that first night I had supper at your place and we talked?"

"And kissed ..." she added, flirting with him.

"And kissed ... Oh, Rhee ... I'll never forget it! I thought heaven would have a hard time competing." He pulled her close. "I love you, Rhea Braemer."

"Rhymer," she corrected.

"Just trying it on for size. It goes really well." Then becoming serious again, he continued, "And that night when we talked you mentioned that maybe your husband would finish the house, so he would feel like he belonged ..."

"I remember only too well how embarrassed I was after I shared that."

"You're adorable when you blush. But is that still an option?"

"Of course," she said as she helped him on with his jacket and they walked out through the backyard. The path wound its way through what seemed to him a small forest. Maples, oaks, cottonwoods and spruce competed for space with scrawny elder, cranberry and fern. Here and there a birch tried to thrust its slender trunk heavenward seeking a little sunlight. They walked in silence for a few minutes.

"This is quite the property," he broke the silence, "is it okay for us to be here?"

She laughed. "Indeed it is."

"It's okay if we trespass."

"We aren't trespassing, honey. It's all a part of my property."

He stopped, looking at her with amazement on his face. "No kidding!"

"No kidding. I have about 30 acres. Dad and I bought the original 10; then the other 20 went up for sale and the price was right so I bought it quick. It's such prime property right here on the lake, that I thought if I didn't buy it maybe Delta or one of the big hotels might wind up being my neighbors."

"Wow!" They had come to a clearing and the lake was just beyond. "This must be a part of the river system somehow," he suggested.

"It's really just a backwater, but it makes a lovely place to swim and fish. I don't really come here very often by myself. Occasionally just to read or to seek a little solitude. I always feel a little closer to God when I sit here and contemplate. Come sit a bit, you look a little winded."

"Guess I'm not ready for a marathon," he admitted settling on the bench beside her.

"So, to get back to your question. Would you like to finish the house, and if so, what would you like to see ...?" She stopped, looking at him.

"Do you still have the original architect's drawings?"

"Yes, but I don't want to follow that design now. I'm not thinking retreat centre; I'm thinking of a home."

"So what are you suggesting?"

"I think we should decide together what our needs are, then you can work on it while I'm in Africa. Do you like to design things, Michael?"

"Yeah, I do; I worked with Dad a lot when I was a kid, but I'd need help with this much. Would you mind if I got him involved?"

"I was hoping for something like that. It will give you time together, and let him know we need him."

"By the way, what are we hearing about Dad?"

"Dr. Clark insists he has to have the prostate removed.

He'll probably stop in before he heads home to make arrangements with Tyler to take over while he's away. Then he's coming back for the procedure. In spite of the circumstances, it will be good to have your folks around. I need to get to know them better, maybe you do, too."

"Do you like them, Rhea?"

"Yes, very much."

"Dad didn't offend you by his forward remarks and offhand comments?"

"Oh, my, no," she said smiling. "He and I will get along just fine. He's really up front. Come," she said getting up, "we need to get you back to the house. I have clinic this afternoon but Jonathon will be here, and then I'm going to prayer, and to the street clinic. I won't be home till around 10:00."

"I really could stay alone, you know, sweetheart. I'm not helpless anymore."

"Give it a couple more days before you get so independent, okay? We don't need any relapses."

"I'd like to get back to work, Rhea. I've been gone nearly five weeks; that's a long time to be out of touch, and a lot of things are just hanging ..."

"I know, Michael, I know. But being impatient won't help. Can you try to relax and enjoy being here? I'm enjoying having you, and for that matter, so is Jonathon. Maybe you can look at the house plans after your nap, and give me your ideas. That might occupy your mind for a day or two. We'll need to decide how much of this property we want for a backyard. I really like having access to the lake, though it makes for quite a big area. Somewhere down the road we will need to deal with developing or selling off the rest."

"What do you think we should spend on the addition, Rhee? I probably have enough investments to pay it outright, but give me some idea."

"We'll have to decide what we want first. So far I've spent upward of $200,000 without the land. But it might be better if we took a mortgage for the rest, rather than cash in your investments and have income tax take half of it."

"So do we want to build before we marry?"

"Good question. Maybe we should decide when we would like to marry," she looked at him questioningly.

"Tomorrow sounds like a good day."

"No it doesn't, Michael."

"Can we get married before winter? I can't bear another winter. Before Christmas?"

"Oh, Michael! Wow! If I wasn't going to be gone for all of September. Let's think on that a bit. Maybe it depends on what kind of a wedding we want, how big ..."

"Big, Rhea. I want the whole world to know you're going to be mine."

"What if we planned for early December. That would give us October and November to get ready. And Lynda will be here to help me. I want her to be my maid of honour."

"And I want Jonathon to be my best man, and Tyler and maybe Jared for groomsmen. I'd really like my good friend, Bob, but I think we should ask him to tie the knot."

"Well you got that all worked out. I'll ask Tracy and my old friend, Racy, from way back." He looked at her questioningly, and she chuckled, "Short for Racine, but Racy really does suit her. I guess she'll be partnered with Jared ... oh dear, that may not be the best; they're an awful lot alike."

"So what's to worry about?"

"She got off to a rough start, but made a commitment to Christ this last few years and is really growing. I would hate to see ... I guess that's not my business.

"Well, that's a lot to decide all in one morning. If we keep up like this we'll be ready before I leave at the end of the month."

"I can hardly bear the thought of another separation ... and for a whole month."

Do you want to move into the house and stay with Jonathon while I'm gone? You two have batched together before ... it would be a lot handier for you to work on the plans when you have the house around you."

"I'd like that; I'd better discuss it with Jon." Then after a moment, he asked, "Do you expect he'll live with us once we're married."

"No. Definitely not. I'm sure he isn't expecting such a thing. Though I would really like for us to have a guest suite on the side of the house. Private entrance and all that sort of thing. My thinking is for my Mom and Dad when they come home; they'll need a place to live until they find themselves. Meantime, if Jonathon needs a place ... or if we just want to keep it open for company ... your family, friends, whatever. What do you think?"

"That would suit me just fine ... any of the above. We'll certainly work it into the plans. Do you want to use the same contractor?"

"I'll leave that up to you, honey. He's quite pushy; probably thought he could get away with it because I'm a woman. Talk to him, and you'll get a sense of oughtness. He does good work."

Chapter 24

Hope Springs

Michael glanced at the phone as it cut through his thoughts. *It's Rhea,* he realized glancing at the call display. *It's unusual for her to call mid-morning. Something must have come up. Maybe she wants to meet me for lunch,* he thought happily as he picked up the call.

"Michael, are you busy?" she asked trying to keep her voice under control.

"Rhee, what's going on? Are you okay? You sound like you're gasping for breath?"

"Are you busy, Michael? I have to see you. Can you come?"

"Yes, of course, be right there."

She sat at her desk, pale and shaken, her breath coming in short gasps.

"Rhea, baby, what...?"

Her hand shook as she pushed a medium-sized business envelope across the desk toward him. It was addressed by hand to Dr. R. Rhymer at St. Michael's Hospital. It was empty. It bore a Congo postmark, nothing more.

He looked at her questioningly, "Your Dad...?"

She nodded as tears let loose and she shook with sobs. In an instant he had her in his arms. "Oh, Rhee, baby, this is wonderful news! The evidence we've been praying for."

She nodded again. "This is the kind of envelope we always used to order supplies. Dad knew I would recognize his handwriting. I wonder what happened to the order. Someone must have taken it out." She paused, then with a fresh burst of tears, "We know they're alive ... they're alive ... Oh Michael!"

He held her close. He had never seen her like this. It was clearly his turn to comfort ... or to rejoice ... he wasn't sure. "Oh, God," he prayed, "thank you for this answer to prayer. Show us how to use this new evidence...thank you for keeping Rhea's Dad and Oh, God, please ... her Mom, too ... alive."

A fresh burst of tears from Rhea. It hadn't occurred to her that the evidence was from her Dad only. What if her Mom ... ? She couldn't think in those terms. They cried together.

"Isn't Jonathon back tomorrow?" Michael ventured. "That's great timing!"

She nodded, sniffling. "And we'll need to call Jonathon Fields. He's been wanting to come and discuss this with us and he needs to meet you. I suggested he wait until my brother gets back and until you're feeling better. But we need to get this information to him. Would you call him for me, Michael? And if he still wants to come, he should come either on the week-end or next week. After that I'm too busy getting ready to leave. Does that work for you?"

She smiled as the two Jonathon's sat discussing the envelope. What special men they were! After Michael and her Dad, they were the most precious men in her life, along with Pastor Bob. *How good God is,* she thought, *to put men like these in my life ... and always at a time when I need them most ... Jonathon coming back from Australia ... Jonathon Fields surfacing again, and Michael... Michael ... to be my husband. Thank you, God, thank you.*

"She's off in another world ..." she heard vaguely as she tried to refocus her thoughts.

"You might try me again," she laughed.

"How soon can we expect Michael?" from brother Jon.

"Probably a half hour. He's instructing a group of students this morning. There is a glassed in area where we can watch without disturbing the class, if you're interested."

She was both surprised and pleased when Jonathon Fields affirmed, "Good idea. Let's do it."

"To avoid confusion, I'm going to call you Jon," she said indicating her brother, "and we'll let you be Jonathon," she indicated Jonathon Fields. Both smiled in approval.

Rhea felt anew her sense of love and pride in this man she had chosen - who had chosen her. She loved the way he dressed ... his dark brown turtle-neck sweater accented his tweed sport coat ... *almost an exact match for his hair,* she thought. She noted the intense interest of the students as he described the inner structure of the bone, the marrow, and the various systems at work H*e's brilliant, absolutely brilliant!* she thought, as she watched Michael field questions from the students on the causes and prevention of osteoporosis. She loved the way he led the student along until she discovered the answer for herself. She had never seen him in the classroom before. *No wonder he's such a favourite with the students*! *I'm so glad both Jonathons get to see him like this. What a neat introduction to Michael!* She smiled as she glanced at Jonathon Fields and noted that he was totally absorbed.

"He's expecting to meet us in my office; we'd best wait for him there," Rhea suggested as the lecture wound down.

"He'll have a few assignments or whatever to hand out before he's done."

So today I get to meet Jonathon Fields, Doctor of Laws, Michael thought to himself as he made his way down the hall. He had promised Rhea that he would indeed try to like him, in response to her plea. He could still hear her voice, *He is a very nice person, Michael, and a good friend to both Jonathon and me. Please ... work at it.* And work at it he would.

More yellow roses, he muttered to himself as he passed the front desk in OB GYN. *This is going to be more difficult than I thought!*

He paused as her office door swung wide. "Jonathon, I'd like you to meet Michael. Michael ... Jonathon Fields," she smiled.

The men exchanged pleasantries as they headed for the cafeteria.

"What do you want me to do with the flowers, Dr. Rhee?" Sandy asked as Rhea started for the door.

"Best leave them where they are for a few days," Rhea replied laughing and shaking her head. "I'll deal with them by the week-end."

"All three of them so handsome, Dr. Rhee. You're gonna have to choose pretty soon," Valida chimed in.

Rhea looked up surprised to find all three girls looking at her. "Don't sweat it, girls; It's not what you're thinking!" She hurried to join a waiting Michael.

"So you're an orthopaedic surgeon," Jonathon began as they settled around the table. "That was quite the lecture you gave this morning ... on osteoporosis. My mom would have benefited from that. And I especially appreciated ..."

Michael looked up surprised, then glanced at Rhea. "We tuned in to the last half of your class from the observation ..." she broke off at the look on his face. "We didn't think you'd mind; it was most informative."

He chuckled. "Good thing it was only a lecture and not something invasive."

"Our time here is really short today; both Michael and I have a fairly heavy afternoon scheduled," Rhea began.

"Now hear ye, hear ye," her brother chimed in. "Cut with the small talk and get down to business."

"Jon, if you don't cut with the nonsense. What I wanted to say before ..." she gave her brother a mock frown, then went on, "what I wanted to say is that we would really like to have you come for supper and an evening at my house. Does that suit you, Jonathon?"

"Sounds just great, but I'd love to treat you all to supper. You're putting in a full day already."

"Actually Michael and Jon have consented to barbeque for us. The rest is already taken care of. It will be a fun time, and maybe more relaxing than a restaurant. Besides, I would like to have the Chief and Joan join us."

"And Pastor Bob Martyn," Michael added.

Jonathon was silent for a moment. "You know it's imperative that we keep this information under wraps?" he looked from Rhea to Michael.

"Indeed we do," Michael nodded. "The Chief was a partner with Doctor Matt, and is aware of the circumstances. Pastor Bob is just a good friend who has spent a fair amount of time in Africa. But I really want him to come because he knows how to pray."

"Well, we'll certainly need prayer," the lawyer agreed, looking questioningly at Rhea. She nodded her agreement.

"None of these folk know about the envelope," she added. "Can we just let you divulge as much or as little information as you choose?"

Jonathon nodded as she rose to go. "See you around 5:30 then."

"You've done it again, Missie. I haven't had ribs like that in a coon's age," the Chief wiped his mouth."

"I couldn't agree more," Jonathon added. "Can't remember when I've eaten like that!" He rose to get his briefcase as Rhea and Joan cleared the dishes and brought more coffee.

Rhea admired the way he presented the information he had gleaned, the conclusions he had come to, and the immediate steps he felt must be taken. Joan cried softly as he spoke of the envelope that had arrived, evidence pointing to abduction rather than land mine. He had several weeks before leaving for South Africa and would pressure the Government to cut off all aid to the Congo until such time as Matt and Rheanne were released. It certainly fell under the category of *international incident* and would qualify for some drastic action. However, in the meantime the new evidence had arrived too late to be of use by September.

"So what would you and Rhea hope to accomplish in September?" Michael's question was not unexpected.

"Actually I would like Rhea to show me exactly where the alleged accident occurred. More than that, it will give me a look at the surrounding area, put me in touch with the officials in charge. I hope to carry some authority to investigate from the Government of Canada to the Government of the Congo. They need to know we are aware of the kidnapping, and that we expect them to co-operate in the release."

"Do you think the Congolese Government knows of the kidnapping?" the Chief asked.

"At this stage it's hard to know. Once we present the evidence, they will have to take responsibility whether they want to or not."

"If we're about done, I'll need to get going," Michael rose from the table.

"What word do we have from your Dad?" Jon asked.

"Procedure went well. He's recuperating nicely at home. Will be back to see Dr. Clark in two weeks, I believe."

"Will you drop me back at my hotel, Doctor?" Jonathon Fields addressed Michael directly.

"Be glad to."

"Can I see you tomorrow? How about breakfast together?" Michael whispered as he took her in his arms and nuzzled her neck. She nodded as his lips found hers. Then they were gone.

They drove in silence for a few minutes. "Did you want to talk?" Michael ventured.

Jonathon nodded slowly. "I ... I ... know you are very special to Rhea."

"Rhea is my fiancee. We will wed in December."

"I'm sorry; I didn't know. I did notice that you're a little stressed about our meeting in the Congo. I want you to know ... I promised Rhea and Jon that I wouldn't use my appointment as their attorney to win Rhea back. That's not what this is about. I loved her folks. They were my other parents, always treated me like a son. I was devastated when they disappeared. I love Rhea, too, and Jon. I want to do this for all of us ... and I'll do the best I can."

"Are you in love with Rhea?"

"Yes. Of course. For years and years. But she made it abundantly clear that she's in love with you ... you lucky wretch! Watching you today, I understand her a lot better. I have only myself to blame. I loved her in highschool. I was an adolescent ... and I acted like one ... let her get away. I think she still sees me as an overgrown kid."

"Not at all. She's not about to entrust her parent's rescue into the hands of an adolescent. She has a deep respect and love for you. More than I appreciate. She warned me that I had better like you, or else!"

"Or else?"

"Never mind that. I like you already … okay!!"

They both laughed, as Michael continued, "I came prepared to like you if it killed me, thought I'd really have to work at it, but," he paused and cleared his throat, "I find you to be all she said, and more. I would really appreciate if we could …"

"… be friends?" Jonathon held out his hand. "I like you too, Dr. Mike. Friends it is."

Chapter 25

Thanks Living

"Thanks for making this a first-class reservation, Rhee," Linda stretched out in the Boeing 747. "I feel like I need to recoup some of my losses."

"I only do first class when I come and go from the Third World. Like you, I feel so battered … so used up. I don't usually pamper myself, but this is a must. This is one month I don't want to repeat!"

Rhea dozed off. They would arrive in New York after breakfast …Toronto by lunchtime … then Riverview … and *Michael.* Her heart jumped at the thought of him … his boyish physique, sandy hair, deep grey-green eyes looking into hers, his arms around her, his lips soft and warm and insistent. *Oh Michael, Michael, I love you, I love you.*

"So who is this that you want me to meet?" Lynda asked as they prepared for touchdown in Riverview. "How will I know if I've met him if you won't give me any clues? I may wind up with the wrong guy."

"Fret not. There'll be quite a few eligible bachelors vying for your attention. You can sift and sort."

Rhea spied them as she came through security. *Leave it to Michael, the rascal; he's not taking any chances that someone else might meet her first.*

"Rhea, my very own Rhea. I thought I'd die before you got here," he whispered between kisses.

"It looks like we won't get an introduction out of them. I'm Bob Martyn, and you must be Rhea's cousin, Lynda."

"Yes, I'm her cousin, and I agree ... I'm afraid they're quite oblivious..." Lynda began.

"Okay, okay, you two. I gather you've met. Bob, we need to get these girls home." Then turning to Rhea, "Have you girls eaten? Shall we get you something? We have supper planned for a little later." *We're not the only ones oblivious,* Michael thought, as he noticed Bob and Lynda absorbed in conversation; *they haven't heard a word. Not much wonder; she's a beaut, a Rhea with long hair.*

"So how was Africa?" Bob addressed the girls as they sat over a bowl of soup.

"Exhausting, stressful, bugs, snakes, heat, AIDS, babies ... babies ... babies ..." Lynda laughed.

"Just the usual," Rhea commented.

"So is she a slavedriver?" Michael teased.

"Well, yes ... and no. The Africans are slavedrivers. The terrible needs drive you to work from early morning until midnight. We never got done. So many pregnant women and girls ... little girls ... pregnant. The old chiefs have harems of little girls, most of them way too young to deliver a child. It almost killed me to see what goes on there. Many of them must die in childbirth when there is no help. I could hardly come home."

"So how do you cope with it? You've been there so many times." Bob addressed Rhea.

"I always do the best I can. But more than that, I'm training mid-wives. Each time I go I add a new level of training. This time four of them got their certification as mid-wives. They're actually pretty good. They'll be effective in their villages and the women won't have to travel so far at such a crucial time. The mid-wives understand the situation better than we do. It's always hard to leave, but totally necessary to preserve life and sanity. I would die of exhaustion if I stayed. There's never enough rest, never enough help to go around. This time I had Lynda to help and they nearly killed us both."

"She speaks truth. I sure learned a lot... not just about Africa and its problems, but about myself ... about life. I came away with a whole new sense of gratefulness to God for my life, my family, my country, my health, the opportunities I've been blessed with. We Canadians are an incredibly spoiled lot."

"That we are. Any news of our folks?" Rhea smiled at the 'our folks.'

"We met Jonathon Fields in the Congo and I showed him the supposed grave site. It had all been cleared away, no sign of a grave. They denied making such claims ... said we were in the wrong place.

"We both really admired Jonathon's negotiating expertise. He was well prepared, knew what he was doing, how far he could go with what he had, and what he needed to find out for future pressure on the governments. We all left feeling that Mom and Dad were alive, and that it's just a matter of time and pressure, not to forget prayer, before they're released. On the way home Lynda and I were laughing about some of the things that went on; we agreed that Jonathon could probably out-negotiate a camel trader."

"Speaking of camel trading, Rhea, I've never really gotten the story of why Jonathon tried to trade you for ten camels. Is that a family joke, or is there more to it?" Michael's eyes sparkled as he looked at her.

"Rhee, you must tell them; tell them the way you told it to me."

"I'm way too tired to tell it with as much flourish as Jon might muster, but the short version is that Mom and Dad had gone to pick up an order of supplies. Jon was bossing me around, as usual, and I just got tired of it and rebelled. He threatened to sell me to the old chief who endlessly tried to negotiate a deal with Dad. They basically buy girl babies, then collect them when they think they are old enough for their harem. Most of them still children. Here I was already ten and still no one had been able to buy me, and the old chief thought it would really be a feather in his cap to have a westerner in his harem.

"Well, I laughed at Jonathon's threat. I knew Dad would never allow it. He warned me that Dad wasn't home and by the time he came I'd be gone. I laughed. He followed through on his threat to scare me and didn't realize how serious it was until the ten camels showed up. I saw them coming and ran into the jungle and hid. They were looking for me when I heard Mom and Dad arrive. I had been praying wildly ... far too frightened to cry for fear I would be discovered.

"The old chief was outraged. At least half of the village had joined his entourage to see him collect his new bride. He lost face. Not that he didn't know better than to negotiate with a boy. He just saw the advantage and knew Dad was gone. He threatened Dad, yelling and screaming.

"As soon as he left Dad called for me and I came running, crying hysterically. The folks never unpacked the supplies. They threw everything they could into the back of the land rover and a small trailer we had used to move supplies. Jonathon and I were packed in on top of our scant sleeping gear. Dad really stepped on it and the old land rover screamed out of there, kicking dust into the air. It was dark already, gets dark around 6:00. When we reached the edge of the village, we saw the old chief had rallied his tribesmen. They were heading toward our little medical facility, long spears flashing in the light of their torches."

"So what happened? Obviously you got away," Michael's eyes were wide.

"Dad had certainly made the right call. He knew what the chief would do to save face. They would either have had to hand me over or ... or ..."

They all sat silently for a moment. "And you went back there? I can't believe I let you go. If I'd known the half ... you're not going again." Michael spoke with a passion fueled by fear.

"Of course I didn't go back there! We've never ever gone back. It's way too dangerous. But we had such a good work, a good ministry there, and it was all aborted by the foolishness of my brother. I had never seen my Dad so upset, before or after. He was beside himself."

"So did you return to Canada at that point?" Bob wanted to know.

"Oh, my, no! We drove most of the night. Mom and Dad had driven all day to get home, so they took turns driving and sleeping. We couldn't bed down in the jungle ... far too dangerous ... so we drove until we came to a village that Dad knew and they just slept sitting up in the land rover. Once the sun was up we carried on until we reached the border and made our way to a large village; actually Lynda and I spent a week there this trip."

"And Jonathon?" Bob asked, shaking his head in wonder.

"Oh, poor Jon. I hardly slept that night in the land rover. I was so fearful of what Dad might do to him. I had never seen my father so angry. I remember praying for them both. I knew Jon really meant me no harm; Dad knew it, too, but he couldn't dismiss it as a childish prank. It nearly cost us all our lives. Fortunately, he knew enough to wait until he was rational. They talked for a long time the next evening; Jonathon was distraught. He cried and asked my forgiveness. I remember Dad asking him what his punishment should be and he suggested a spanking. We all cried and cried and cried. It's been a painful memory for him. We have never spoken of it in the last 20 years until I mentioned the camel trading the night of our engagement. I was pleased he was able to joke about it … some healing there obviously."

"My experiences in Africa were never that exciting," Bob offered as they rose to go. "We'll need to have you girls share some of your experiences in our missions service next week. I'd love to hear more."

Just bet you would, Michael grinned to himself as he watched him exchange smiles with Lynda.

"Good to see the house is still standing," Rhea teased as they pulled into the garage. "Is there a bed for each of us?"

"You bet. Jon moved in with me for now so Lynda could have the guest room. You really don't have enough guest rooms, you know," he said laughing. "You could easily fill a half dozen or so."

"We'll see how you feel about that once we're married," she grinned impishly. "How are the house plans coming along?"

"Great. At least I think so. Dad has been coming for radiation therapy and we've been working on structural details. I'd forgotten just what an incredible architect he is. We're enjoying each other more and more …" he broke off, then regaining his composure, he continued, "We've got the foundations all laid. If we finish our room, my office and the guest suite by December, I think we can leave the rest of the interior and finishing work until spring."

"Sounds great."

"How late would you girls like to sleep? Bob and I would like to come back and prepare supper. Jon will join us.

What if we eat about 6:30? Would that give you time to catch your breath?"

Rhea glanced at Lynda, who nodded her approval, "Sounds good to me."

"Rhea, is that him?" she asked as they heard the garage doors close. "The one you wanted me to meet? Cause if it's not...you don't need to bother ..."

"Wow! I thought I saw some sparks flying back and forth ..."

"Sparks nothing!! You two nearly started a forest fire. Just answer my question. Is that him?"

"You might never know. Glad your first impressions were favourable. Wait until you get a second; he just keeps getting better and better. Did you happen to notice Michael at all? Did you see him, I mean?"

"Stop it, Rhee. You know I did. He's gorgeous! Rather in love, I would say." They both laughed softly as Rhea showed her cousin to her room.

Supper ... I'm going to see him again at supper ... and apparently he can cook, Lynda mused as she stretched out in the wonderful comfort of a real bed, and drifted off.

Chapter 26

Family

❝I had no idea you guys could cook like that; but now that I know…" Rhea teased as Jon and Bob took their leave. "Will you be at the church tomorrow afternoon, Bob? I'd like to show Lynda around … provided we're coping with the jet lag, of course."

"In that case, I'll be there," he said with a wink.

"I'm so glad you're home, Rhee," Michael murmured as they snuggled on the couch. "Promise me you won't run away on me again."

She chuckled softly. "I haven't run away the first time. I was only gone a month … about the same amount of time you spent in New York … only you didn't visit me at the half way point. Did you feel abandoned?"

"Not really. Just missed you terribly. I really appreciated being here in the house, enjoyed your bedroom, felt close to you.

"I must say it's been really positive connecting with Dad. We're playing catch up, getting to know each other. He brought me a bundle of letters he had written to me. Guess he wrote me one every Christmas for the last

11 years, then couldn't bring himself to mail them. He contributed pretty heavily to most of my research projects, anonymously, and kept up on all my accomplishments. I cried for hours as I read his letters and saw his heart. It's helped me grow in my understanding of where he's coming from. He listens pretty carefully to everything I say, to our likes and dislikes with the house...doesn't try to make me see it his way. It's quite humbling, really."

"Sweetheart, that really makes my heart smile. A relationship like that is a gift from God. Are you feeling okay? You look a little weary, maybe stressed. Have you lost weight?"

"Yeah, a little. I've been awfully tired. Jonathon thinks I need my blood checked again. But I have been really going. Putting in too many hours at the hospital, a few too many on the house plans. I wanted to get some things done before you got back so we could have some time together. I think I'll be okay now that you're back; I'll slow up a bit and get more rest."

"I think you'd better eat suppers here with us from now on. We can all chip in on the prep and you'll eat better if you're not alone."

"That sounds great. I'll take you up on that." Then as an afterthought he added, "And I worked in the street clinic one night."

"You did what?"

"Well, Jeremy called. He was a little strapped so I went to help him out. And you know that girl, Brandy, the one you're encouraging to apply for a job at the hospital? She was on the street again, and she propositioned me."

"Poor thing! It's all she knows. How did you respond? I hope you didn't get angry."

"No, I was too surprised for that. I just told her there were better things she could do with her life."

"Thank you, sweetheart, for being so gracious. By the

way, do you know if Tracy and Tyler are coming for Thanksgiving? We'll need to count pretty soon."

"Yes, he called yesterday. Would it be okay to include Jared? He's always alone at special times, just like I used to be. My heart kind of hurts for him."

"You know that would be okay with me; we've been wanting to have him in," she planted a kiss on his cheek.

"Oh yeah, I forgot to mention that Jonathon would like to bring a couple of friends."

"Jonathon? Jonathon Reimer? Really! He hasn't said a word to me. Course I've hardly seen him. Do you know who?"

"No. But the lines have been pretty hot between here and Australia."

"Oh my! Sounds exciting … a lady friend … and from Australia!"

"Darling, can we have a time together, just the two of us, you know … a real date? Maybe tomorrow night … supper somewhere?"

"Mmmm, I'd love it. I've missed you so … our times together."

He seemed almost a little shy as they smiled at each other across the small table at Wilhelm's. He had asked her to wear the burgundy sweater and slacks she had worn that first time they went up Olympia together. *Deja vu* she thought. They were obviously expected; Michael must have made a reservation.

"You're married now?" Willie asked as he seated them by the fire.

"Not quite, not till December," Michael replied.

"This was a wonderful idea," Rhea smiled. They ate their Beef Wellington slowly, savouring the time together, catching up on each other's lives, planning for the future, loving every minute.

"When we came here last time, sweetheart, I ... I ..." he looked down as his eyes misted, "I knew I had never met anyone like you before. By the time we stopped in on our way home, I knew I wanted to make it long-term. I fell in love sometime over that weekend." He took her hand gently in his, and slipped his ring on her finger. "I love you, my beautiful Rhea, my love, my friend, my soul mate ... my bride! This ring is my promise to love you forever!"

"I'll love you forever, too, my dearest Michael," she murmured, then gasped as she looked at the ring. "Oh Michael! It's beautiful ... it's beyond words. Did you design this?" He nodded as she continued to examine the huge diamond embedded in reddish gold, the dozens of tiny diamonds swirling around it and down toward the band. "This is incredible ... it's ... it's like a ski run. It's Olympia!" she squealed, looking at him. "Is that it? Am I right?"

He laughed, delighted that she recognized the ski hill, relieved that she loved it.

"You really are very creative, you know. This is a masterpiece!"

"I have another one that goes with it," he smiled.

"You are something else!" Then becoming suddenly teary, she added, "I'm looking forward to our life together, Michael ... to having some little Michaels ... just like you."

Chapter 27

The Ball

H e stood looking, his eyes soft and warm. Then, a long, low whistle. His gaze took in the long black sheath with side slit, the scoop neckline that accommodated the chain he had given her, the earrings from her parents, her engagement ring, her hair piled high. "Rhea ... Rhea ... my lovely Rhea ... you are ravishing. I don't think I've ever seen you in black before; you look marvellous!" His voice was husky with emotion.

"And you! You my love are the handsomest man I know. Is that a new black suit?"

He nodded. "Sure enough. Had to be special if we're announcing our engagement tonight" he whisked her around the room.

"Okay, okay you two, the dance hasn't started yet." Jon stood in the doorway. "I'd like you to meet two lovely ladies; Lucinda and Miranda Robinson ... or you could say Luci and Randy. This is my sister, Rhea, and her fiancé, Michael Braemer."

Rhea was struck by their sheer beauty ... identical ash blondes ... peaches and cream complexions ... tall and willowy. Finally, finding her voice, she extended her hand, "I'm so pleased to meet you, so glad you could be here for this special evening." Then turning to Jon she remarked, "Why, Jon, you haven't been nearly generous enough in your comments. You must bring these ladies for Thanksgiving dinner."

"Indeed, I will, and I have another guest for you as well. Jonathon Fields will be joining us."

She noticed Michael's jaw tighten slightly but he nodded his approval.

Lynda joined them as the doorbell rang. "It's for me," she smiled as she opened the door for a radiant Bob.

The great hall buzzed with conversation as Michael seated her at the Chief's table. She noted that it had grown considerably since last year. In addition to the Chief and Joan and the Board of Directors and their spouses, it now accommodated the entire Braemer family, her brother Jon and his fair lady, her sister Randy (obviously paired with Jonathon Fields for the evening), Pastor Bob and Lynda, herself, and a couple she had not seen before. It was usually the centre of attention as the Chief would be announcing and welcoming any new staff members, giving accolades, commendations, jokes, stories. The Chief loved every moment of it, and was good at this sort of thing. At the end of the evening when the donations were all in, he would announce the amount raised for the new equipment to be purchased. This year it would go to orthopaedics.

From time to time Rhea caught sight of the girls who worked in her department. She had given them tickets for the banquet, and was glad to see that Sandy had brought her husband this year.

Conversation and laughter filled the hall as great platters of turkey and stuffing, roast beef and bowls of mashed pota-toes, vegetables and salads were depleted and replenished from time to time. *If the hungry could even have the leftovers,* Rhea mused.

"They're certainly enjoying each other," Michael commented as he watched the Chief and his father sparring with each other on any topic that came to light. "Probably like old times; something we don't know anything about." Rhea nodded and smiled.

"I hope we're not too full to dance," he glanced at her hopefully. The orchestra had finished tuning and started on a slow waltz. Several couples were already on the floor.

"I'm not sure I can manage it," she teased, as he pulled back her chair and she stepped onto the floor. Bob and Lynda were next, Jon and Luci, Jonathon and Randi, the Braemer's Sr. *I'm surprised he's well enough; he's pretty frail after all those treatments, but it does look like they've enjoyed dancing with each other for years,* Rhea mused. Tracy and Tyler held each other closely as they danced. The Chief and Joan were on the floor now, loving every minute. He wouldn't let too many dances pass him by, she knew.

They were almost at their table when the music suddenly became frenetic. "Sorry, ol' boy, this one's mine," her brother Jon laughingly led her back to the floor.

"No, Jon, no," she pleaded, but he was already dancing Africa style, the frenzied gyrations they had learned as children in Africa. There was no time to point out that they would be a spectacle. The floor cleared as dancers watched from the sidelines. No time to ponder how he got that music to the orchestra ... what a character he is ... she had forgotten ... or maybe she thought he had grown up. *No chance of that,* she decided as he spun her around. She remembered to duck in time, as he swung first one leg over her, spun her around, then the other.

I can't believe I'm doing this ... and in front of my staff ... the entire hospital ... the Braemer family!

"Jonathon, you are a wretch!" she said laughing, as the onlookers clapped and cheered. Jonathon took a bow. "I haven't done that in 15 years. I'm amazed I remembered anything."

"I knew you'd be able to do it. Something like that just grows on you. You never forget it." He was terribly amused by her reluctance. "Besides," he continued, "you're far too dignified to be my sister. With me here now, folk will get to know you much better."

She made a face as he popped a kiss on her nose and held her chair for her. She noticed Valida watching from the sidelines, her eyes wide with astonishment.

"Michael isn't the only Braemer that knows how to dance, you know," she looked up to see his father offering her his hand.

"I've already noticed that,"she smiled as she got up. The two-step was fast paced and she marvelled that he could keep up along with a running conversation; she marvelled that *she* could keep up after that performance with Jon.

"Your brother is a man of many talents," he offered.

"You don't know the half," she laughed. "It's risky just having him around. However will I cope with him on a full-time basis?" She noticed Michael and his mother whirl by. They were obviously enjoying the dance and each other.

"Now then, do I dance as well as my son?" he asked as he deposited her back beside Michael.

"You're definitely cut from the same cloth," she managed before Jonathon Fields approached and glanced at Michael for permission.

"I just wanted to dance with *the belle of the ball*," he smiled as they glided easily over the floor.

"Oh, but you already have! She's just gorgeous!"

"Yes, she is that. And intelligent, too. She is working on a doctorate in music."

"Oh my! Oh my! Oh my! Where is she studying?"

"She has been at Laurier in Waterloo. Soon to be in Montreal."

"Sounds good. Was that a little chemistry I was seeing there?" She smiled encouragingly.

"Maybe we'll just give that a little time," he suggested as Jared cut in.

He stood on the sidelines watching as the dance finished and Michael claimed her. He noticed her lovely corsage … white roses with soft burgundy centers … matching the one on Michael's lapel. *Another man's roses,* he thought sadly, *another man's smile … another man's arms … another man's kiss … another man's ring … another man's bride.* Would he ever get over it, he wondered as he made his way back to the table.

"Dance?" he asked, without even noticing the sadness in the beautiful grey eyes that had watched him from across the room.

It's always my luck, Randy thought to herself as he danced with her like an automaton. *Just when I meet dream boy, he's dreaming about somebody else!*

The music slowed, then faded out, as the Chief rose to introduce his guests and the new staff members. He proceeded with his usual enthusiasm as each newcomer was introduced and applauded.

"He really enjoys this," Rhea whispered to Michael.

"I think everybody enjoys watching him enjoy!" he whispered back.

Spontaneous applause burst forth as the Chief introduced Dr. Jonathon Reimer as the brother of Dr. Rhea Rhymer. He explained the name change for the curious, he said.

Last of all he introduced Dr. Michael Braemer, and announced that the fund for the new aorthopaedic equipment had topped $300,000. "St. Mike's has been good to you, Dr. Braemer … God has been good to you. I doubt that this company knows just *how good ...*" he handed over the microphone, obviously pleased with himself.

Michael smiled as he rose and acknowledged the generous gift to Orthopedics. *I bet at least a hundred grand came from Michael Sr.* Rhea mused, noting it was that much higher than last year. He went on to thank God for the opportunity and privilege of working at a small research hospital like St. Michael's, then pausing, he looked down at Rhea. Her eyes shone with love and pride as he continued, "I would be remiss indeed, if I did not share an even greater blessing that has come to me since arriving at St. Michael's." He paused. Then taking Rhea's hand, "The lovely Lady Rhee has consented to be my wife." She rose as the cheering and catcalls began. When the crowd quieted, he added, "We would be pleased to have you join us at The Chapel on December one; reception will be here ... in this hall."

As he finished the music cut in with *Let Me Call You Sweetheart, I'm in Love With You,* and the dancers moved slowly toward the floor, clapping, singing, dancing.

"Sweetheart, I'm so sorry to suggest this, but would you mind if we left?" he asked as they neared the end of the dance. "I seem to be a little drained."

"I'll just let Joan know in case they're wondering," she said as she picked up her wrap.

"Thanks for being so understanding," he said as they drove. "Guess I'll have to have that blood check that Jonathon suggested."

She said nothing as she snuggled into his shoulder, but the dark circles around his eyes at the end of every day sent chills up her spine.

"I guess I need to get some sleep," he admitted as he pulled her close and nuzzled her neck. "You know in just about six weeks, we won't have to say 'good night' any more; I can hardly wait. What time would you like me to come and help tomorrow? How many are coming on Sunday ... for Thanksgiving Dinner, I mean?"

"Why don't we both sleep in and you can come for brunch around 10 or 10:30. We can play in the kitchen off and on all day and not have to rush. If I get the turkey in the oven by 6:00 on Sunday, it should be ready by the time church is over. There should be about 15 or 16 of us. Jon has promised to peel the potatoes, so we'll let him do that."

He took his leave slowly, reluctant to let her out of his arms. "I love you, Rhee Braemer," he whispered over and over between kisses.

She smiled and didn't bother to remind him she was still *Rhymer.*

Chapter 28

Thanksgiving

"Darling, why don't you take your coffee and relax by the fire while I clean up here and organize the kitchen?" she suggested as they finished brunch. "You look like you could use a few more winks."

"I really don't understand what's going on with me. I slept really well last night. It just never seems to be enough."

It seemed only minutes before she heard his deep, even breathing. "Oh God," she prayed. "Oh God ... Oh God ... I hardly know what to ask for ... watch over him for me."

He woke to hear Jonathon and company boisterously enjoying the kitchen. *He's quite a guy,* he mused, *everything's a game with him.* He lay listening as he instructed Luci and Randy how best to hold the knife to remove maximum peel from the potato. "It would go much better if we got some rhythm going," he suggested as he introduced one ditty after another. Finally a jig was added to increase oxygen levels and ensure maximum performance. Michael laughed to himself, and wondered what happened to Rhea. What could she possibly be doing in her kitchen in the midst of all that commotion?

"Hi, sweetheart," she said from her favorite chair. "How was the nap?"

He laughed. No need to worry about her. Obviously she knew her brother pretty well. She simply curled up in her chair with a good book ... totally out of harm's way. By dinner tomorrow, all would be in order.

———

"Michael, I'm glad you had the good sense to pick such a good cook. Chip off the old block there, eh?" Michael smiled and nodded at his Dad's remarks. "Now this wedding banquet; is she cooking for all 500?"

Laughter and banter continued around the table with much advice for the soon-to-be newlyweds. Brother Jon with his gift for story telling and outrageous embellishment kept the entire table rocking with laughter.

Rhea noticed that Jared was enjoying himself next to Randy. *All that charm and attention isn't lost on her,* she thought. *I hope it isn't lost on Jonathon Fields either. He better get on with it or he may be too late.*

"I want to thank you, Pastor Bob," Michael began as the conversation slowed, "for the excellent message this morning ... for the reminder of all that we have to be thankful for. When I think of all that God has blessed me with, I realize how ungrateful I am, and how quick I am to take His goodness for granted. I thank God today for all that he has built into my life ... for bringing me to Himself when I was just a kid ... for a family that loves me ... for bringing me to St. Mike's ... for good friends along the way ... for Rhea ... for letting her live ..." he paused, "and for giving her to me." He paused again, as some nodded and others murmured their agreement. "I just want to thank God today, and I'm wondering if any of you ..."

The Chief broke in at once with much praise and

thanksgiving for the blessings over the past year including good health, new staff added to St. Michael's, and finally persuading both Michael and Jonathon to get on board.

Rhea was deeply moved as the *thanksgiving* continued around the table ... some in tears ... some with much joy. Tyler gave thanks for his relationship with Tracy; Tracy gave thanks for Rhea; Mom Braemer for Dad's cancer being in remission; Dad Braemer for special family relationships. *Oh, Michael, I think we might be putting some folk on the spot, here,* Rhea thought as she glanced at Jonathon Fields and Jared McCaig. *They're probably not used to this sort of thing. I hope they don't feel obligated to participate.*

As if reading her thoughts, Michael interjected, "We don't want anyone to feel obligated to participate here; I realize this is probably a little different for some of you."

"Well, it is different for me," Jonathon began, "but I have known the Reimer family for a great many years ... they were my *other family* when I was in high-school. I was always welcome at their house; they treated me like a son. I am richer for having known both Jon and Rhea, and today I just want to say *thank you* both to them, and to God for bringing them into my life."

The *thanks continued around the circle.* Rhea noted that only Jared remained silent ... as if afraid he might somehow reveal the depth of his emotion.

"Lynda, why don't you play for us?" Rhea suggested as the guests drifted toward the large family room with the piano. "We could sing ..."

Murmurs of consent followed as Lynda tried a few scales.

"Michael, hon, will you lead us?" she asked.

"Actually I think Jon would enjoy that," Michael responded with a twinkle in his eye.

"Indeed, I would," he offered and set about instructing Lynda how to play *The Old Grey Mare* in a round.

It can only get worse, Rhea mused, noting he now had everybody on their feet learning a new step to go along with *She'll be Coming Around the Mountain.*

"Sweetheart, do we have any of that punch left? I think we may need a thirst-quencher before long," Michael joked.

"Punch, nothing," Rhea retorted. "I think we'd best roast another turkey." They laughed from the kitchen, as Jon started on yet another safari.

"I haven't had this much fun in years," Lillian Braemer squeezed Rhea as she took her leave. "Michael certainly is marrying into the right family. I hope you'll join us for Christmas. It's been years since Michael has been home for Christmas. And bring Jon, too."

Two by two the guests left, slowly, as if reluctant for the day to end. Only Jared lingered.

"I want to thank you, too," he began, then cleared his throat, "for including me. I know I'm not family, but I felt like I belonged today. Thank you, Mike ... Rhea." Then he was gone.

"That was quite a day," Rhea mused as they cuddled on the couch. "That Jon ... I keep hoping he'll grow up a bit ... you know? But he seems to get worse with the years!"

"Guys like Jon should never grow up. The world needs more of his kind ... look at all the fun he brought to everybody today, and he does it so naturally ... it's a part of him. Good thing, too, with the awful responsibilities he carries. I don't think I could work with death like he does, watching patients disintegrate and fade away. I really don't know how he copes. God has certainly given him something special; that sense of humour must stand him in good stead!"

"You're right. Guess I hadn't consciously put all of that together. He has a strong faith and a terribly soft heart. I know it affects him terribly when his patients die ...

especially the little ones ... and so many of them don't make it."

"I have an appointment to see him this week. We both think I need some blood work done. By the way, I got the confirmation for our reservations in Mauii. Air Canada had a pretty good deal on, so I took advantage of that, too, and we're booked for the night of the third."

"Wonderful! That'll give us a couple days to rest up at home; Jon is the only one who knows we're going to be here. Lynda moves into her own suite at the end of this month, so we'll be all alone. How will we ever cope??" They looked at each other with roguish grins.

"And I've asked Randy Robinson if she will play for us. I'll have to get the music to her before she leaves. She says she can take time out of her studies to come a day or two early and be here for rehearsal. Flowers are ordered; caterers will get me their price list this week. Hall has been arranged for. My dress should be ready for final fitting in the next week or so, and the bridesmaids will be gorgeous; seamstress tells me their dresses are done. Invitations should be out this week."

"You've been busy. It always amazes me how you accomplish so much ... and have all that company and keep up a full-time job. You really are amazing!"

"Actually, I picked up the materials and patterns, and made some of the arrangements before I left in September, so it really isn't as incredible as it looks."

"Bob would like to see us a few times; I suggested once a week in November. Will that work for you?"

She nodded. "Sounds good. Have you asked your groomsmen?"

"I've talked to Jon and Tyler. I'll meet with Jared this week."

"And I've asked Lynda and Tracy and Racine.. They were thrilled. I'd like the Chief and Joan to walk me down the aisle; but I want Jon to give me away. Of course, you understand you may need a fleet of camels on hand ... just in case ..."

They both chuckled. "I'll call tomorrow, sweetheart," he whispered as he reluctantly rose to go.

Chapter 29

Challenge of Faith

He sat quietly sipping his tea, absorbed in his own thoughts.

"Sweetheart, you look tired. How did things go today with Dr. Jon?"

He started as though his thoughts had been exposed. "He's not sure yet," he hedged.

"Michael," she forced his eyes to meet hers. "You had better be up front with me; this is no time to play games. What does he suspect?"

"He has to do more tests. He wants to ..."

"Michael," she interjected. "You can speak more plainly than that."

"He suspects cancer, Rhee. I was having some problem urinating, then I discovered this lump ... guess it puts pressure on the urethra."

"Lump?"

"Yeah. Its in my lower abdomen. Jon thinks it's about the size of a tennis ball. Rhee, I didn't want to tell you all this; I'm not sure I know what I'm talking about."

"What tests?"

"I'll probably go in on Monday for a needle biopsy and bone marrow. He's booking me for a CT scan."

"So he's pretty sure ... Oh, Michael!" her eyes were wide.

"At this point he's thinking lymphoma, since it's growing so fast."

"Will you give Jon permission to talk to me about this, Michael? We need to work through this together."

He nodded. "It certainly has come at an awkward time. Of course, if I'd gotten on it in August when I had pneumonia and Jon wanted me to ..."

"Oh Michael," her voice was almost a whisper, "I hope we haven't waited too long."

They sat in stunned silence as the realization hit them ... *it may be too late.*

"We need to pray about this or fear will immobilize us," she whispered and he nodded and took her hand.

They bowed together as Michael talked to God. Tears flowed freely as she heard him commit his life into God's hands and asked Him to have His way in their lives, their future. He prayed for wisdom for Jon and his team, and for themselves on the eve of their marriage.

Jon came in quietly as he finished. "Sorry I'm late. Luci wanted me to look at a car she's considering ... it took longer than I thought."

"So she must have gotten on at St. Mike's? She'll be working with Merle Jacobson."

"Yes, indeed she has, and she will be working with Merle. I'm not sure it's the best thing for her ... to be here, I mean."

"Jonathon," she spoke with surprise in her voice, "I thought you'd be thrilled to have her here ... to know that she'll be able to stay in Riverview!"

"Sure," he said with an air of finality, signalling the matter was closed.

"Rhea and I would like to ask you some questions … if you don't mind talking shop over supper. We think it would be best if we both discussed my situation with you."

"I'll go with whatever you're comfortable with. Fire away!"

"What makes you think Michael has cancer?"

"Rhee, I'm *sure* Mike has cancer. And I'm almost certain its a type of lymphoma; nothing else could come up that quick and grow that fast. The blood tests back that up. It has attacked his stamina …"

"So why are you planning to check the bone marrow? Do you think it has metastasized?"

"Possibly. But mostly its routine precaution. His blood doesn't show an elevated PSA but I'd like to check the prostate. The CT Scan should give us a pretty good idea what we're facing. The biopsy will tell us if it is in fact lymphoma, what kind, and what stage the cancer's at."

"Tell Rhea what you told me about the stages."

"Stage one and two are very treatable, especially if it's an early stage two. If it's in the bones, it most certainly has metastasized and is at least a stage three."

"So?" she asked, her eyes wide.

He sat quietly, concentrating on stirring his tea.

"So?" she asked again.

"Stage three is harder to treat … chances aren't nearly as good. Stage four …" he broke off, not wanting to continue.

"So how will you treat this?" she asked in almost a whisper.

"Probably with chemo. Let's wait until all of the evidence is in and see what we have."

"What does this mean for our marriage?"

"Rhea, you're too far ahead of me. Ask me next week."

"We've less than four weeks left, Jon. It's getting to be too late to cancel."

"You'll need to cancel the honeymoon trip. Chemotherapy will have to begin as soon as we know what we've got; we can't take a chance and wait ... we can't play games with his life. And everybody reacts differently to chemo; some seem to breeze through the first few; others get horribly sick. Mike's blood is pretty low. I'm sorry, I don't mean to paint such a ..."

"Thanks, Jon, for levelling with us," Michael spoke calmly. "I know I speak for both of us when I say we want to know the truth ... and the consequences. I know this is hard for you; we both appreciate your willingness to look after my treatment. I gather it may get a lot harder as we go along."

"Hello, Valida," Rhea caught the phone on the first ring. "Yes, of course, tell Dr. McCaig I'll be right there."

"Babies, babies, babies!" Jon smiled as she took her leave.

What beautiful little babies, Rhea mused as she sat at her desk. *It isn't often we have four. Glad our fears were unfounded; she delivered beautifully. Jared gets so proud you'd think he was the father. Wonder if Michael will ever get to be a proud father. "Oh, God, let it be,"* she pleaded as the ring of the phone cut through her thoughts.

"Rhea, I have to see you. Can you see me tonight or tomorrow?" It took a minute to recognize the strained voice as that of Luci.

"Luci, why yes, of course. I'll be here for a half hour or so. Come on down."

"May I pour you a coffee?" she offered as the shapely ash blonde sat nervously on the edge of her chair.

"Oh, please do. I could use something. I'm sorry, I should have mentioned that this isn't a professional matter; it's personal - very personal."

"That's just fine. How can I help?" Rhea looked at her quizzically.

"It's about Jon. I don't think he loves me anymore. He used to say such wonderful things - that he loved me ... that he wanted to be with me always - and now ..." the tears spilled over washing her mascara into little rivers.

"Now?"

"I don't know about now. I gave up my job in Sydney to come and join him here. I was away in Melbourne on an assignment when he came back from his vacation and he never even left me a note. He just left." She paused as sobs shook her slender frame. "Now he acts as if I'm just a casual acquaintance ... treats me like he treats my sister."

"How is that?"

"Very courteous ... kind ... friendly ... helpful."

"That's it?"

She nodded, reaching for the box of tissues on the desk. "That's it. I'm sorry I'm in such a state, but the hospital has offered me a job, and now I don't know ... I don't think Jon is excited about my being here ... and I don't know if I should take it."

"What would you like from me, Luci?"

"I'm not sure. You always seem so kind and helpful, and I guess I thought you approved of Jon and me," Rhea nodded as she continued, "Maybe I need some advice about Jon. Did he ever tell you about me, before I came, I mean?"

"Yes, of course. He told me he was crazy about you."

"That's what he led me to believe ... so what do you think the problem is?"

"Did you let him know you're crazy about *him*? Give him reason to believe you loved him?"

"I thought I did," she sat quietly for a few moments, "but I was so busy trying to finish my residency. I thought he understood ... he's done a fair bit of this himself ... he knows you can't take time off because you have a boyfriend.

I do remember him getting really impatient with me sometimes. Guess I never realized how he was seeing things."

"Have you talked to him about this?"

"No. Actually, he avoids being alone with me. Like he doesn't want to open himself to a relationship with me."

"Do you think you are both on the same wave length?"

"Definitely. Both of us want something permanent."

"Meaning?"

"Marriage."

"Then why don't you call and invite him for supper, or take him out somewhere, just the two of you. Tell him you want to talk, and see what he does with that?"

"Guess I'm afraid he might refuse, and then I'd know. Maybe I'd rather not know."

"Do you think that sounds like Jon?"

"I don't know. You know him better than I. Do you think he still cares for me?"

"I'm sorry I don't know. He hasn't confided in me lately."

"May I ask if there's someone else in his life?"

"I can't answer that either. Certainly no one that I know of. If he seems preoccupied, it could well be that he has ... he has a really difficult situation at work right now ... a good friend of his ... has cancer ... and he will be the oncologist. I know it's giving him a lot of stress. Call him anyway. A good supper and a lovely lady might be just what the doctor ordered." They both chuckled as they rose to go.

"How are the wedding plans coming along?"

"A little rough in spots. Some uncertainties."

"Anything I can help with?"

"Let me put a little thought into that and I'll be in touch. Thanks for the offer."

"Thanks for seeing me. I really appreciate your suggestion."

222

"Keep in touch. I'll keep you in my prayers."

"Hi hon, I just got an e-mail from Randy. She would like to know if you want her to play for your solo at the wedding, or if you have other plans."

"Maybe we could just put a hold on that for now, Rhee. We need to talk. I got the test results this afternoon, and …."

"And?"

"And we need to talk," he finished lamely.

"What does that mean, Michael?"

"Rhee … sweetheart … I don't know how to say this. I really don't think we can get married right now."

Chapter 30

For Better... For Worse

R hea sat in stunned silence. She had sensed his reticence ... his uncertainty the other night. Whispering a prayer for guidance, she dialled Jon's number. His voice-mail answered. She glanced at her watch. *It was just after 12:30. Of course, he'll be in the cafeteria. I can't face that crew down there right now.* She hesitated a moment, then left a message, " Jon, I need some answers. Can we get together?"

Her phone buzzed loudly interrupting her troubled thoughts. *An outside call. Who could that be?* She answered reluctantly, "Dr. Rhymer."

"Dr. Rhymer, indeed! And how's our little bride-to-be?" She recognized Jonathon Fields. "I am a bearer of good tidings of great joy that shall be to all the Reimers ... yes, and the Braemer's too."

"Oh, Jonathon, you are a breath of fresh air. Tell me please. Tell me quickly. I can use some good news."

"I have tried both your intended and your brother, and I get only recordings. Honestly, don't you have any real people around there anymore? I'm afraid one of these times I'm going to get *for English press one.*"

"Jonathon! You rascal! Stop it! You know I'm dying to hear what you have to say."

He chuckled. "I don't suppose I could tempt a new bride to desert her beloved and accompany me to Africa to see her very-much-alive parents?"

"Jon! Oh Jon! Are you joking?"

"Not at all. We have finally gotten confirmation that they are *both* alive."

"Oh, that is wonderful news. Thank God!! Thank God!! Do we know where they are?"

"No. That has not been forthcoming. But we need to keep the pressure up, and I think we'll know soon enough. It's one of the reasons I think we need to go to Africa as soon as possible."

"So you aren't kidding about that?"

"Not at all! Not at all! If I were to arrive in Riverview tomorrow, would you and Michael and Jon have time for a meeting of great minds?"

"I'm sure we would take the time. Can we make it over the supper hour at our house? That would work for all of us, I'm sure. Thanks for all your efforts on this. I can hardly wait to tell Jon."

She looked up as her brother's handsome frame swung through her door. "Sorry I'm unannounced," he grinned. "No one at the front desk seemed to mind."

She smiled. He probably had charmed the girls on his way by. "Well, that was fast!"

"I arrived back from lunch just as you finished your message, so I came straight away. I know you're concerned about Mike. I thought he took the news pretty well, actually. What can I tell you?"

"Tell me everything. All I got from him was that he can't marry me, and I'm still in shock. But I've just had a call from Jonathon Fields and they have confirmed that Mom and Dad are both alive." Her eyes filled with tears as she continued, "Jon, I can't stand too much more in the way of surprises. I'm about done in."

He rose quickly and put his arms around her. "Rhee ... my dear little sis. I'm thrilled to bits about Mom and Dad! But the timing! Sometimes things just come all at once!"

"Jonathon wants one of us to accompany him to Africa as soon as possible. He'll be at our house tomorrow night to discuss details."

"Wow! Wow! Do you think you can go? I'm not sure I can ... I've only been on the job a couple months and my roster is overloaded. On the other hand, these are my folks ... and they're *alive!!!* Bless the Lord! Let's both go, no matter what."

She nodded. "Tell me about Michael's condition. He's pretty distraught. I don't know how to talk to him about this."

"It was as I suspected. He has Non-Hodgkin's Lymphoma, intermediate grade. The tumour is localized, making it a stage two. It hasn't metastasized, thank the Lord. But it is growing daily, and has worked its way between the intestines, near as I can make out, sort of with long tentacles. I can't tell whether it has attached itself to the intestine. If so, we may be in for trouble. When we hit this thing with a massive dose of chemo," he noticed her grimace as he continued, "it may pull away and rupture the bowel. We'll have to keep a very close eye on it."

"And the prognosis is?"

"Usually good. I think he should do okay, though a lot depends on how he responds to the chemo. Some seem to breeze right through. Others get terribly sick ... their blood count goes down ... they need a few units to top them up. Mike's blood is pretty low again. He needs to get this treatment immediately to stop that wretched thing from growing and sapping his strength."

"So, this chemotherapy. Tell me what it consists of and how it will be administered."

"Doctor, doctor, doctor, doctor! Nobody ever asks me that. We'll give three drugs intravenously: Then he'll have to take prednisone orally on a daily basis."

"And the side effects? ALL of them?"

"They vary with the individual: low blood counts, hair loss, weight loss, fever, chills, sore throat, cough, mouth sores, nose bleeds, upset stomach, nausea and vomiting, diarrhea, constipation, numbness in hands and feet, joint pain, muscle or bone pain, increased appetite or none at all. I think that about covers it."

"So will he have any or all of these after the first treatment?"

"I doubt he'll know he had it after a few days. We'll give him something to make sure he doesn't throw up. His hair should remain intact at least until after the second one. The tumour will shrink very rapidly which will free up his bladder function. He's really hassling with that right now."

"When will he have to start treatment?"

"Should have started weeks ago. How about tomorrow?"

"And when will he have the second one?"

"In three weeks, though we can delay for a few days if he isn't well enough."

"So why can't we get married?"

"You can."

"Michael says not. What's he afraid of?"

"Well, there is a possibility that he may be impotent for a time. I don't see it as a big deal; he'll probably be too weak to care. It will probably ... more than likely ... clear up once the treatment is over, though he may or may not be infertile."

"Who will look after him if we don't marry?"

"Maybe you should ask him. I have a few other questions for him. Is it possible to cancel all of the arrangements you've made? What about all the folk who are coming from a long distance, like his relatives? They will all have made travel arrangements."

"Jon, I would like to keep his condition under wraps until we know whether we will cancel the wedding. If we cancel, that's one thing, but if we don't ... I don't want the guests feeling sorry for us ... I would like them to rejoice with us. It will be a blessed event and should be enjoyed."

"How do you feel about marrying him in his present condition, Rhee?"

"Well, as I tried to explain to him the other night, when I said 'yes' to his proposal it included *for better - for worse, in sickness and in health.* I believe the Lord brought us together and he knew all this would be in our path. I think he intends for us to see it through together. I am most concerned about his care during the chemo. As you mentioned, his resistance to disease isn't that good right now; once he starts the chemo he may be ..." she looked up tearily, "he may be unable to care for himself."

He sat quietly for a moment. "My dear little sis. How like you to think about him at a time like this. You have a mountain of cancellations, not to mention thousands of dollars to pay for a banquet that you can hardly cancel at this late date, a hall, an orchestra, the florist - and all you can think about is Michael. Is he one blessed bridegroom, or what? He must be nuts to even think about cancelling! Would you like me to talk to him?"

"No. No. Please no. We talked for hours last night in his apartment. He didn't come for supper. He thinks he's doing me a favour by not imposing his illness on me. He wants to wait until he's well and 'in charge of his manhood,' and then we'll marry. He wants to keep up the payments on the mortgage while he lives in his apartment. I tried to explain that the house belongs to both of us. He should be there enjoying it and letting me look after him rather than holed up in that apartment ... which he hates. I told him if he wouldn't marry, that I would take over the mortgage payments. I gave the ring back. He cried terribly ... so did I."

"Wow! I didn't realize it had gone that far."

"He just doesn't seem to be thinking clearly."

"I agree. I think the shock will wear off in a few days and he'll come to his senses. Meantime, keep praying ... I know you have been."

She nodded as he rose to go. "See you at supper." He gave her a quick squeeze, and was gone.

"So, where's the bridegroom? Marriage plans a little too much for the boy?" Jonathon Fields joshed Rhea in his usual manner.

"Could be," she replied nonchalantly, "he hasn't been feeling too well lately. Actually, he had an appointment after work. I suggested he come when he's through, even if he's late. He didn't commit."

"Not even to hear about your folks?"

"He doesn't know about this. I didn't want to burden him with anything further. He really isn't feeling well right now."

The lawyer sat silently. Obviously something was not quite right here, but he had already put his foot in it, and he'd best let it be.

Michael arrived as they finished asking the Lord's blessing. He looked pale and uncertain as he apologized for being late. He was apprised of the situation as they ate.

"So, who will come to Africa with me in mid-January?" Jonathon asked as they considered the evidence he had presented.

"Both of us," Jon offered.

Michael looked up surprised, the colour rising in his face.

Rhea avoided his eyes. She knew what he was thinking, *She didn't even ask me.* His heart sank as his thoughts focussed, *She doesn't have to; she isn't my fiancé anymore.*

He joined her in the kitchen as she prepared the tea. "Rhee," he said softly coming up behind her. She stiffened slightly as he put his arms around her waist. "Can we talk tonight ... after the meeting?"

"About?"

"Us."

She looked at him questioningly.

"Please?" he asked, his voice pleading.

She turned toward him tearily, removing his arms. "Michael, I don't know how much more stress I can handle. I'm in way over my head ..."

"Please," he repeated. "Can we work on it together? One more time?"

She nodded, handing him the teapot and trying to deal with her tears.

"Will you sit beside me, Rhee?" he asked as she settled in her chair across from him. "I can't talk when you're way over there. You know we always talk better when we're close."

She hesitated, then moved almost reluctantly to sit beside him on the loveseat. He slipped his arm around her and eased her head back against his shoulder. "Rhee, Rhee sweetheart," he began. "I don't know where to begin. I'm so sorry for what I have put us both through these last few days. I guess ... I guess I thought it would just be easier for you if I got this wretched chemotherapy over with before we married. I really thought that I was thinking of you, and of your welfare. Then tonight I had a session with Bob. He came down on me pretty hard ... said I was more concerned about myself and how I might look to you, than I was about your well-being. I guess ... I guess I have to admit that I am concerned about that. I've been concerned that maybe I wouldn't be able to consummate the marriage ... then we'd be married in name only ... and if I didn't recover from the impotence ...," he stopped and she felt his tears on the side of her face. "I'm afraid you might fall out of love with me when I'm all emaciated, and I can't really be your husband."

"Michael, dear Michael," she whispered softly, "I told you that when I said *yes* it meant *for better - for worse ... in sickness and in health.* This isn't just your problem; it's our problem. We don't have to perform for one another; we'll just love each other with the grace God gives. Marriage is more than sex, as important as that is."

"I know, sweetheart, but have you ever worked with anyone on chemo?"

"Yes, a number of times. Actually, Lynda and I tended her Mom for the last few months before she died. She had breast cancer ... it spread to her bones, her lungs, finally her liver. We took turns ... day and night. It was pretty gruelling ... especially dealing with her Dad besides. Poor little lady was almost not there by the time she died. I know what we're facing, Michael."

"I've thought a great deal about what you said ... you know about living in this house instead of the apartment ... of having you care for me instead of hiring someone if I got really sick. Oh Rhee ... Rhee ... I am so sorry, will you forgive me?"

She nodded, reaching for a tissue.

"Can we start over again, Rhee?"

"Do you really want to do that, Michael. You really don't see me as very trustworthy ...   you don't trust my love to be long term ... to look after you ..."

"Do you think my failure to trust might come under the *for better - for worse* that you were talking about?"

"You're sneaky!" she said sitting up suddenly.

"Does it?"

She smiled and nodded. "I guess it better."

"So I'm forgiven?"

She nodded.

"And we can start over?"

She nodded again.

He turned her face gently, his mouth seeking hers. She turned away.

"I thought you said I was forgiven?"

She nodded.

"And we can start over?"

She nodded again. So what's the problem? Why can't I kiss you?"

"I'm waiting for my emotions to catch up with my good intentions," she explained.

"Will it take very long?"

She smiled. "Not more than a couple of months."

He took her face in his hands and looking into her eyes, he asked, "Rhea, my lovely Rhea, will you marry me?" She nodded and he gathered her into his arms, pausing only to slip his ring back on her finger.

"Did you cancel any of the wedding arrangements?"

She shook her head. "I didn't have the presence of mind to know where to start or what to tell people. That wedding cake … honestly Michael … who would want a cake that covers half an acre and is shaped like Mount Olympia?"

"So it's still in the works? Wonderful!! Oh Rhee, my beautiful Rhee!" She could feel his heart pounding as he held her close.

"I asked Jon about your chemo treatments. He mentioned that you might need to be hospitalized for the first one. So, is that happening tomorrow?"

"Actually, he has arranged for me to have it tomorrow after I'm through work. He's invited me to stay with him in the suite so he can keep an eye on me, rather than putting me in the hospital. He doesn't seem to trust me to look after myself. Apparently, if it's attached to the bowel, it may tear when it pulls away."

"So we have about 11 days till the wedding ... then we should have nine or 10 days for a honeymoon ... before the next chemo."

He nodded. "If the tumour pulls away cleanly, Jon thinks I should be okay after this first one. He expects it to shrink rapidly, giving some relief to my urinary function. That will be a blessing. Apparently, I'll keep most of my hair until after the next round. He thinks I'll be able to work at least two weeks out of every three, though I think we'll let the rest of the crew do the operating. That will be hard for me ... to be on the sideline."

"Yes, it will. But it's a small thing in light of everything else. Have you told your team about all this?"

"Not yet. Course I had to tell the Chief. He's very understanding ... concerned. Wants me to take off as much time as I need. I've already given Jeremy a lot of responsibility. He's one sharp little character ... loves what he does and is good at it. Doesn't leave too many stones unturned. I like the way he does things. He's a Chief of Surgery in waiting. I'll call them all together and tell them the situation when I go for my next treatment."

"So you'll live with Jon until we're married? Why don't you move out of your apartment? Bring your things here. At least we'll have that done. And we can all eat suppers together?"

He was quiet for a long minute as he held her close. She was back in his arms, his ring was back where it belonged, wedding plans were on target. In 11 days he would move in completely and she would be his ... his to love ... to live with ... forever and ever. He closed his eyes and breathed a prayer of thanks.

"Is it a time to dance?" he asked noting the music had switched to *Winter Wonderland.* They slipped easily into each other arms and moved together as one. Then mindful of what lay ahead of them tomorrow, their voices blended with the soloist:

> Later on, we'll conspire, as we dream by the fire -
> To face unafraid, the plans that we made -
> Walking in a winter wonderland.

(Dick Smith, Felix Bernard)

Chapter 31

Whatever Will Be

S he shuddered as she watched her brother and the nurse adjust the bulging bags of fluid and start the intravenous. *Poison ... poison to kill the cancer cells ... poison that will kill all fast-growing cells ... not discerning the good from the bad.* Her mind whirled as she watched the heavy black fluid drip and ooze into Michael's veins. *Oh, God, I don't think I can handle this!*

"Dr. Reimer, maybe you could take your little sis for a bite to eat. She hasn't had supper, and my guess is that you haven't either." Michael suggested.

Glancing quickly at Rhea's stark complexion, Jon took her by the arm, "Come. He's in good hands. Meribelle's the best. We'll be back in a half hour. You'll feel a lot better with a little food in your tummy." Then turning to Meribelle, he asked, "Did you check on that blood supply?"

"Yes, indeed! Dr. Paulson has donated a number of times. I asked them to hold a few units for us just in case."

"He's really going to be okay, Rhea," Jon began as they sat in the cafeteria. "I'm going to monitor him very closely for a few days. If his temperature goes up, we'll deal with it within the hour; if his blood goes down we have a supply on hand. He'll be at my place tonight so I'll be sure he gets his medication and doesn't throw up."

She sat silently, toying with her soup spoon.

"What are your fears?"

"They're nameless. They're out there like a big black blob ... like that black bulging bag dripping poison into his veins."

"I'm sorry about that, Rhee. You really shouldn't have come, you know."

"I couldn't stay away."

"I know. I know. I wish we had something better to offer. There is a new treatment in the pipeline that apparently kills only the cancer cells, and spares the healthy ones, but it'll be years before it's on the market. Mike, and hundreds like him, can't wait for that."

"I know," she whispered.

"What's this?" he reached over and turned the diamond on her finger.

She smiled. "Looks like we're back on target ... if ... if ..."

"He'll be well enough, Rhea," he answered her thoughts, "and he should have all of his hair. He'll be a handsome groom. I'm glad he's going to be my brother at long last. I would have picked him for you ... if you had let me," he grinned.

"Can I ask what's going on with you and Lucinda?"

"Actually, not a whole lot. She plays games, and I'm really tired of the whole scene. Guess I just don't want to open that bag again."

"But she came all the way here from Sydney, to be near you. Doesn't that mean anything?"

"Not much. It's like her. She hates to lose ... likes change ... likes to be pursued ... waited on. I'd like to meet somebody who cares about me like you do about Mike."

"Well, you know, Jon, I inherited a lot of that from our Mom and Dad ... I guess we both did. I'm not sure it's fair to expect it from somebody who comes from a broken home and has been on her own for years. Trying to make your own way in the world makes one a little self-centered."

"She's more than a little. I don't really know what to do, Rhee. I can't say I'm not attracted to her. I just wonder what marriage to her would be like. A zoo ... and I'd be the grounds keeper."

"So you aren't seeing her?"

"Well, I am ... sort of. She invited me for supper but I'm too busy with Michael right now. Told her to make it Sunday or next week. That should be interesting ... I don't think she knows how to boil water."

"Now, Jonathon! Aren't you being a little judgmental?"

"Knowledgeable!"

"Can't you give her a few tips? You've managed a healthy diet for so many years."

"Actually, I was thinking of sending her over to you, so you can teach her to cook."

"I think we'd enjoy getting together like that. A lot would depend on how she was approached."

"She knows she can't cook ... though I think she'd like to. She'll probably ask me to barbeque ... that would be okay, too; at least we'd get something to eat. Says she'd like to talk to me. It will be an interesting evening, I'm sure."

"Do you think Michael will want to eat tonight?"

"He probably will. Soup would be a good choice. Do you have any on hand?" he asked as they rose to go.

"There now, that wasn't so bad," Michael rose and rubbed his arm. Then smiling at Rhea, he asked, "So when do we eat?"

Chapter 32

Till Death...

S he paused as the double doors opened and the organ burst forth, *Here comes the bride!*

Her glance took in the full pews, her bridesmaids in their floor-length burgundy gowns with bouquet's of soft pink roses and lily of the valley, the groomsmen in their black tuxedos, Pastor Bob waiting, smiling, and ... Michael ... Michael in his white tuxedo ... waiting ... waiting for her, his face radiant, his eyes filled with love and promise. *What a handsome groom! My groom! My wedding day! Thank you, God, thank you!*

The guests stood to their feet as one as she moved slowly, gracefully down the aisle, the tiny crystals hidden in the folds of her rich silk gown and matching train sparkling with each step.

"She's elegant, she's regal," Michael's Mother whispered to Michael Sr.

The Chief proudly escorted her on the right, Joan on the left. They paused as the organ ceased. It began again as Michael stepped forward and in a rich baritone sang to his bride, *I never knew how much I really needed you.*

I wonder if the chandeliers are tingling as much as I am, Rhea wondered as she listened and watched her beloved. The fear she had felt for his lack of strength had completely dissipated.

"Who will give this woman to this man?" the clear voice of Pastor Bob.

"I will," her brother responded as he moved toward her, shook hands with Joan and the Chief, and taking his *little sis* by the arm he escorted her to stand beside her groom.

"Michael Braemer," he began as Rhea looked at him in surprise. "Michael Braemer, my good friend, soon to be my brother. It gives me a great deal of pleasure, on behalf of our parents, Matthew and Rheanne Reimer, to entrust to you my best friend, my confidante, my buddy, my sister." Then pausing to regain his composure, he added, "I charge you to take good care of her." Carefully lifting her veil, he kissed her softly, before placing her hand in Michael's. Rhea sighed with relief, *No camels!*

Pastor Bob's message to the couple was as powerful as they had come to expect ... brief and to the point. *I wonder how a single man can know so much about marriage*, Rhea wondered, then wished it were possible to steal a glance at Lynda.

As she handed her enormous bouquet of burgundy and creme roses to her maid of honour, she turned toward Michael. They faced each other now, holding hands and looking into each others eyes.

"Rhea Ann Rhymer," he began. "I want to thank you today for consenting to become my bride ... my wife. Today in the presence of God and in the company of these witnesses, I promise to love you always. After God Himself, you will always be first in my life. I will keep only unto you as long as we both shall live ... I promise to be faithful to you in good times and bad, in sickness and in health, in times of plenty and times of want. I will seek always to protect you and respect you, to be a kind and loving husband, to provide godly leadership in our home, and ... God willing ... to be a good father to our children. Your family will be my family and we will love them and care for them together."

"Michael ... Michael Lee Braemer," her eyes were soft as they looked into his. "It is a special joy and privilege for me to become your wife today. In the presence of God and of all these, our family and friends, I promise that I will never leave you nor forsake you. You will always be first in my life, after my relationship with Jesus Christ. I promise to love and respect you, to care for you ... in sickness ..." she paused, "and in health, for better or for worse, in plenty or in want. I will always be faithful to you, Michael; I will keep myself only for you till death parts us. I look forward to being a part of your family. Your people will be my people. Together we will love and enjoy and care for them."

The organ began softly and soon her rich soprano filled the auditorium as she sang her own arrangement of the love song from the Book of Ruth,

> *Where you go I will go,*
> *And where you stay I will stay.*
> *Your people will be my people*
> *And your God will be my God*

(Ruth 1:16)

"Michael Lee Braemer," Pastor Bob began, "do you take this woman ....?" It seemed only moments and vows and rings had been exchanged. Carefully Michael lifted the veil and turned it back over her crown of white roses; then taking her in his arms, his eyes sparkling, he kissed her softly.

They knelt together then, as Michael's parents and the Wahl's came forward and laying their hands on their bowed heads, committed them to the Lord in prayer. Rhea felt Michael's tears on her hand as slowly, softly, his mother, in her beautiful contralto, sang *The Wedding Prayer.*

Again Pastor Bob's voice, "Ladies and Gentlemen, may I introduce Mr. & Mrs. Michael Braemer."

They smiled into each other's eyes as Miranda began to play the recessional. The future would hold many unknowns, but after today they would face them together.

Comments floated around them as they made their way to the door: "A wonderful couple ... beautiful ceremony ... lovely bride ... handsome groom ... talented couple ... exceptional way to do things ... wonder what her parents would have thought? Almost sounded like they were alive the way Jonathon gave her on their behalf ..."

Some were all smiles, others in tears. No one noticed the tall gentlemen in the black suit slipping out the side door to hide the tears he could no longer control. He would have them in check in time to dance with the bride and to wish her well. He had just heard her promise Michael that she was his until death. *Oh, God, I never really knew I could hurt this much,* he breathed as he made his way to the car. He would see that Miranda got a ride to the banquet hall and act out his part as he ought. *With a little practice ...*

The banquet hall was already filled to capacity. Great platters of turkey, beef and whole-baked salmon awaited only the arrival of the bride and groom. The bridal party entered first, slowly taking their places at the head table, then mid much cheering and clapping, Michael escorted Rhea. She had shed her veil and the long train, and her gown, beautiful in its simplicity, sparkled with her as she walked.

"I've just never seen a lovelier bride ... a more beautiful couple," Joan whispered to the Chief with all the pride of a parent. "If only her Mom and Dad could have been here to see this. They would have been so proud! I wish they could have waited."

"We know why they didn't." he replied. "I hope those cameras got every jot and tittle, There were enough of them."

"I wish you hadn't asked Jon to toast the bride," Rhea whispered to Michael as her brother got to his feet. "He just enjoys this sort of thing way too much."

Michael grinned. "That's why I asked him. Anyway, who knows you as well as he does?"

"I am surprised," he began, "that my sister asked me to give her away again today." A ripple of laughter as he continued. "It isn't the first time I gave her away; actually I didn't really *give* her away; I *sold* her." Those who knew him were laughing in anticipation. It promised to be a real *vintage Jonathon* story. He proceeded with the account of the camel trading with all of the embellishments native to his personality. "Of course it was a lousy thing for me to do, selling my lovely little sister for a measly 10 camels; I should have asked at least 50." As he came to the end, amid much laughter and thumping of tables, he paused, "My father was not a violent man," he commented, "but the violence that he inflicted on my anatomy that day has only to be remembered to be felt."

As the applause slowly died down, he went on to honour Rhea, telling stories of her childhood, her middle years in Africa, her passion to help the hurting, her high school and medical studies, her accomplishments. "Rhea is a warm, caring, loving, *forgiving* person," he stressed, turning to Michael. "You're lucky, Mike; you need somebody like that!" A smiling Michael nodded his agreement. Then holding up his glass, Jon invited, "Join me in toasting ..." his voice caught as he finished, "... our lovely bride, Mrs. Michael Braemer!"

Michael's reply was both witty and charming. Clearly he knew his brother-in-law very well and had anticipated his remarks. "I am a little surprised, too," he began with

245

a slight grin, "surprised that my brother Jon would lead you to believe that he *gave* his sister to me today. He neglected to mention that the price had now gone up to 50 camels;" he paused as laughter erupted, "he cited her beauty ... her education ... her earning capacity ... her caring ways ... inflation." Looking down at Rhea, he smiled, "He knew I wanted her at any price! Her price is far above rubies ... never mind camels!

"Today I want to acknowledge the debt I owe to the Reimer family. Most of you do not know that Rhea's father, Dr. Matthew Reimer was my mentor for many years. Next to my own father, he influenced my life more than anyone else. He kept his eye on me when as a young pre-med student, then a very green intern, I could have taken many wrong turns in my career ... my life. I met his son, Jon, whom you already know ..." he paused for the laughter, then went on, "and we became best friends. He always told me to find his sister and marry her, that she was what I was looking for. I didn't find her till ten years later. I would have to say that with this family I have been thrice blessed." He went on to thank his own family, Jon, all those who had a part in their lives, and in their special day; then taking his bride by the hand he escorted her to the dance floor.

"My dearest, I think we need to head for home," she suggested after they had completed the necessary dances with family and wedding party.

"Do I look like I'm fading?"

"Your eyes have taken on that glassy, vacant look; I really think we need to go."

"You're right, beautiful, but it's our big day. There's probably at least a dozen guys out there that would enjoy a few steps with you, and I know you're having a good time."

She turned her head in time to see a signal from Jon. He hadn't missed the signs of Michael's fatigue. "I'm about done in, too. Why don't you talk to your folks and just tell them we're going and ..." she broke off as Jonathon Fields approached for a dance with the bride.

"Were you leaving already?" he asked curiously as they glided across the floor. "Isn't it a bit early? Do you need a ride to the airport?"

"Yes, yes and no," she said laughing. "Yes, we will leave right after this dance. Yes, it is early to be doing so. No, we don't need a ride. Thank you, though."

"So?" he asked.

"Michael hasn't been feeling well for a while. We both think he needs more rest than he's been getting."

"Rhea, can I ask ... is it something serious?"

"Yes," she replied as the dance ended and Michael claimed her.

"Well, I'll be!" he said under his breath as he watched them walk away.

"They are one beautiful couple! He certainly married well! Handsome rascal!" Michael's father noted with pride as he watched his son escorting his bride from the hall.

"Handsome ... yes ... like his father," his wife mused. "So you're happy with our new daughter-in-law?"

His face showed his surprise. "Well, I guess! She's not only beautiful, she's a mover and a shaker. Guess it was her care and concern for Michael when he was sick that really got to me. She loves him! Incredibly! How could any man ask for more than that?"

She nodded her agreement. *Rheanne's daughter ... my old and best friend's daughter. I wonder if she knows about this from Up There! I bet she's smiling and thankful like I am.* Aloud she murmured, "I'm so glad we have our son back ... and his wife. God has been outlandishly generous in his gifts to us!"

"Yes ... yes ... yes ..." he replied. Then looking at his wife, he added, "But I'm asking for more, you know." Noting the surprised look on her face, he added, "Grandchildren! Can't you just imagine grandchildren from those two!"

"Oh Michael ... oh my dear!" she whispered as they rose to enjoy an old-time waltz.

"Well, we haven't seen any from Tracy and Tyler," he continued as they danced.

A sharp pain stabbed at her heart. *If he only knew how desperately Tracy longs for a child,* she thought, then a silent prayer, *Oh God let it be.*

"She certainly is one beautiful bride," Randy whispered to her sister. "I can't help but be glad that she's married."

Luci nodded knowingly. Maybe now Jonathon Fields would get over his infatuation as Randy was hoping. "You're at least as beautiful as she is, and you have just a much to offer," Luci encouraged. "He'll come around."

"I sure hope so. I'm afraid I'm getting a little too fond of him for my own good."

"I don't know what's gotten into that Jonathon Reimer tonight," Luci remarked. "Honestly, he's spent half of the evening dancing with his sister. Hope he knows I'm still here now that she's gone."

They broke off as the two Jonathon's came to claim them for a dance.

Chapter 33

In Sickness and in Health

The glow from the fireplace in the master bedroom high-lighted the warm glow in his eyes as he entered the room. "My beloved!"she murmured moving gracefully toward him in time with the music, her filmy white negligee flowing softly about her. "Is it a time to dance?" she enticed, looking up at him through her lashes.

She lay awake long after she heard his deep, even breathing. "Thank you, Lord," she whispered. Thank you for my husband; thank you for sustaining his strength today, for making it so special for our first night together, for letting me become Mrs. Braemer." She would remember this night for years to come ... his tender care for her in spite of his boyish eagerness ... his joy at being her husband ... his prayer of thanks to God before he drifted off. She glanced at the bedside clock ... 10:30; the wedding dance would go on until midnight. *Wonder what Michael told his Mom*, she mused as she, too, slowly drifted off.

"Rhea!" his voice sounded strained.

"I'm here, love," she hurried to the bedroom, coffee cup in hand. "I woke an hour ago and didn't want to disturb you; you were sleeping so soundly."

"Sweetheart," he said as she sat on the edge of the bed. "I had the most wonderful dream ... I dreamed we were married, and we ..."

"I know, darling. I had the same dream." She set her cup hastily aside as he pulled her back into his arms.

"We're married, Rhee! You're my wife!"

"Mmmmm. Shall your wife fix you some breakfast before you fade away?"

"In a few minutes," he nuzzled her neck as he held her close. "Actually, I had something else on my mind."

"Mmmmm," she murmured, as she snuggled closer.

"Let's always stay married," he suggested at length, as they relaxed together.

"Definitely," she smiled against his cheek. Then, "what did you leave your Mom with?"

"I told her we'd still be here on Monday and asked them to drop in before they left for home. I thought we could tell them about the cancer, and maybe about your folks."

"Good thinking."

"If I'm feeling okay by Tuesday, do you think we could hit the slopes for a couple of days? It will give us some time away and it may be the only skiing we'll get this year."

She smiled. "Great idea, sweetheart; I was thinking the same thing. We don't have to ski all day; maybe we could sleep in in the morning and take the afternoon runs. Just so it's relaxing ... and fun."

"I'm a little surprised that you're still here; I guess I thought you were heading somewhere warm," Michael's father commented as Rhea poured his coffee.

"Well, Dad, that was our intention, but you know ... *the best laid plans of mice and men!*"

"Most folk thought you were leaving to catch the plane after the banquet ..." his mother began.

"Actually, we hoped they'd think that, but you know, Mom, that's not why we left. We left because I ran out of steam. Mom ... Dad ... I'm really sorry to tell you this ... but I have cancer."

"Oh, no!" his mother's hand went to her face. "Oh, Michael! Rhea!" she looked from one to the other.

"Prostate cancer?" his father asked, his face showing the stress he felt.

"No, thank God! It's lymphoma ... stage two ... quite treatable, but a bearcat for coming back in a year or two."

"And the treatment is ...?"

"Chemotherapy. Actually, I had my first treatment almost two weeks ago. My next one is due early next week."

"Oh, Michael," his mother repeated in stunned amazement.

"And you kept this from us, son?" His father's voice had taken on that authoritative tone he used when Michael was a lad.

"Yes, Dad. We only found out about three weeks ago. We kept it from everyone except those who had to know ... the Chief ... Dr. Jon - he diagnosed it of course, and is the oncologist. We didn't want all of our family and friends feeling sorry for us on our wedding day. It's a time for rejoicing!"

"I guess that makes sense. How do you feel about marrying him with cancer, Rhea?" he looked at his new daughter-in-law.

"It was the only thing that made sense to me. I love Michael; I could hardly look after him if he stayed in his apartment. It wouldn't even be decent. He may need round-the-clock care if he doesn't respond well to the chemo. His blood took another nose-dive after the first one and he had to have a couple units ..." she paused realizing his mother had turned pale. "I'm sorry, Mom, I didn't mean to frighten you, but chemo can be really hard on the system, and he has five more to go. Michael didn't want to go ahead with the wedding, but ..." she paused as his father looked at him questioningly.

"Well, I hated to inflict her with my condition, but finally came to my senses and realized it would be harder on her not to marry. I was afraid the chemo might leave me impotent; it could well leave me sterile."

"And you knew all this?" he addressed Rhea.

She nodded.

"Dad ... Mom ..." Michael began, then paused. "You need to know that I'm still okay. The real side effects are yet to come. I'll lose most of my hair after the next treatment. I'll probably become impotent as my body weakens."

"Oh God! Oh God!" Lillian moaned. "I can't believe this is happening."

"It's okay, Mom. We aren't looking forward to it, but we're looking forward to having it over with. Rhea's a real trooper ... the Lord sure gave me the right helpmate!"

"Will you let us help ... I mean if there's anything at all that we can do, will you call ...?" she glanced at her husband and he nodded his approval.

"Actually, we probably will need some help. Rhea has some really big news ..." he stopped as they both looked at him in surprise.

"I do ... I do indeed! Jon and I have always been of the opinion that our folks, Matthew and Rheanne, were never killed in a land mine," she paused as their eyes opened wide in disbelief. "We thought they were kidnapped by the Congolese army and forced to treat their wounded. Last summer we engaged the services of Jonathon Fields. You remember the lawyer that came for Thanksgiving Dinner? Jonathon and his father do a lot of international lobbying for our Government, and he offered to go to work on this. He was of the same mind, and had collected all manner of information concerning the incident. A few weeks ago the Congolese Government finally admitted that they are both alive."

They sat speechless, unable to deal with the sudden shock.

"So far they have refused to give us their location, but Jonathon feels we need to keep the pressure up. He would like Jon and me to accompany him to the Congo in mid-January."

"Oh my! Oh my! Oh my!" Lillian's voice came out in thin raspy whisps.

"And you think this is for real?" Michael Sr. asked skeptically.

"We really do, Dad. Jonathon is nobody's fool. He met Rhea over there in September and got a really good handle on things. They both came away convinced that they were on the right track. He probably won't give in until he locates them in January."

"Oh my! Oh my! Oh my! And I thought we were coming to talk about Christmas!"

"Yes, yes, that too," Rhea smiled. Since we don't know whether Michael will be feeling well enough to travel that far, we're wondering ... well ... I know how much you've planned on having us at your house, but would it be possible ... I mean would you mind terribly ...?"

"If we came to your house?" his father finished for her, then looked at his wife.

"Of course we can come ... we should come. I'm sure Tracy and Tyler will make every effort ..."

"Actually, I was wondering whether you and Joan might make the celebration at her place. I haven't asked her yet, but they are always included in our Christmas, since they're our guardians, and think of us as their family. If Michael is really ill, he won't appreciate the house filled with guests. He'll be looking for a quiet place. We have a lot of unknowns here ... of course; Christmas will be about two weeks after his next chemo."

They nodded as she continued, "And I'm wondering whether you could both come and stay here with Michael while I'm in Africa. I expect to be gone about a week or 10 days, but right now it's open ended. He will be half way through his treatments by then, but you should know that he'll have to have one while you're here ... unless his blood is dangerously low. What do you think? Could you come?"

"Would you be comfortable with that arrangement, son?"

"Very," Michael nodded, noting how often his dad addressed him as *son*.

They sat quietly, each trying to process the information that had just been forthcoming.

"We need to be on our way, Lil," his father said quietly, looking at his wife.

"Yes, yes, dear. But Rhea ... Michael ... I know you said no wedding gifts ... just donations to the hospital or the street ministry, but ... well ... we are your parents you know ... and we needed to ... I mean would it be okay ... we have something ..."

"Oh, Mom, I'm sorry. When Rhea and I decided on this we should have let you know it would be okay. We just didn't want folk bringing arms full of things we surely don't need, when the hospital is always short of funds, and there are so many folk who are cold and hungry. We knew folk would want to give, so we just made way for it."

"I'm so-o glad," she glanced at her husband as he rose to get their parcels from the car. "This one is from us; this one from Tracy and Tyler."

Rhea gasped as Michael opened the solid oak chest with sterling-silver flatware. "Mom ... Dad ... this is beautiful!"

Rhea sat in stunned amazement as Michael handed the second parcel to her to open.

"Matching candlesticks!" she found her voice. "How did you know ...?"

"I asked Joan. She really knows quite a lot about you, you know. We know you love to entertain and always have a house full. She remembered your choice of pattern. We thought ..."

"Well you certainly thought very well. These are almost too lovely to use. What a treasure, Michael. What a lovely, lovely treasure from your family!" He smiled, obviously delighted that she was so pleased with the gifts from his loved ones.

"I've been using my Mom's lovely things. What a joy it will be helping her to make a home and get established again. I get beside myself thinking about it."

"Well, we'll certainly be keeping you both in our prayers, with all you have on your plate in these days. Why don't we just pray before we go," and bowing his head he asked God to undertake for his precious son and his wife, her brother as he treated Michael, her folks wherever they were, themselves as they journeyed home.

"What a precious time!" Michael remarked as he watched them drive away.

"What a precious family!" Rhea smiled.

"Dr. Mike! Dr. Rhee! I didn't know you were coming skiing. I thought you were going some place warm." Jeremy stood before them ready to head up the hill.

"Hello, Jeremy. You guessed right. We were planning some place warm, but ... well, we've had a change of plans. Do you have time for a coffee? I'd like to talk for a few minutes."

"Sure thing," the young skier replied as he stuck his poles in the snow and clomped into the ski lodge behind them. He looked questioningly from Michael to Rhea as they sipped their coffee.

"Jeremy," Michael began. "I ... uh ... I ... I don't quite know how to tell you this, but we found out a few weeks ago that I have cancer."

"Cancer! Oh Dr. Mike! Dr. Rhee! Oh no!" Then after a moment, "Can I ask ... is it leukemia?"

"Yes, you can ask. No, it isn't leukemia. It's lymphoma. I bet you wondered because of the amount of blood ...?"

Jeremy nodded. "I guess I've been wondering why you needed to be transfused. You haven't looked terribly strong for a while ..." his voice trailed off. "So, do you have to have surgery? Chemo?"

"Just chemo. Actually, I started two weeks ago, and will go again next week. I expect to meet with you and the rest of the staff and tell them the news and lay out a plan for the days I may not be there. I'd appreciate if you'd just keep this information under wraps until then."

"Yes, yes, of course." He sat quietly, as if trying to think his way through the shock. Then finally, he offered, "I guess that's why you handed some of your responsibilities and surgeries over to me in the last few weeks. Guess at the time I thought it was because you'd be gone on your honeymoon."

Michael smiled, "That, too. But I won't be operating while I'm on chemotherapy; though I'll try to be there for consultations and help in any way I can."

"Well, I'll be!" Jeremy repeated over and over as he rose to go. "I'll sure be praying for you, Dr. Mike ... both of you."

"Thank you, Jeremy." Rhea smiled, " We know you will, and we need prayer more than anything else."

"You really do ski like a pro," she smiled at Michael as

they stopped mid-way. She noticed his face was flushed and he was needing to catch his breath.

"Look who's talking. Rhea, you are something else! I'm glad we got to do this together, and I'm praying there'll be many more times like this," he paused as tears stung his eyes.

"Yes, Oh yes," she responded warmly. Then, noting he was ready, she shoved off with a spray of soft white powder.

"I guess I'm about done in," he offered after the second run. "I can hardly believe how weak I am. Guess it's preparing me for the main event."

"I could use a little nap, a quiet supper and a lazy hot-tub myself. I think it would be great to sleep in, have a late brunch, and then catch the afternoon runs again tomorrow."

He nodded in agreement as they stepped out of their skiis and moved toward the chalet.

"You know, sweetheart," he smiled as they sat at supper, "in spite of my lack of strength, I don't think I have ever enjoyed skiing this much. I never thought I could ever be this happy! Rhee, I'm so glad we married!"

"So am I, darling," she offered a tissue as he wiped at his tears.

"I really don't understand you, you know, Jon." Luci addressed him directly as they finished the steaks he had barbequed.

"What is it that's bothering you, sweet lady?" he asked in his usual bantering tone.

"Just a whole lot of things."

"Such as?"

"Well, for one thing you have been promising to come to my place for supper; and after putting me off for a few weeks, I wind up at your place."

"Heh, come on! We've already discussed this. You didn't have a barbeque and you wanted steaks, so you made the supper and I brought you here so we could barbeque."

"Because you didn't trust my cooking?"

He chuckled. "You made a lovely meal, my dear; I was just trying to make it easier for you. And I didn't really put you off; I had a very good reason for postponing our supper."

"You thought you'd like to postpone indigestion?"

"Stop it, Luci. I have to admit I didn't remember that you liked to cook."

"I didn't. But I took lessons as soon as I finished my residency."

"Wow! Why did you do that?"

"Because I know you like to eat," she smiled impishly.

"Well, I'll be ..." he looked at her admiringly.

"And another thing," she went on, "your behaviour at the wedding dance was quite unusual for the brother of the bride."

"What do you mean by that?"

"Well, I wasn't the only one who noticed how often you tagged the groom and took the bride. Honestly, Jon, doesn't the groom have first rights? I didn't even get to dance with you until they left?"

He sat silently as if trying to decide just how to answer her. Finally, resolving the matter in his own mind, he replied, "I guess I need to share with you the real reason for my unusual behaviours, though I must ask you to keep it quiet until it becomes public knowledge. I know that Rhea and Mike won't mind my telling you. Michael has cancer. They only found out a few weeks before the wedding. He had asked me to tag him whenever the music got a little frenzied because he couldn't keep up. He had his first chemo about 10 days before and was pretty shaky. He did awfully well at that wedding ... God gave him something extra."

"Oh Jon! Oh Jon! How absolutely dreadful! I am so sorry ... so very sorry."

He went on as though she had not interrupted. "And the reason we couldn't come here sooner is that they were still here, in the house. They didn't go to Hawaii. Mike needed some time to recuperate."

"So where are they now?"

"They went up Olympia this morning. My guess is they'll stay only a few days and give Mike time to rest again before his next chemo ... next week."

"Oh, dear Jon. Forgive me for thinking badly of you. I am indeed sorry. I should have known that behaviour wasn't characteristic of you. Actually, I found myself quite jealous of the love you have for your sister, and the time and attention you lavish on her. Will you forgive me?"

He nodded, smiling.

"And can you tell me about the cancer? What kind it is and what his chances are?"

Her beautiful gray eyes filled with concern as he described the disease, the chemotherapy process, the side effects, the chances for complete remission. "I'm glad they married anyway," he finished, "she'll look after him like nobody else, and besides ... she'll make him want to live." He chuckled.

"You really love her, don't you, Jon?"

"You bet! And I love Mike, too. I've never had a friend like Mike. I couldn't wish anybody better for her. They were surely meant for each other." He paused, then looked at her, "But I don't think that's what you wanted to talk about, is it?"

She looked down, now suddenly embarrassed. She was seeing a side of Jon that she had not heretofore known existed, and she was suddenly shy.

"Come," he said, "let's take our tea over to the sofa, and get comfortable."

He put a careless arm about her and drew her casually against his shoulder, "So tell me, Lady Rob. What's on your mind?"

"You're not making it easy for me, are you?" He looked at her surprised, as she continued, "Jon ... you used to tell me ... that you loved me. Do you still?"

He sat quietly, his arm still loosely about her. Finally he looked down at her as he spoke, "Would it matter to you if I did, Luci?"

"You know it matters to me, Jon."

"No, I don't know that. It never made any difference to you before ..."

"Don't say that!" she interrupted. "I told you that I loved you ..."

"What does love mean to you, Luci?" he asked at length. "It seems to me that our definitions are worlds apart. To me, love means commitment, it means marriage, it means a lifetime together, loving and serving one another, having kids ..."

"It means that to me, too, Jon, but you just went off and left me ... without even saying goodbye."

"You weren't there, Luce, and nobody seemed to know where you were. I left because I couldn't stand it anymore. Remember how often I tried to talk to you about the future, and how many times you put me off. You didn't have the time of day for me ..."

"Jon, don't!" She put her hand to his lips. That's not true ... at least not the way you're seeing it. I had all of those deadlines and internships to complete for my specialization. I guess I thought you'd understand ... you've been through that process yourself. I wanted us to be together and to talk about the future, but my mind was so preoccupied. Oh, Jon ... dear Jon, I am so sorry. I've hurt you, haven't I?"

He sat silently. This was a turn of events he had not considered. At length he turned her face toward him and looked into her eyes for a long time. "You want to marry me?" he asked with a note of incredulity in his voice.

She nodded, "but not in that tone of voice," she whispered.

She lifted her mouth to meet his. His kiss was warm and caring, then suddenly his arms tightened and they embraced passionately, as though to make up for the intervening months. "I love you, Lady Rob," he whispered, then slipping to his knees, he asked, "Will you marry me?"

She nodded as she slipped to the floor beside him and into his arms. Tears mingled with kisses as they held each other close.

The hours flew as they caught up on each others lives, and laid plans for their own.

"Do you want me to take the job at St. Michael's?" she asked.

He nodded. "You bet. I really can't have my wife working in Australia."

He told of the news of his parents. They agreed they wouldn't marry until Matt and Rheanne were safely back on Canadian soil, especially since they had missed Rhea's wedding.

"Will you come home with me for Christmas and meet my Mom?" she asked.

"Ouch, I've promised to spend it with Rhea and Michael. Could we ask your Mom ... I mean does she ever have Christmas Dinner on Boxing Day? Maybe we could leave here late on Christmas Day and get there. You know I'd love to meet your Mom, and I need to. I need to ask her permission, and your Dad's, to marry you. I don't want to offend her before I get there. Tell me what you think."

"I think I'll just call her and find out. Randy plans to be there. She apparently asked Jonathon Fields to join us for Christmas and he declined. Said he needs time to find himself, or something like that. Something about getting over another relationship ..." She looked at Jonathon with a question in her eyes.

"Yeah, I guess he had it pretty bad for Rhea ... an old highschool thing. It's years ago; I'd have thought he was over it by now."

Chapter 34

The Honeymoon is Over

"**H**oneymoon over already? That was short lived!" Jared quipped as they waited for the rest of the staff to gather in Rhea's office.

"Yes, I would have to say it's over. And, yes, it was way too short. Guess we'll have to make it up another time." She continued to ignore his questioning look as the staff filed in.

"I'm sure you're all wondering what I'm doing here when I expected to be honeymooning in the deep south." They nodded as she continued, "A few weeks before our wedding, Michael was diagnosed with lymphoma. He had his first chemotherapy about a week and a half before the wedding. His second one will be today ..." She looked from one to the other as some faces registered shock, others gasped.

"Rhea ... I am sorry," Jared managed at last. Then asked, "You obviously thought it wise to marry in those circumstances?"

"Yes ... yes we did! It was the only thing that made sense. He is showing signs of responding badly to the chemo and it would have been difficult to look after him if he continued in his apartment. Neither of us thought it would be right to cancel all of our plans, all of the arrangements for the wedding ... and for our lives together."

They nodded, as Jared continued, "Can I ask what the chances are for recovery? And whether Dr. Reimer is the oncologist?"

"Yes, Dr. Jon is looking after him, and his chances for recovery should be good, barring unforeseen circumstances. It's in the second stage. Are there further questions?"

"So you didn't have a honeymoon, Dr. Rhee?" from a pale-faced Valida.

"Well, yes, we went home early from the wedding celebration ... Michael was exhausted ... and after a few days to recuperate, we went up Olympia and enjoyed the slopes for three days. It was enough for us right now. We'll do the south seas another time when we can enjoy it more.

"I guess it goes without saying that if he is really sick the first week after each treatment, I won't be here. Jared, I would like you to be in charge for the next three months. I should be in at least two weeks out of every three, but that isn't guaranteed as the treatments progress."

He nodded as she continued to outline the plans for her department during her expected absences.

"Would it be okay if I dropped around sometime this week to see Mike?" he asked as he rose to go.

"Yes, of course. He'll need a few days to recoup from his chemo but I know he'd like that. Why don't you give him a call and come for supper? Want to make it for Friday? He should be able to enjoy his food by then."

"I'll just leave you two if you don't mind," Rhea suggested as she cleared the last of the supper dishes from the table, "I have a few things to attend to in my office. Perhaps you might find a more comfortable spot," she motioned toward the chairs by the fireplace.

"That was a great supper, Rhea," Jared complimented. Turning to Michael, he remarked,"You sure didn't do it justice; guess I made up for you."

Rhea smiled as he turned away, but she had noticed that already Michael's face was beginning to look gaunt, his eyes seemed to have that sunken look. Of course, with his hair thinning so drastically … She forced herself to think more positively. *We have only two-thirds left to go*, she told herself. *In a few short months we'll put this behind us.*

"So, how's it going for you, ol' buddy?" Jared ventured once they were seated.

"I guess you can pretty well see for yourself," Michael commented, wondering just where Jared was going with this.

"I … uh … I wanted to come and see you. I have a few things I've been wondering about. Could I just run them by you?"

"Sure. Go for it."

"Well … remember when we were kids … ?"

Michael nodded, wondering again where he was going.

"And we went to camp together quite a few times … and then that one campfire when we both …?" He stopped, looking at Michael, then added, "Tell me what we did there. How come it seems to have worked for you and not for me?"

Michael was taken by surprise. After a few moments, he offered, "I can only tell you what I did … what happened to me. I had felt the need for sometime for forgiveness and for a relationship with God. That night at the campfire I asked Christ to forgive me and come into my life. I thought you did, too, Jared, as I recall. In fact, you were a changed boy for a long time after that. Am I right about that?"

"Yeah," he replied hesitantly. "I remember doing that, and I remember being wildly happy at first, and for quite a while after, but how come it doesn't work now?"

"What do you think happened to your joy? When you were a boy, I mean."

"I'm not sure. I know my Mom and Dad really disapproved of my 'getting religion.' They told me it was a lot of mind-game stuff and that if they had known what Bible camp was all about they wouldn't have sent me. I really think they would have sent me anyway; they wanted to get me out of their hair so badly. I remember trying to pretend I was just the same as I had always been, and using bad language around them. Pretty soon, I guess, I was just the same as I had been before. I guess maybe that's what happened," he finished lamely.

They sat silently, Michael trying to absorb what it must have been like for Jared to be persecuted in his own home as a boy. He thought of the spiritual encouragement his Mom had always been to him, and suddenly his heart went out to his old friend. How little he had really understood him in their growing-up years!

"I guess that would do it all right," he managed. "When I think of all of the encouragement I got at home ... and I still struggled ... I can hardly imagine what it must have been like for you. I am devastated to think that I didn't know ... or care ... what you were going through."

Jared was visibly moved. He struggled for words. "I guess you must be wondering why this is important to me right now?"

"I really hadn't gotten that far yet, but, yes, I would like to know. You do project that devil-may-care image ..."

"Well, quite a number of things have been playing on my mind. I guess I've never really dated a Christian girl before, I mean one who really believes what she claims she does. Then I tried to date Rhea and she absolutely refused to have anything to do with me. She laid it all out in no uncertain terms. She said she was a one-man woman ... looking for a one-woman man ... she had no intention of joining my harem. She cut me to the quick." Michael smiled as he continued, "I guess she found that in you, huh?"

"We think a lot alike in matters of faith, marriage, family ..."

"I'm sure you do, but I'm really thinking of renewing my faith ... coming back to God, or whatever ... but I have some questions that I'm wondering about."

"Such as?"

"Well, I know that you always intended to wait for marriage to have sex, and I assume that you did ... wait, I mean?"

Michael nodded.

"Doesn't it seem to you to be ironic ... more than that ... devastating ... that after you waited all those years to have sex ... that God would lay cancer on you just about the time you're ready to enjoy?"

Michael chuckled. "I guess it depends on how you look at it, Jare. If you're accusing God of the cancer, then it doesn't make sense. However, cancer comes to those most susceptible whether Christian or not. Sickness is a part of our inheritance from the Fall in the Garden of Eden. God doesn't play favourites. He doesn't promise to protect us from every pitfall or sickness that could possibly come upon us, but He does promise to be with us in it.

"As I look at my situation, I see the goodness of God in giving me a wonderful, loving, and caring wife just at the time when I needed one the most. Rhea is incredible ... she changes from doctor to nurse as required. She is God's gift to me ..."

"And you think that you're being fair to her? I've looked up the side effects of chemo and, honestly, Mike ..."

"Which of the side effects are you concerned about? Rhea knew them all and insisted we marry anyway."

"Well, I know that you could very well not have a sexual relationship ..."

"That's a possibility, of course; it may well happen as my body weakens. We haven't been dwelling on it, in fact Rhea and I agree that these past two weeks have been the happiest of our lives to date, notwithstanding cancer. We're very compatible."

"But what about the future?"

"Whatever the future holds, we will deal with it when we get there, trusting God that His grace will be sufficient for us. We have so much in common ... our faith first of all ... our love of family, music, sports, travel, medicine, reading, dancing ... it goes on and on. We're enjoying getting to know each other ..." He broke off at the look on his friend's face. "You seem to have more on your mind than Rhea and me?" he commented.

"Yeah." He sat quietly, gazing into the fire. Then, "I guess I'm surprised at how up-beat you both are, knowing what you're facing and all. I'm sure it's your trust in God ... and I wish I had it, but ... I'm not sure I'm ready ..." He broke off again and sat staring vacantly into the fire. "I guess I have another reason for pursuing this faith thing."

"Is she from around here?" Michael joked.

"No. Actually she's Rhea's friend, Racine. You know ... her bridesmaid," he explained as he noted the surprised look on Michael's face.

Finding his voice, Michael whistled, "Well, she's certainly a lovely gal! Tell me what you're thinking."

"I was pretty taken with her. She was attracted to me, too, but when I asked her if we could keep in touch she asked me a few pointed questions, and then refused. Says she is very committed to her faith, and since I'm not, I didn't qualify. What is it with these babes?"

"Hold on there a minute, old buddy. You're hardly qualified to decide who's a *babe* and I resent your including my wife in that kind of a statement, because she believes in God, and ..."

"Sorry ... sorry ... sorry ... I didn't mean to imply that. Just an old slang term from years agone that I'd do well to get rid of. I'm not trying to be derogatory. And I am interested in renewing my faith in God ... not just for Racy ... but because I'm feeling a need in my life to get straightened around. I'm not sure I'm ready for that step ... don't know how to get ready. Guess I'm not sure that God still wants me ..."

"You don't need to worry about that," Michael assured him, then reaching over he pulled a book from the shelf. "Like to read?" he asked, handing him Yancey's book, *What's So Amazing About Grace?*

"Wow, looks like something I could get into," Jared replied, scanning the jacket. "Thanks, Mike, for hearing me out, and for this. Can we get together again, after I've had time to ponder, and maybe to digest this?"

"Any time, as long as I'm lucid," Michael smiled, as his friend rose to go. "Meantime, I'll keep you in my prayers. Do you mind if I share this with Rhea?"

"I guess I do mind ... but maybe you should anyway. Thanks again," he replied as he made his way out.

"You okay, sweetheart?" Rhea asked, noting his weariness.

"Yeah, just tired. Can we sit for a minute? I'd like to share a bit about Jared and maybe we can include him in our prayers tonight." She nodded as he went on to share their conversation, and his surprise at some of Jared's open and honest revelations concerning his hunger for a relationship with God, and his attraction to Racy.

"Wonderful how God takes our natural desires and uses them to draw us to Himself," Rhea smiled, then added, "Oh, God, let it be so with Jared."

Chapter 35

Come What May

"Sweetheart, I'm concerned about you; we shouldn't have stayed so long."

"Nonsense. I'm just sorry to disturb such a lovely Christmas when we were all having such a great time. I just couldn't stand the noise; the chatter and laughter started to grate on my nerves. Why don't you go back for a while, Rhee? I'll be okay ..."

"I'm just fine with being home, Michael. It was a special day. I'm glad that Jon and Luci got away in good time. Wasn't that special the way they announced their engagement?"

"No kidding! That Jon is unique! A really special guy!"

"I'm really glad we didn't try to have it here; it would have been far too exhausting for you. How did the turkey sit with you? You ate like a little bird."

"Yeah, I know, but I kept it all down. I'm glad the smell didn't nauseate me, like it does sometimes."

" Maybe we need to get some of that Ensure that Jon's been talking about. It has a lot of nutrients ... I'm concerned about the amount of weight you are losing this early on. Come, sweetheart, you look all in, let's get you into bed."

"You won't get any argument from me," he joked as he headed for the bedroom.

"When is your next blood test?" she asked with a note of concern in her voice.

"Just before chemo. Next one is Dec. 31."

"Do you think we should ask Jon to check your blood as soon as he gets back? I'm concerned you may need …"

"More blood? Please, *no.*"

"No, to have it checked? Or *no* to have more blood?"

"I'd really like to avoid the transfusions if I can. They'll be calling me *Jeremy* pretty soon. Seems he's supplied me every month since October."

"We need to be thankful for that, Michael."

"I know, and I am," he said as he sank wearily into bed. "Can I have a glass of water? Really cold water, I mean?"

"Of course, sweetheart, but you know it makes you shiver so badly."

"Let me risk it, okay. I hate when it's not quite cold."

He heard her at the fridge and in a minute she returned with the ice water. She left as he sipped it slowly, savouring the cool refreshment. She returned as the shivers began. "Let me just tuck you in,"she suggested as she pulled back the sheets and covered him with a pre-warmed arctic fleece, then replaced the bedding.

He snuggled gratefully under the warmth, then grinning sheepishly, he suggested, "No wonder I'm always sick … whatever will I do when I have to *take up my mat and walk*?"

"We'll get you out of here soon enough," she smiled, as they held hands and prepared to pray together.

"We'll have to postpone the chemo for a few days, I'm afraid," Jon remarked as he scanned the lab report. "Mike, I know you won't like this, but we do have to have another couple units of blood. Yours is below the acceptable level ... just for living ... never mind for chemo. Sorry, old buddy."

Michael nodded.

"I think we'll need to have you in hospital for a few days ... once the blood gets to work we'll want to give you the chemo and keep a close eye on it. How do you feel about that?"

Michael nodded. "Do what you have to."

The doctor looked at Rhea. She nodded thoughtfully. "How long do you think it will be before his blood will be at an acceptable level for the next chemo? I'm concerned about heading to Africa ..."

"I'm hoping it won't be more than a few days ... maybe by the third of January. If we leave on the 15th ... that will give us ten days ... he should be doing well by then."

———

Rhea leaned back and closed her eyes as the jumbo jet roared down the runway and lifted off. So easily it soared through the cloud cover and into the endless blue; she wished her heart could be lifted so easily. In fact she had left it behind ... behind in the sickroom where her beloved lay wasting away. What a terrible time he had experienced this past two weeks ... sleepless nights ... endless bathroom stops ... throwing up ... intravenous. *Oh God,* she prayed, *Oh God ... Oh God ... Oh God!*

As if he heard her prayer, her brother reached over and took her hand. "It was hard to leave him, wasn't it, sis?"

She nodded tearfully.

"He's going to be okay, you know. Sometimes I think

it's harder for the loved ones who watch than it is for the patient. Let's pray together." And pray he did, asking God to care for Michael and to give grace and stamina to his folks, the Chief and Joan as they cared for him. His prayers for Rhea asked for grace that she might let go of her anxiety … that she might leave Michael in God's hands … that she could relax and enjoy the trip. He added a petition for success with their mission and asked for his parents well-being. Then, as had been his usual practice in the past two years, he poured out his heart to God for his beloved Luci and her family.

Rhea felt the heaviness fall away as he prayed, and squeezed his hand gratefully.

"So where are we meeting Jonathon Fields?"

"He should be arriving in Cape Town shortly after we do. I've made arrangements with Dad's old friend, Dr. Ben Wyman … remember him from the clinic there? We'll stay with them for a day or two until Jonathon arranges the rest of the details. I've stopped over with the Wyman's a few times on some of my forays. They're quite wonderful folk … always warm and welcoming. They'll be delighted that we're pursuing this investigation. I'll want to call home before we leave Cape Town. No access to a phone where we're headed."

Chapter 36

In his Time...

"**B**ut I must tell you the ones you seek are not here."
The pompous, Congolese officer eased his considerable bulk into the chair behind the desk. Rhea delegated him 'lieutenant' in keeping with the authority he assumed, as he went on, "You have been misinformed. We do not know of such a doctor in these parts." He had reiterated these statements for over an hour, his dark skin no longer able to hide the red that crept from under his collar and flushed his face. From time to time he wiped the sweat that rolled down his forehead and into his eyes, while his damp shirt clung to his bulging body. Still he persisted.

Rhea was glad for the presence of Jonathon Fields. The lawyer was nobody's fool. Again and again he caught the lieutenant contradicting himself ... there had been no doctor there ... there had been no accident... someone must have misinformed Dr. Rhymer ... well maybe there was an accident ... he wasn't sure about that point ... he hadn't been there that long ... well four years ago when he came ... It went on and on. He became more frenzied as the questions continued; the lawyer was relentless.

"We have this assurance from your own Government, and we will not leave until you have delivered Dr. and Mrs. Reimer into our care," he stated calmly and firmly. "We are prepared to stay until such time as …"

Suddenly Rhea rose and exited the small stuffy room. The official's stress increased noticeably; he wanted to object but could think of no way to do so without rousing further suspicion. Slowly she made her way up the small dirt path praying fervently for an end to the impasse. Then, feeling desperately lonesome for the parents she had not seen in three years, she suddenly burst into song, the one she and her Mamma had sung the first time she came to Africa as a tiny girl of four. Her powerful soprano carried down the dusty path and around the dirty compound; it carried into the tense room where the army man rose in astonishment and hurried outside, followed by the two Jonathons.

> Jesus loves the little children
> All the children of the world
> Red and yellow, black and white -
> All are precious in His sight;
> Jesus loves ….

As she paused, unable to control the tears in her voice, an answering echo issued forth from the small, dirty building to her right. No mistaking that clear, beautiful contralto:

"Jesus loves the little children …" she sang as Rhea ran, sobbing wildly.

"Mamma, Mamma," she cried as she lifted the heavy latch that held them prisoner. Mother and daughter fell into each others arms crying hysterically. A moment later they felt themselves lifted off the dirt floor in a gigantic hug as Jonathon joined the reunion.

"Mom ... Dad!" he cried out as he spotted his father on a make-shift cot against the wall in the dilapidated shanty.

Only the lawyer stood in the doorway, coldly eyeing the embarrassed official who looked up and down and everywhere to avoid the accusing gaze.

"Is that really you, my son?" the elder Reimer murmured feebly. "And my girl ... my little girl!"

"Oh, Daddy ... Daddy," she cried as she gathered him in her arms. "Oh, Daddy, you are so-o hot! You are so sick! Is it malaria? I have medications in my bag on the plane."

"We'll get you out of here at once," Jonathon spoke with authority.

"Not so fast, there! Not so fast!" the army man spoke up in an attempt to regain the loss of face and take charge of a situation that was suddenly out of control.

"We'll carry him to the plane," the lawyer stated emphatically, ignoring the remark. "Take hold of the sheet there; we'll make a hammock. Good enough!" The men proceeded with their plans as the official roared and threatened.

"I'd put that thing away," the lawyer growled, nodding at the pistol the army man brandished. "There are two governments involved in this rescue, and if they don't hear from us by tonight, guess whose head is going to roll. I'd think you're in trouble enough, going against orders from headquarters."

Sitting quietly on the small dirt strip not more than a few hundred feet from the hut, the pilot watched the proceedings and gladly opened the door and lowered the small steps. He had made many forays into the African wilderness for many reasons, but this was definitely a first.

Hurriedly, Rhea helped her Mom gather their few personal belongings. As they moved toward the door Rhea spotted her Father's medical bag. It was tattered and worn, and in a burst of fresh tears, she scooped it into her arms and together they ran through the intense heat toward the small refuge waiting on the runway.

"Now, we'll need some identification and a couple of passports," the lawyer straightened up, as they finished making the patient comfortable. "I won't be long."

"Hold it! I'm coming!" Jon jumped from the plane and prepared to follow.

"Get Daddy's watch," Rhea called. "The lieutenant is wearing it." Then turning to her Mom she explained, "That's one of the reasons I knew he was lying. That's the Seiko I gave Daddy for Christmas the year before you came here. I could hardly keep quiet ... seeing him with Daddy's watch while he sat there denying any knowledge of you. Besides he was here when I came three years ago and his story was totally different."

"They had probably moved us out into the jungle before you came last time."

"What a filthy, dirty hole they put you in," Rhea remarked. Why not the clinic?"

"We were in the clinic until yesterday; then they moved us in here. We thought someone official must be coming, but we had no windows to see anything," her Mom replied, as Rhea quickly opened her medical bag and prepared to make her Father more comfortable.

"Careful not to mask my symptoms, Little One," he murmured, "I may have meningitis ... it came on awfully sudden ... we didn't have any medications left ..." the weak voice trailed off.

Rhea smiled. He would always be Dr. Reimer - the teacher - instructor - mentor. He would always be Dad, helping and instructing his daughter no matter how many degrees she had, how old she was, or how many years of experience she might have. "I'll be careful, Daddy," she responded.

"Now," Jonathon Fields confronted the officious army man, "we would like Dr. and Mrs. Reimer's papers ... passports ... money ... Dr. Reimer's wristwatch ..."

"You should know that we have none of those things; they would not be kept here on the station," he remarked haughtily.

"I beg to differ," the doctor remarked. "That's my father's wristwatch you're wearing; his name is on the back. I ask you to remove it at once."

Obviously flustered, the man removed it, kicking himself that he had been so careless. He had merely intended to show these Westerners that he also had status, but had quite forgotten from whom he had lifted it.

"Now, we'll have the passports and anything else you have," the lawyer ordered in his most authoritative tone.

"We have no place to store anything like that..." the lieutenant tried again.

"Perhaps we might start with that locked cabinet," the lawyer went on. "If you have no key, I'm sure we have enough manpower ..."

"Well, I suppose we could give it a try," he pulled a ring of keys from his pocket and in no time the door opened revealing among other things, a purse.

Springing to his feet, the lawyer helped himself, turning the contents upside down on the desk ... passports ... family pictures ... birth certificates ... "This will do nicely," he said as they hastily gathered the contents and replaced them in the purse. "Thank you for your co-operation," he added with a smirk as they headed for the door.

"Not so fast ... not so fast!" the lieutenant yelled after them. "There are a few releases to sign here."

They laughed as they headed for the aircraft. "I just bet there are!"

"So where are we going, my son?" his mother asked as they got underway.

"We're heading for Cape Town; Dr. Ben Wyman has offered us refuge for a few days. We'll get Dad to the clinic and get a diagnosis as quickly as possible. Dr. Wyman will see to that."

The elder doctor nodded. His illness was begging him to rest, but in the joy of seeing his family and finding himself a free man, he could not. "My little girl ... my little Lady Rhee ... is that a wedding ring I'm seeing?"

"Yes, Daddy," she moved closer, holding up her left hand with the gorgeous diamond rings. "You'll have to call me *Mrs.* from now on."

"*Mrs. Who,* may I ask? He looked expectantly at Jonathon Fields.

"I wish it were so," the lawyer attempted a smile.

"She's Mrs. Michael Braemer," her brother filled in quickly to stem the embarrassment.

"As of about six weeks ago."

"Well, I declare. That's wonderful. I always said he's make somebody a great son-in-law. Congratulations to you both!" Her father was obviously delighted.

"Oh, my darling daughter," Reanne chimed in. "My little girl - a married woman. And where do you live now?"

"Same place, Mamma. Michael and I finished the house. But right now Michael has cancer ... lymphoma. He's on chemotherapy and very sick."

"Oh, honey!"

"We found out about three weeks before we were married, but we went ahead anyway. Jon is his oncologist ..."

"Oh, my dear ... my dear! But how can Jon be looking after him from Australia?"

"I just moved home a few months ago. I'm at St. Mike's too, along with Rhea and Michael. Just one big happy family. Can't wait for you to get back home where you belong.

"Now I think we need to thank God for this miracle of His grace, and then we'd better leave a little catching up for another time so Dad can get some rest. He's had far too much excitement for one so sick."

They nodded and gathered around the sickbed for prayer. As her mother and the Jonathons returned to their seats, Rhea gently sponged her father's fevered face, his neck, his hands, his arms.. He smiled and whispered softly, "My little girl ... my little Rhea ... I knew you'd come ... in His time ... I knew you'd come!"

Rhea could hardly wait to call home. She trembled as the stress of their recent experience caught up with her. *This has been a nightmare,* she thought, *a three-year nightmare. What must it have been like for Mom and Dad? I can't wait to hear. Please, God, bring speedy healing to Dad so they can come home.*

Her hand shook as she placed the call. It would be 9:00 a.m. in Canada. They should be up by now, she mused as she waited. His mother picked it up on the second ring.

"Rhea, Oh, Rhea, it's so good to hear your voice. Michael has been so sick. We had to take him back to the hospital ... he hasn't been able to eat or drink. They've put him on intravenous again ..." She paused as Rhea gasped.

"Oh, honey, I'm so sorry to give you such news. Dr. Clarke thinks he's doing better ... you know ..." she tried to encourage, "but he'd like Dr. Jon to call him as soon as he can. Tell me how your trip went. Do you have news of your folks?"

"Yes, yes we do," Rhea managed. "Actually, we have found them and brought them out to Cape Town. Daddy is very sick with malaria; we thought for a while it might be meningitis. His old friend and colleague, Dr. Wyman is treating him, but they will have to stay here for a few weeks of recuperation before they will be well enough to travel."

"What about you, sweetheart? Will you stay too?"

"Oh, no! I'll be on my way home shortly. Is Michael well enough to talk if I call the hospital?

"Oh, yes, I'm sure .. .and he'll be so glad to hear from you. He asked yesterday if you'd called."

Rhea's fingers clicked the phone numbers with a mixture of excitement and anxiety. She hoped Michael would be in his room. She was sure he would be awake.

"Good morning," he answered sleepily.

"Good morning, Michael, it's Rhea. How are you, sweetheart?"

"I just knew that was you!. I could tell by the happy little jingle the phone made when it knew you were on the line."

"Tell me how you are. You're back in hospital. Your Mom says you couldn't eat or drink."

"Yeah. Greg Clarke thinks I have an obstruction of some sort ... took me off everything by mouth till I quit throwing up. Guess he would like to discuss this with Jon before he does anything more. But, tell me where you are ∴. and how you are. Any word of the folks?"

"Oh, Michael! God has been so good! We've found Mom and Dad and brought them to Cape Town. Dad is terribly sick with malaria ... they had run out of meds. The officer at the army camp gave us an awful time. Good thing we had Jonathon Fields ... he didn't take *no* for an answer to anything. I can hardly wait to tell you all the details."

"Where will they stay in Cape Town?"

"They'll stay with Dad's old friend and colleague, Dr. Ben Wyman. He made short work of a diagnosis and put Dad in hospital. The rest of us are here with the Wymans."

"Sweetheart, I want you to do what you have to do there, and not rush home on my account. This is a monumental experience; you need to take time to process and enjoy before you leave there."

"I know you're right, sweetheart, but I am aching with loneliness for you. Getting a husband was pretty monumental, too, you know ... cancer is pretty monumental..."

"I know, Rhee ... I know ... but we'll both still be here when you get back ... both your husband and the cancer."

She smiled at his attempt at humour. "I have to tell you how thrilled Mom and Dad were to hear that we had met and married. Dad said he always knew you'd make somebody a great son-in-law. He's glad it's him. They were devastated to hear about the cancer."

"Give them hugs from me. I can hardly wait to see them again. We'll have lots to share."

"Have you lost more weight, Michael? I assume that you have if you haven't been able to eat or drink."

"Some, I'm sure. Not much left of me. But we're past the half-way mark, Rhee. We're going to make it!"

"To that end we pray," she said softly.

"Now then, my little Lady Rhee. Tell me, how is my new son-in-law?" her father asked as she entered his room.

"Well ... Jon tells me that he has ordered another CT Scan. Michael hasn't been able to eat or drink for almost a week. Something must be obstructing the digestive system."

"My dear little one," he took her hand gently in his. "You have gone beyond the reasonable in coming after us at such a time as this ... to say nothing of that daring rescue. God has blessed us with such a daughter and son. Now ... you know I am in good hands ... and I know that your heart is back in that hospital bed at St. Mike's ... and we both know that a wife's place is by her husband's side ... especially when he is so sick; that's why you find your Mother always at my side."

"Thank you, Daddy," she said softly, as tears escaped and started down her cheeks.

"I know Michael well enough to know that he'll be needing you. Oh, he'll say otherwise ... so as not to disturb our time together ... but we men weren't built to go it alone. Besides we'll get together in a few weeks ... and that for a very long time. Your brother will soon be on his way. I know him pretty well. Duty calls ... he answers. You both must go - with our blessing!"

Chapter 37

Doctor... Doctor

"Rhea ... Rhea ... Rhea ..." he murmured, trying to hold her close in spite of the intravenous and oxygen tubes. "I can hardly believe you're here already!"

"Dad sent us home," she said laughing. "He's still *Dad* you know, and tells his kids what to do no matter how old they are."

Jonathon stood by smiling quietly. "It will be interesting adjusting to having them back," he mused. "If they weren't so gracious ..."

Rhea and Michael nodded, understandingly.

"So how're you feelin', ol' boy? Are you still throwing up? Or have things settled down?"

"I'm feeling better since they took that tube out of my throat. Still won't let me eat or drink, except for that cocktail I had before the CT scan this morning. I didn't throw it up," he made a face.

"I'm off to get a look at that scan, and I'll report back in the morning. If Rhea can tear herself away," he said mischievously, "you really should get to sleep before midnight."

"Like father … like son," she chirped, planting another kiss on Michael's gaunt cheek.

"I'm so glad you're back, my sweetheart, and so glad your mission was successful. Won't it be something to have Mom and Dad back!"

"Mmmm, and I'm going to get you home and fatten you up before then. With Dad around, you'll need all the extra energy …" They laughed softly together, remembering her Dad's boundless energy. "Of course, he wasn't going on any safaris when we saw him this time," she added, "but he really is in good hands with his old friends and Mom there to make sure they do it all right."

"Like mother … like daughter," he teased, lovingly bringing her hand to his lips. "I can't wait to get home."

"You know Jon … he won't fudge on what he thinks is right. My guess is that you'll have to be able to eat and keep it down … and then another chemo is due …"

"Yeah, I've thought of all that. I'll be interested to hear his report on the scan. I doubt it can be more cancer. How could anything survive?" he chuckled.

"I think we're going to let you out of here. Your scan is clear; my guess is that when that tumor pulled away from between the bowels, it may have stretched something … allows the bowel to double over on itself so nothing gets through."

"Wow, any chance of a recurrence?"

"Oh, sure, that's always a possibility, but if it happens again we'll do the intravenous thing and allow the system to rest. You'll be more relaxed at home with Rhea looking after you and monitoring your intake. Nothing gets by her."

Michael grinned. *Home … with Rhea … warm blankets … milk shakes … special meals … homemade soup; home*

... where the heart is ... where my own bed is ... with Rhea in it. What a lot to be thankful for!"

"But I have even better news than that! The tumour is gone; I would say we have achieved remission."

They both looked at him in stunned amazement.

"Tell us that again, Jon," she found her voice. "The cancer is gone?"

"Yep! Looks like it."

"So we're finished with the chemo?"

"Nope! We have a rule ... *remission plus two chemo ...* and ... I'm sorry to have to tell you this but ... we have a second rule ... *with lymphoma, always give six."*

"Oh Jon! Oh Jon! Really? Really?"

"Sorry, sis," he gave her a brotherly squeeze. "I really am sorry, but this is the best kick we will ever get at this thing; if it returns, it won't be nearly so treatable." He looked at Michael.

"Just do what you have to do, Dr. Jon," Michael responded. "It's okay, sweetheart; we're going to make it!" he added, noting Rhea's white face.

"And we'll do your next chemo Friday afternoon; I've asked Meribelle to schedule you in. Your blood looks good right now, and you'll have a couple of days to enjoy home and hearth before then." He looked questioningly at Michael.

"Good enough!" Michael responded as the nurse prepared to remove the intravenous.

"I'll pick him up at the front door," Rhea instructed the orderly with the wheelchair; that's a pretty raw wind out there this morning.

"Come, sit by the fire," she encouraged a shivering Michael as she helped him off with his coat. "We'll get you warmed up. How about a warm blanket and some hot tea and a muffin?"

"Sounds like I'm home. Feels wonderful," he smiled as she tucked him in.

"Are you warm enough?" she asked as she came with the tea.

"I could use my little toque and bed slippers that Lynda knit for me."

"That's why they looked so familiar. I remember she made a set for her Mom when she was on chemo. She's one special cousin ... the sister I never had. Has she mentioned how things are going with Bob?"

"No, but he has. He's been to see me quite a few times, and just gets happier all the time. He tells me they're in love."

"Wow! A June wedding?"

"Hasn't said anything. And I have other news."

She looked at him questioningly.

"Tracy thinks she's pregnant. She's beside herself. Sure hope it's true ... it will be an awful let-down if she isn't. They've waited so long."

"Wowee! What excitement! Dr. Clarke must know his stuff. Glad he was able to help Tyler, whatever the problem."

"Rhee, tell me about your Mom and Dad. How are they? Did they survive the jungles okay ... except for the malaria, I mean?"

"Well, they're pretty resilient, as you know. They know how to do with almost nothing for months on end. However, I think this was way past their endurance. Supplies were scant, meds ran out, threats to heal prominent army leaders or else ... were quite common. They were pretty rag-tag when we got there. Their clothing had been pretty much taken away, in case they would attempt escape. They had some old hospital garb from somewhere ... disgraceful. Poor Mom was so embarrassed! I had her change into my extra pants and blouse on the plane. Her hair was really long, and she had it in braids around her head ... actually looked quite elegant. Dad's hair was long too, and his beard. Said they really couldn't justify using hospital scissors for such things; they were already old and dull, and no way to sharpen or replenish them."

"How were they mentally? Spiritually?"

"Better than I imagined. They were trusting completely in the Lord to bring them out... *in His time*, Dad said. He went on to tell of all the young men who accepted Christ ... some on their death bed ... others who thought they were dying. Some of those young men recovered, and went on to live for Christ. They all knew of Mom and Dad's abduction and several offered to help by smuggling letters out for them. Dad knew they weren't getting through when nothing changed in their circumstances ... until he got malaria and they had to bring him to the clinic. Of course, they had nothing to treat it with. God's timing was perfect; I'm sure he would have died without medication. They had only been there about 24 hours before we arrived."

"God is never late!" Michael smiled. "How long do you think ...?"

"I don't know. Dad is dying to get home, but he knows his limitations. He'll have to be really on top of it physically before Dr. Wyman will let them go. He looked a lot better with a bath and shave and haircut. They'll need to do a little shopping. We got Mom some new things and got her hair cut. She is still as trim and beautiful as ever!"

"I bet she is ... just like her daughter!" Rhea smiled as he went on, "The Chief and Joan have collaborated with my folks to have a city-wide *welcome home* ... with their kids approval, of course."

"Sounds great! Hope they give us all a little recovery time. Speaking of recovery ... do you need to get horizontal?" Noting his nod, she added, "In the chair, or shall I help you to bed? I should slip down to the hospital for a couple of hours and re-orient myself."

"In that case, I'd best head for bed. Not sure I can make it there on my own ... no food makes one rather wobbly. When will we have lunch?"

"I'll be home by one o'clock. Want to try a beef-vegetable soup?"

He slipped his arms around her as she arranged his bedding. "Just hold me close for a few minutes before you go, sweetheart; what's left of me is really lonely for my better half."

He felt her smile on his cheek. *Still has that wonderful sense of humour,* she thought as she planted a kiss.

"That's number four," he reminded Rhea as she picked him up in the Oncology lounge.

"We'll be done with this in no time. Jon says I can stay home as long as I behave - no throwing up."

"We'll take it really slow then ... no big meals with meat ... just small lunches ... lots of milkshakes with straw-berries and bananas ... lots of Ensure and yoghourt. I'm so glad you'll be home, my love, and I'm going to do my best to see that you stay here. I sure hope you feel good in the morning. I'd like it if we could call my folks first thing before I leave for the hospital. I'm anxious to hear how everybody is doing. Of course, if you're under the weather ... I'll just stay home ... I've alerted Jared ..."

"I'll be okay, Rhee. I can certainly manage by myself for three or four hours. You need to be able to plan your schedule without so many uncertainties."

Rhea smiled as she helped him from the car. *This is what Dad would call 'he-man talk'* she told herself. *Manage by himself, indeed! He'd have an awful time getting his own lunch when he can hardly walk!*

"I've suggested to Jonathon that he come by and join in

the call. It's good if he can hear them first hand. I'm sure they must be doing well, or somebody would have called us by now," she added as she picked up Michael's buzzing cell phone and handed it to him.

"This sounds like my new son-in-law came the booming voice of Dr. Matt Reimer."

"It is indeed, and how is my father-in-law? We were going to call you in the morning."

"Well, it seems to me that you were scheduled for another chemo today and we were just wondering how that went."

"You don't miss much, do you Dad?" Michael chuckled. "Actually, Rhea just brought me home from the hospital. I had it about an hour ago, and haven't had time to get sick yet. That will come later, but I'm doing pretty well ... a whole lot better since Rhea's back. Thanks for sending her home. Now, tell us, how are you, and when can we get excited about having you home?"

"We are both doing well. I'm sure I'm over this malaria business, but you know what doctors are like ... always keep you longer than they have to ... more medications than necessary ... all the extra precautions ..." They enjoyed a chuckle. "Ben has hardly given me clearance to leave the bed, never mind the country. Won't even talk about letting us go. Not that we aren't enjoying the luxury of civilization ... good friends ... good food ... a good bed ... hot water ... electricity ... a newspaper ... It goes on and on. Never realized just how much I took all these things for granted until about six months into the jungle." He chuckled again. "But we're anxious to get home, and we'll be there at the earliest possible moment."

"We're having a hard time waiting, Dad. Rhea is standing here waiting to talk to her Mom, so I'll sign off. Take it easy."

"I will son, and now you go and take your own advice. Here's Mom."

"So how are you and Dad doing, Mom?" Rhea asked after they had exchanged greetings.

"Apparently not as well as Dr. Ben would like. We're both pretty run down. Your Dad's fever comes and goes. Ben is checking both of us for any possible parasites, disease ... as well as trying to build us up ... looks like we'll be here for at least three or four more weeks. We're both too weary to offer any objection. Can hardly believe the kindness of Dr. Ben and Vera ... precious people. Maybe it's for the best that we stay a while ... I'm feeling some stress about getting back to Canada ... looking for a place to live ... finding our way again."

"Oh, Mom, we hope you'll stay in our guest suite until you're ready to start making decisions. Jon is in there right now, but he plans to move in with us for a few months until he gets married. The suite is really large ... you can do whatever you like with it ... stay as long as you like. Please try not to feel stressed about all this. We're all in this together and will be thrilled to have you home again. We have three years of catching up to do, so we won't want to rush anything."

"I must admit that we're more than anxious to meet our future daughter-in-law. If she's half of what Jonathon describes, he'll be blessed. We can hardly wait to meet her."

"She really is a special girl, Mom. The more I get to know her the more I love her. Oh, Mom ... sorry ... I have to run ... looks like Michael needs me." She signed off quickly, trying hard to keep her tone matter-of-fact.

Her Mom had not missed the awful crash. She would call back later to enquire whether Michael was okay.

She struggled to lift him to the bed as his arms and legs trembled convulsively. *He must be having a seizure of some sort*, she thought, as she murmured, "Oh sweetheart ... my poor sweetheart ... my dear Michael."

"What's going on?" he asked as he came to.

"You seem to have fallen. Are you all right?"

"Yeah. Sure. I was just going to the bathroom. Guess I must have gotten a little dizzy. Help me, okay?"

"You should have buzzed me; you know better than trying this yourself," she lectured softly as she supported his feeble effort to walk. "You'll need to use that urinal when I'm not here. We can't have you falling and breaking something."

"Only two more to go," he encouraged. "In six weeks or so, the worst will be behind us. Maybe I'll be up and about by the time your folks arrive. Wouldn't that be something?"

"It would ... it would indeed!" she joined in his enthusiasm. "Joan and your Mom would like to set the welcome-home party for early April. You'll need to be able to dance by then," she smiled encouragingly.

Trembling inwardly, she thought, *I'm afraid the worst is still ahead of us ... two more chemos ... in your condition ...* Her heart sank. She must talk to Jonathon. Surely ...

Chapter 38

Made in Heaven

"So, you believe matches are made in heaven?" Michael quipped to his old friend, Bob Martyn as they enjoyed a cup of tea by the fire.

Bob smiled. He had come to expect this sort of question from Mike ... the ones with no definitive answers. "I'm not sure how to answer that," he began, "but since all of us are *made in heaven* so to speak, I'm sure God prepares compatible personalities; then gives us differing gifts so we can serve each other and serve others together."

"Like Rhea and I? Do you think our marriage was made in heaven?"

"God gave you the right to choose. Then He gave you the good sense to choose each other. Your marriage is made on earth ... it is what you make it."

"Wow! That was a whopping dose of theology ... all in one paragraph." He chuckled. He was used to Bob's cryptic answers. His spiritual insight was always refreshing.

"So, does that apply to you and Lynda?"

"You betcha! Compatible personalities ... giftedness ... goals ... a heart to serve God. AND ... He gave me the good sense to see it that first night at the airport." Bob smiled. "Isn't she something? Remember the conversation we had in the hot tub that night at Olympia? I was really broken up about Rhea. Nothing had worked out. She obviously did not want to be more than a good friend ... then I almost got her killed ... then you came along. It was as though God had forgotten how badly I wanted ... and needed ... a wife. Looking back I can see that God was preparing Lynda and me for each other. I needed to trust Him and to wait."

"She really is a special girl. Rhea calls her the sister she never had. The girls are certainly close."

"You know that we'd like you and Rhee to stand up for us. We're thinking about early September. Lynda would like the wedding and reception to be outdoors ... she loves the fall colours and all that sort of thing."

"Sounds fun. We're blessed. You know that Jon and Luci are planning for June. Don't think it will be here ... possibly Montreal where Luci's Mom lives."

"So how are you doin', Mike? That was number five, right? You're looking a lot better than you did last time."

"Yeah. Dr. Jon put me on Neupogen. It stimulates the bone cells to produce the right kind of blood cells, wards off infection, that sort of thing. Cut back a bit on the chemo. All in all, I'm feeling better than I have since I started the treatment. Side benefits are forthcoming as well ... I'm starting to grow a little hair," he pulled off his toque as he spoke, "and I even have an appetite. Rhea is starting to enjoy cooking for me. She's had a hard time finding anything that I would eat. I'm finally gaining back some of that 45 pounds I lost. It's been a circus. Nothing that I want to repeat. We're both looking forward to having a marriage!"

"I must say I've been praying and watching you two with amazement. You seem to be so in love ... in spite of all the difficulties you've been through."

"I'm blessed. Rhea has never complained about all the sleepless nights ... the messes ... the uneaten meals ... the disrupted schedule at the hospital. It would have been a different ball game if she had resented what God allowed in our lives. I don't know how I would have managed without her. I'm glad I took your advice and got married in spite of the cancer. I was afraid it would tear us apart ... it's turned out just the opposite. We are very close."

"You mentioned a while back that you might not be able to have a family?"

"That's something else we're just leaving in God's hands. We both just love kids. You know my sister is pregnant; they'd been trying for a few years. We're just thrilled for them! We'll probably adopt if we don't have any of our own. Rhea is such a little mother hen; she says it's hard for her not to bring home a few of those little African orphans every time she goes over." He paused, "So, do you think babies are made in heaven?"

Bob smirked, "You bet I do ... you just bet I do!"

Chapter 39

A Time to Dance

"**N**ow that's the man I married," she smiled as she saw him adjust his tie in front of the mirror.

"Not really," he responded. "This one is cancer free."

"Oh, Michael … Michael …" she slipped into his arms and lifted her mouth for his kiss. "You are even more handsome that I remembered. I can hardly believe how quickly you gained back that weight. It's hard to believe … after what you've been through."

"Are your folks riding with us?"

"No, I gave them my car … actually it's their car." She laughed. "Now you can get me that new one you've been wanting me to have. Or maybe we should get them a new one. This sifting and sorting thing will be fun."

"I'm glad they put this off for a couple more weeks … gave my hair a chance to look half normal, and who knows … maybe I'll even last for the whole evening. That will be a first for a while."

"Sounds good to me. Your hair is just beautiful. That grey makes you look so distinguished … more than usual, I mean," she laughed. "Jon says it will come back to its natural colour once the pigment cells rejuvenate."

"Your Dad still has such a full head of hair. I didn't remember him having any grey ... guess Africa must have done that."

"Yeah, I would think so. Mom, too. But they wear it beautifully, don't they? Course they're almost seniors ... time for a change of colour."

"Indeed! They're wonderful parents, Rhee. No wonder I fell in love with you so quickly; I'd already loved them for so long, and Jon, too. I have been blessed thrice over."

"I'm hoping the Chief will keep the formal part of this thing to a minimum; poor Mom and Dad ... they've had enough accolades and speeches to last them for years. I told him that all we need now is to enjoy dining and dancing. I understand the caterers are prepared to feed at least two thousand. They've really pulled out the stops on this one ... set up extra dining rooms and dance floors."

"No kidding! I'll be surprised if that's all ... the hospital ... the church ... the town ... that's a lot of people."

The main dining room was already full when they arrived. Rhea thought she had never seen such opulence. The Chief bustled about among the guests with his usual air of importance, seconded by Michael Braemer Sr.; Michael and Rhea exchanged quiet smiles.

They were ushered at once to the family table and seated next to her parents. Rhea was pleased to see her Mom and Lillian Braemer making up for the thirty-plus years they had been separated. She smiled remembering the tearful reunion ... the forgivenesses asked for and received by both couples. *God, you really are a miracle worker. Thank you, God ... thank you for both of our parents ... and the Wahls, too ... three sets of parents. We are blessed.*

"This meal is beyond belief; I've never seen so much beef ... turkey ... ham ... salmon ... in one place at one time in my life," Matt Reimer commented. "No one in

Riverview ought to go hungry tonight."

There were quiet murmurs of agreement around the table, as the Chief quieted the guests and called on Pastor Bob to offer thanks to God for the feast before them.

They dined leisurely ... enjoying the festive atmosphere ... enjoying the occasion that brought them all together ... enjoying the renewed relationships with old friends. Rhea was pleased to see that Jonathon Fields seemed to be enjoying himself and that Miranda Robinson had come to join in the festivities. The Chief had been more than generous in his praise of the lawyer and the prominent role he had played in the rescue. It gladdened her heart to remember Jonathon's modesty ... the downplaying of his involvement.

True to his word, the Chief was brief ... at least he was brief for him, Rhea thought. He spent about a half hour expounding on the the Reimers, their faith, their work, their return from the other end of the world. Repeatedly, he thanked the Lord for their return to health and to Canada.

As he took his seat, her brother Jonathon took the microphone. She gave him her best *keep it brief* look. He smiled acknowledgement. "Ladies and Gentlemen," he began. "This is indeed a special occasion for all of us ... we have welcomed back our loved ones that have been dead to us for the past three years. Since Rhea and I were children we have been taught to celebrate such joyful occasions in two ways ... firstly, to offer praise and thanksgiving to God; this we have done for the past three months; secondly, we follow the pattern we find in the Scriptures where the people of God danced for joy on special occasions when God had poured out his blessing. I submit to you that tonight is such an occasion ... God's blessing in the life of our family is without precedent. We find in the Scripture in Ecclesiastes Chapter Three that there is a time to mourn and a time to dance. We have had our time of mourning ..."

He turned to his parents, extending his hand as though inviting them to lead the way, as he continued, "Friends ... family ... special guests ... let me ask you ... is it a time to dance?"

Michael turned to Rhea. Happy tears flowed freely down her face. He offered his hand, "Come, my love, it's time to dance!"

Printed in the United States
58742LVS00002B/100-123

9 781591 605287